KISS THE SUN

Vicki Childs

Kiss the Sun

a novel by

Vicki Childs

Paperback edition

Copyright © 2023 by Vicki Childs

All rights reserved. No part of this book may be reproduced or used in any manner without written permission of the copyright owner except for the use of quotations in a book review. For more information, address:
vickichilds.author@gmail.com

DISCLAIMER
This is a work of fiction. Names, characters, places, and incidents either are the product of the author's imagination or are used fictitiously. Any resemblance to actual persons, living or dead, events, or locales is entirely coincidental.
First paperback edition July 2021

ISBN 978-1-7373077-2-3 (paperback)
ISBN 978-1-7373077-3-0 (ebook)

www.vickichilds.com

To my patient husband, and my wonderful children. Thank you for all your support, I love you more than I can say.

1

Birthday Wishes
Saturday, April 18th - Pasadena

Emily stared out the kitchen window, her fingernails digging into the smooth ceramic surface of the butler sink as she forced the mask of blissful contentment back into place.

Outside, the birthday party was in full swing. Sunlight glinted across the brightly colored helium balloons as they bounced in the breeze, metallic orbs of childhood joy, tugging at their anchors in a desperate attempt to break free. Behind them, an azure blue California sky, stretching to infinity, filled with the gleeful squeals of children playing on the water slide just out of sight.

She touched her hair to check it was still in place.

"It's getting hot already," she said, watching the balloons.

"Yeah," said Ed. "I'll take some more water out. And some juice boxes when I go."

He stood behind her at the kitchen island, cutting up fresh strawberries and dropping them into paper bowls, before placing the bowls on a glass platter.

Emily shifted her weight and swallowed.

"Do you think I should take the cake out of the freezer?" She asked, not shifting her gaze. "The instructions say to let it sit out before you serve it, so the ice cream isn't too hard."

"Maybe. It's 1pm already, so it's probably a good time," replied Ed, his voice hollow.

Oppressive silence filled the room once more.

Emily took a deep breath and sighed, before turning towards the fridge-freezer.

As she stepped towards Ed, he moved aside, his eyes flickering to her face for a moment, before returning to the fruit.

"I'll top up the snacks while I'm out there," he said, turning and reaching for a bag of chips.

"Ok. Do you want more guacamole?"

"No, I think there's still quite a lot left, but I'll check when I'm out there."

Emily looked at him. His gaze slid to the floor.

"Do you want a beer?"

"No. Thanks. I'm good."

"Are you, though?" Emily said, turning to face him. "Are you? '*Good*?'"

Ed's jaw tightened. "Let's not do this now. Please."

"We have to talk about this. You have to tell me what's going on."

"This is not the time nor the place. Let's just focus on Harry, OK? This is his day, after all."

"There's always something, though, isn't there? You're never willing to talk to me anymore. I know I've been busy with work, but you're so distant, even more than normal," her voice trailed off.

Opening the bag of chips, Ed turned to her, his expression guarded.

"OK. I hear what you're saying. Let's just get through today and then we'll talk, yes?"

Emily clenched her teeth.

"Get through it?" she said in an icy tone. "I'm sorry if this is such a hardship for you. Is there somewhere you'd rather to be?"

"For Christ's sake, Emily, just stop, OK? This isn't helping," Ed said, dumping the chips into a bowl.

"Helping what, Ed?" she spat, folding her arms and squaring herself towards him. "What is it exactly that needs help? Your attitude? Our marriage? There are so many options to choose from, after all."

"Keep your voice down," Ed hissed. "People can hear you."

Emily slammed a hand down on the counter.

"You know what, Ed? I don't give a shit anymore. Let them hear me. I'm sick of pretending to be this perfect family with a perfect life, when it's obviously just bullshit. Do you even love me anymore?"

A thought raced through her mind. *"Did you ever really love me?"*

Ed saw her expression, and the unasked question it held, and he looked stunned.

Reaching towards her, he whispered, "Don't say that. You know I love you. I've always loved you."

Emily stepped back, her breath catching in her throat.

"Do you, though? Because you have a funny way of showing it."

Ed reached out again.

"Don't touch me!" Emily said, jerking her hand away.

It caught the edge of the glass platter and they both turned to see it spin.

They stared in horror as it spun around and around.

Before they could react, it reached the edge of the counter, tipped, and smashed onto the tiled floor.

Shards of glass flew everywhere.

Emily gasped and dropped down to a crouch, picking up the broken glass and strawberries, trying to see through the tears that streamed down her face.

Ed was beside her now, holding her elbow, gently lifting her to her feet.

"Stop. I'll get the broom. You'll hurt yourself if you try to pick it up by hand."

"Too late," Emily said, as a scarlet bead of blood grew on her fingertip.

It trickled down her finger and into her hand, mixing with the juice of the strawberries.

Ed wrapped a paper napkin around it and squeezed.

"It's OK. We can fix this," he said. "It was just an old platter, no harm done. Now let me get the broom and I'll clear this up."

As he turned to go, Emily held his arm.

"Ed? We're going to be OK, aren't we?" she asked.

Concern flickered across his face before he said, "Yes, everything is going to be fine. Now go freshen up, while I clean up this mess. Everybody's waiting for the cake."

As the children gathered around the table, the chattering subsided, replaced by an expectant hush.

Harry sat at the center of the group, his eyes gleaming as he admired the huge Transformers ice-cream birthday cake set before him.

"Ready, everyone?" asked Emily, lighting the candles and beginning to sing.

A chorus of 'Happy Birthday' rang out, everyone smiling as Harry beamed with joy.

He knelt up in his chair. Leaning forward, he blew with all his might.

Everyone cheered and there were shouts of, "Make a wish!"

Harry screwed up his freckled face and grinned.

"I wonder what he's wishing for?" thought Emily, a hard knot forming in her stomach.

She cleared her throat and said brightly, "Let's cut the cake, shall we?"

Cheers rang out, and cake was distributed to a multitude of small, grabbing hands.

One mother patted Emily's arm and said, "What a lovely day. Just perfect. You must be so proud."

Emily smiled. "Yes, it's been wonderful. Thank you so much for coming."

"It was a pleasure. We wouldn't have missed it for the world."

Emily turned to the table to collect the discarded paper plates, trying to swallow the lump in her throat.

She glanced over at Ed, who was laughing as he swung Harry around and around in circles. Harry screamed with glee and shouted, "Faster, Daddy, faster!"

She watched them collapsing into a heap on the grass, laughing and hugging. Philip and Sophie stood watching and laughing as well. They had grown up so much over the last year, now they looked more like young adults than her precious babies.

"Mum," Philip shouted, "come here and let's take a family photo."

She put the plates down, adjusted her hair, and walked over to her family.

They leaned in together and smiled at the camera.

"Say cheese!" said Ed.

"Cheese!" they all shouted, and Emily did her best to smile for the photograph.

2

Groceries
Tuesday, April 21st - London

Liz pushed her shopping cart around the empty, cavernous grocery store. It was late and most of her fellow commuters had gone home hours ago. They were now tucked away in their warm, cozy homes, eating dinner and relaxing in front of the TV.

She was dog tired but, as per usual, there was no food in the house, so she had come directly from work to get some essentials.

Her feet ached in her high heels and she couldn't wait to kick them off, throw her suit on the bed, and put on some sweatpants.

As she rounded the corner into the cereal aisle, the tinny, anemic sound of 'Africa' by Toto played over the loudspeaker.

She nodded politely at a fellow shopper, an older gentleman wearing an ill-fitting suit and a bleary expression. He blinked in acknowledgment as he stood wilted over his cart, staring, uninspired, at the various types of granola.

Her mobile phone rang, and she pulled it out of her

handbag, clamping it between her ear and shoulder as she reached for the Cheerios.

"Hi Liz, it's Lauren. Are you coming home?"

"If only," thought Liz, as she said, "Yeah, in a bit. I'm in Tesco's buying essentials."

"Nice! Can you get cereal?"

"Yup. And I'm getting milk and pasta too. What else should I get for Naomi's lunchbox? Do we have fruit?"

"I'm not sure. Let me check."

Liz could feel the low throb of a tension headache forming in her temples as she reached for a large carton of milk.

"So," said Lauren. "We have one moldy banana, but that's it. Can you get some wine as well? Oh, and we need bread. And more dishwasher tablets."

Liz raised her eyes to heaven in frustration.

"Weren't you supposed to do a grocery shop at the weekend? How come we're out of everything already?"

"I did!" said Lauren. "I went to Tesco's on Sunday after I got back from Gary's house. But I forgot the list, so I only got the stuff I could think of at the time."

Liz clenched her jaw, gripping the shopping cart hard as she turned onto the wine aisle.

"Um, actually," Lauren continued, "Gary asked me if I could go to the pub tomorrow night to watch the match with him and some mates. Can you watch Naomi? I know you'd normally go to pilates on Wednesdays, but this is a big game and I really want to go. Please?"

Liz took a deep breath, aware of how tired she was, and not wanting her voice to reveal her frustration and concern.

"Lauren," she said, carefully, "I get that you guys are having fun, but you're spending a lot of time together and I'm worried that it might start interfering with your work. You've only just started this job and you need to make a good impression."

Silence. Then came Lauren's sullen voice.

"The job is going great. If you don't want to babysit, then just say so. You don't have to get all passive aggressive about it."

Liz reached for her favorite Cabernet Sauvignon.

"Sorry, I didn't mean to piss you off, it's just that.."

"I'm not pissed off," snapped Lauren, "but every time I talk about Gary, you get all 'high-and-mighty', telling me what to do. If you don't like him, then tell me. I'm a grown-up, I can handle it."

Liz rubbed her neck. She was stiff and tired, and she wanted to get home and relax.

"It's not that I don't like him. I just think things are moving very fast between the two of you, and don't want you or Naomi to get hurt."

"Leave Naomi out of this."

"Fine," Liz said, throwing her hands up in the air. "I don't want you to get hurt. You've only just qualified and got a steady job. You've worked so hard for this and you've wanted it for so long. I simply want some stability for you."

"Gary's a good guy, Liz. You need to give him a chance."

"I know, I know," Liz conceded, putting a hand to her forehead and sighing. "Maybe I'm overly protective of you guys. We should all spend some more time together. We could invite him over at the weekend for a barbecue if you want?"

"Yeah, that would be nice," Lauren said, her voice relaxing a little.

"Ok, you invite him and I'll buy some chicken and ribs while I'm here. And sure, I'll babysit tomorrow. I just need to move a couple of meetings around so I can be home on time."

"Thank you! You're the best!"

"Yeah, well, it'll be nice to spend some time with the little monkey," Liz said, grinning. "Is she still awake?"

"Mmm, not for long. She's had her bath and her story and I've put her to bed. She'll probably be asleep by the time you get back. Sorry."

"That's fine," said Liz, the tiredness returning to her body. "I won't be long. See you soon."

She grabbed the last couple of items, paid the checkout clerk, and stepped out into the dark drizzle of the night.

As she hauled the shopping bags out of her cart and put them into the trunk of her car, she heard the laughter of a small child. She turned to see a mother, illuminated by the overhead yellow-tinted street light. She was lifting her toddler out of a cart and buckling her into her car seat. The little girl held out her arms, and the mother gave her a quick kiss on the forehead before closing the car door.

Liz stood, one hand on the open trunk, while a sharp pang of sorrow cramped her heart. The breath caught in her throat and she swallowed hard.

Slamming the trunk, she swung herself into the driver's seat and turned the car towards home.

As she drove through the rain-washed streets, she thought of Lauren and little Naomi. She loved them both, but she couldn't shake the uncomfortable feeling she had about the future.

The treadmill of work and cooking and laundry and dishes wouldn't let up. Maybe she needed some time away to clear her head, but Lauren and Naomi needed her.

She realized in that moment that she had felt off-kilter ever since her brother's wedding in December. It felt as if she had been carrying an invisible weight that she'd neither wanted to carry nor set down.

She smiled to think of David and Billy though, if ever there was proof of a 'happily ever after,' they were it.

As she sat at the traffic lights in the drizzling rain, her

windshield wipers squeaking back and forward, waiting for the light to change to green, she thought back to the day of the wedding.

That crisp, cold, December morning, the wedding party had awoken to find a light frost coating the grass and trees surrounding the beautiful stately home, their venue for the occasion. The glittering ice crystals added to the magic of the special day.

Liz had pulled her fur wrap tightly around her as the moisture of her breath hung in the chilly morning air. Standing on the balcony, she'd looked out across the rolling countryside, marveling at the quiet beauty of this pristine winter's day.

As the guests arrived, the venue hummed with joy and laughter, and everyone settled into their assigned rows, waiting for the ceremony to begin.

A hush fell over the room as all eyes turned to watch David and Billy walking down the aisle arm in arm.

As they said their vows, the radiant smiles on their faces and the deep love in their eyes made Liz's heart overflow.

Later there had been mulled wine, followed by a delicious, hearty meal. Speeches were given and friends and family danced and laughed and cried with happiness.

A tear rolled down Liz's cheek. And then another.

She jumped, shocked by the sharp car horn from behind her.

Glancing at the light, she realized it was green.

She pulled away, her heart hammering and her breath coming in short bursts as she wiped away the tears streaming down her face.

Lauren greeted her at the front door and together they brought in the shopping bags. Liz unpacked in silence as Lauren talked animatedly about the patients in her pediatric ward and the days' various ups and downs, triumphs and tragedies.

They ate their beef stew and drank a glass of wine while watching Lauren's favorite soap opera.

The images flickered in front of Liz but she was a million miles away, on a hillside somewhere looking into the distance, searching for something just out of reach. But what was it she craved so badly? What would it take to fill this emptiness?

3

Query Letters
Friday, April 24th - Pasadena

"Hey mom, it's so great to hear from you," Chrissy said as she transferred her cell phone from one hand to the other so she could unlock the front door. Doogie pushed past her into the house, jumping and wagging.

"Perfect timing. We just got home from our morning walk."

"I got your text," said Trish. "What's the big news?"

"Oh, my god. I can't wait to tell you. Hang on a second, though."

Chrissy kicked off her flip-flops and headed to the kitchen for a much needed glass of water.

"So, you know I've been sending out all these query letters to literary agents? It's the first step to getting my book published, but until now all I've been getting are rejections. Well…"

"Did you get a bite?" Trish cut in. "How exciting!"

"No. Well, yes. But not in the way I thought."

"What?"

Chrissy sat on the couch, tucking her feet up under her and

sipping her water. She took a deep breath and continued.

"Ok, so yesterday I got an email from an editor at a huge publishing house in New York. Mom, they're a household name. It's a dream come true! They said they were aware I was looking for representation, and that they would be interested in talking to me directly about publishing my book. Seriously, it's insane. A publishing house of this size and reputation never reaches out directly to unknown authors. I'm so excited I could scream!"

There was silence on the other side of the line.

"Mom? Trish? Did I lose you?"

"No, I'm here honey. That's great news."

Chrissy was taken aback.

"You don't sound very excited. Are you OK?"

"Yes, I'm good. But I wonder why they would do that?"

Chrissy rolled her eyes. Why couldn't her mother just be happy for her?

"Well, it gets even better. I called the editor to thank him and ask what the next steps would be. It seems a famous author has taken a particular interest in my work and wants to mentor me. A mentor, Mom! A bestselling author wants to help me!"

Another silence.

"Chrissy, what's the name of this author?"

"It's Joseph Graham. I have to admit that I hadn't heard of him before now, so I had to look him up. He's an American writer in his mid 70s. He writes military spy novels, you know, testosterone filled 'men being men' stuff. Although he hasn't written anything for decades now. I have no idea how he heard about me. In fact, it's kinda weird, isn't it?"

Trish sighed.

"Darling, I think I might know why he reached out."

Chrissy felt the excitement draining from her.

"What is it, Mom?"

After a pause, Trish answered in a quiet voice.

"Chrissy, he's your father."

Chrissy felt the floor drop beneath her. She reeled, grabbing the arm of the couch to steady herself.

"What?" she stammered. "That can't be true. He's the guy from the music festival? But you said it was just a fling. You said you never really knew him. Why are you even saying this?"

"I'm so sorry," Trish said, her voice breaking. "I should have told you a long time ago, but I never thought—"

"What?" Chrissy spat, the anger catching her by surprise. "You never thought what, Mom? That he might show some interest in me one day?"

"I didn't think it would be a good idea. You didn't need to know. I did what I thought was best for you."

"Hang on a minute," Chrissy said, standing up and breathing deeply. She walked to the window and leaned on the bureau, looking out onto the sun dappled street. She took a breath, fighting the tears that threatened to rise and break free.

Once she'd regained her composure, she walked to the kitchen, drained another glass of cool water and said, "OK, Mom. Let's start from the beginning, shall we? How on earth did you end up having an illegitimate child with a famous American author?"

Trish chuckled before taking a deep breath and exhaling.

"He wasn't a famous author when I met him. He was just a shaggy, idealistic boy trying to prove himself in the world."

Chrissy listened as her mother's voice took on a warm, wistful tone.

"It was Glastonbury, back before it was a huge event, back when it was just a group of kids sitting in a field. It was 1979. A precious moment out of time, fleeting, filled with love and acceptance and music and connection. I went with a group of friends and we pitched our tent near the main stage. We brought nothing with us but open hearts and warm blankets, and we lost ourselves in the rich currents and psychedelic music of Steve Hillage and Mother Gong."

"So, how did you meet my father?" Chrissy asked, the words sounding strange in her ears.

"Hmmm," Trish said, drifting back to that summer evening so long ago. "Well, one night we were cooking up sausages for dinner, and the smell wafted over the campground. Like a stray dog, he appeared at our side looking friendly and hopeful, and when we offered him some food, he made himself at home. He was wiry, with the muscles of a runner, and he had floppy dark wavy hair he would push back out of his eyes now and then. It was obvious from the start that he wasn't interested in small talk, and pretty soon the two of us were arguing about politics and ethics and philosophy. It was strange because he wasn't threatened by my political opinions like most of the young men were back then. Quite the contrary, he relished an intellectual sparring partner, and as the sun set over the hillside, we listened to Peter Gabriel singing 'Solsbury Hill' as we drank potent homemade scrumpy cider and pulled a blanket around us to keep warm.

"He had the most intense, beautiful eyes. One moment they were flashing and defensive, the next searching and vulnerable. They were the darkest chocolate brown color. A color you could swim in, lose yourself in. I suppose it was fate, and he gave me the most precious gift of all, a baby daughter."

"Mom! Really? I can't believe this. How could you have kept this from me?"

"I don't know. I just... I didn't want you to spend your life looking for him, needing his acceptance and validation. You are so much more than that."

Chrissy sat down heavily on the bench by the kitchen

table. She felt winded. The earlier elation of the morning sucked out of her as if through an airlock, leaving only emptiness.

"Baby girl, are you OK?" asked Trish in a small voice.

Chrissy paused for a moment before answering, "I don't know. I don't know how I should be feeling right now."

Trish cleared her throat.

"What do you think you'll do? Will you meet with him? Work with him? Whatever you want to do, I will support you."

"I need some time to process this. I'll call you later in the week. I have to go now."

"OK, I understand. I love you Chrissy."

There was a pause, and then Chrissy answered.

"I love you too, Mom."

Chrissy walked around the kitchen in a daze. She cleared away the breakfast dishes, loaded the dishwasher and sorted some laundry.

Then the tears began to fall.

She wept. Big, wracking sobs shaking her body, without knowing why she was crying.

She curled up on the sofa and listened to the silence surrounding her. Doogie softly licked her hand and looked at her with worried, searching eyes.

After a while, she pulled herself off the sofa and out of her funk. She reached for her cell phone and called Scott.

He listened as she sobbed, recounting the conversation with Trisha. He was sympathetic and supportive, as always, the rock she needed in this storm, and she loved him all the more for it. They agreed to talk about it some more when he got home that evening.

Around lunchtime, her mood was brightening and as she ate her salmon and veggie bake, she scrolled through her emails. She stopped abruptly as one email caught her eye.

Her breath caught in her throat as she saw the name of the sender.

> From: Joseph Graham
> Subject: Meeting in Los Angeles
> Dear Christina,

I understand that my people at the publishing house have already reached out to you with regard to your manuscript. I would be interested in meeting with you in person to discuss a mentoring relationship.

I will be in Los Angeles on Wednesday, May 6th. I suggest that we meet at Musso & Frank for dinner. I will see you there at 6pm. Please confirm so my assistant can book my usual table.

> Regards,
> J. Graham

Chrissy sat, speechless, staring at the email.

4

Time
Tuesday, April 28th - Pasadena

Ed looked up from the screen of his mobile phone as the door to the coffee shop opened.

He waved at Emily as she scanned the tables.

She headed over, and he stood to greet her.

"Hi," he said, pulling the chair out for her.

"Hi. I'm sorry I'm late. The traffic on the 405 was the worst," she said, hanging her purse on the back of the chair and taking off her suit jacket.

"I ordered you a spinach and feta croissant and a latte. I figured you might not have had time to grab lunch yet. They might be a bit cold by now, though," Ed said, pushing the plate and mug across the table towards her.

"You're a lifesaver! Thank you so much. I've been on the go since I left the house this morning and I'm starving. I don't have much time, though. I'm meeting Brody in downtown in an hour and parking is a bitch, so I need extra time to find somewhere to leave the car."

Emily grabbed the croissant and took a big bite, shutting her eyes as she appreciated the delicious flavors.

Ed cleared his throat. "So, um, how was the factory tour?"

"It was good," Emily said, covering her mouthful and reaching for the latte. "They definitely understand our requirements, and I like their QA processes. They specialize in small product lines with MOQs under ten thousand, so that will work in the short term, but I need to look at whether they can scale as we grow."

"What? You lost me at MOQ's. I can't keep up with all this jargon," Ed said with a smile.

"Shit, I'm sorry. I forget that not everyone lives and breathes this stuff like I do. It stands for 'Minimum Order Quantity'. At the beginning we want to be able to order in small batches, maybe five to ten thousand SKU's at a time, but as we grow, the business we'll need more, so we need to know they can scale when we need it."

"That makes sense," Ed nodded.

"Anyway, enough about work. What did you want to talk about?" Emily said, tipping her head slightly in an enquiring manner while opening her mouth wide to take another huge bite of the croissant.

Ed swallowed. Taking a deep breath, he said,

"Emily, we both have to acknowledge that things haven't been going well for a while now. I mean, they've been 'fine', but something has been missing. Agreed?"

Emily put down the croissant.

Ed moved in his seat, and then continued.

"I've been trying to talk to you about it, but you're so wrapped up in this new job that…"

"I know, it's been crazy," Emily said, cutting across him, "but hopefully in the next couple of months…"

"Can you let me finish, please?" Ed said in a steely tone.

Emily stopped, a shadow of concern crossing her face.

Ed cleared his throat and continued.

"As I was saying, I've been trying to talk to you for a

couple of weeks now, but it looks like this might be our only opportunity. I've decided that it would be best if we took some time away from each other to work out how we feel."

Emily frowned, perplexed.

"What do you mean?"

Ed looked down at his hands for a moment, turning his coffee cup this way and that.

"Ed? What do you mean?" Emily said, the sharp edge of alarm in her voice.

Ed raised his eyes to hers, tears welling in them. Emily's heartbeat began to quicken as she felt a cold shiver run through her.

"Emily," Ed said, slowly. "I'm moving out."

There was silence as Emily stared at him, uncomprehending.

Ed continued, "I've found an apartment in Pasadena. It has three bedrooms, so there's room for the kids. We can split childcare responsibilities, and I can still pick them up after school every day."

Emily was stunned.

"Wh-what the hell are you talking about?" she stuttered. "You can't just move out. How are you going to pay rent? I'm the only one working!"

Ed sighed as he looked at her, his eyes uncharacteristically cold.

"Wow. That's where you go to first, is it?" he said, a sharp edge in his voice.

Emily could feel the anger rising in her. "Yes it is. Because supporting this family has been my responsibility since you lost your job, remember? I have no idea what the hell you're talking about, or where all of this is coming from."

Ed sat forward in his chair, his eyes flashing. "Thank you for that, Emily. Really nice. But I seem to remember that I was looking for another job when this opportunity came along for you, and before we knew it, here we were, part of the 'Emily Show' whether we wanted to be or not."

Emily's jaw clenched as she met his glare.

"Fuck you, Ed." she hissed, trying to keep her voice low, aware that several customers around the coffee shop were starting to take notice of them. "Don't twist this to make it my fault. You were more than happy to come out to sunny California and let me take the wheel. How do you plan to pay for this apartment of yours?"

"I got a consulting job," he said with venom. "Apparently my skills are still relevant in the market."

Emily felt the wind go out of her. This was happening. It was real. Her anger cracked and turned to grief.

"Do you really mean this?" She said, her breath becoming ragged. "This can't be happening. You're right, things haven't been right for a while, but maybe we could go to counseling or something? It's just so fast, I don't understand."

Ed's face softened. "I'm so sorry, Emily. I never intended to hurt you, I promise. But I need this. We both do. We can't go on like this."

"Yes, we can," argued Emily. "We have it better than most couples out there. We have fun as a family and at least we care about each other, don't we?" she pleaded.

The pain in Ed's eyes was evident. "Yes, of course I care about you. I love you. You and the kids. But I can't do this anymore. I need some time on my own to work things out."

"What 'things'? What are you talking about?"

Ed dropped his eyes.

"My lease starts this coming weekend," he said quietly.

"What the fuck, Ed?" Emily said, her voice loud and sharp.

Ed looked around self-consciously. "Keep your voice down. People are looking at us."

The hot rage was back, as Emily said, "You know what? I

don't give a shit. Let them look! My whole fucking life is imploding around me right now, so excuse me if I seem a little agitated!"

"I've been trying to tell you for weeks, it's just never been a good time."

Emily suddenly felt a stab in her heart as the faces of her children flashed into her mind.

"If you're really going to do this, then we need to tell the children sooner rather than later. We don't have much time as it is."

Ed rubbed a hand across his face.

"I know. Maybe we could tell them tonight? I never meant for it to be such short notice. It's just been so hard to find the time to sit down with you alone and talk."

Emily took a deep breath.

"I'm not going to make this any harder on them than it needs to be. I don't know why you're doing this, and I can't fathom what it could possibly be that you need to 'work out', but let's at least be civilized in front of them, shall we?"

Ed's eyes filled with tears again.

"Thank you, Emily. And I'm sorry for everything."

Emily could feel the tears rising in her own eyes, but before they could take hold, she stood and collected her jacket and purse from the back of the chair.

"I gotta go. I'll see you at home later, yes?"

"Yes. It's almost pickup time anyway, so I should leave in a minute. Drive safely, Emily." Ed's eyes glistened.

Emily turned and headed to the door.

She sat in her car in the parking lot and wept. Hard, angry sobs shuddered through her body as she bashed the steering wheel.

Then she took a long, stiff breath and shook herself. She didn't have time for this right now. She needed to pull herself together for her meeting with Brody.

5

Sandcastles
Wednesday, May 6th - London

Liz sat on the bench under the gigantic oak tree, watching as Naomi played in the sand.

It was late afternoon, and the park was empty. The earlier symphony of children at play, laughter and squeals as siblings chased each other around the play structure, had now dissipated, leaving only the sound of Naomi's soft, sing-song voice drifting on the breeze.

She sat alone in the sandbox, engrossed in a complex imaginary game with witches and townsfolk made from twigs and leaves.

Liz felt her heart swell to see the imagination flowing out of this little angel before her. She pictured her as an adult; tall, elegant and self assured. She would be well read, with a passion for both justice and possibility. This little girl would change the world.

Liz closed her eyes and tilted her face to the sun, catching the last warmth of the evening's rays. The weather had been so changeable recently, bitter and blustery one day, soft and forgiving the next. But today had been beautiful; a glorious,

English Spring day with all the hope and promise of new life and happy summer days to come.

Naomi looked up from her game, her eyes shining as she called to Liz to join the fun.

Liz smiled as she stood.

Walking over, she kicked off her shoes and sat next to Naomi in the warm sand. They chatted and laughed as they schemed the next exciting chapter in Naomi's epic tale.

Liz traced the edge of the township where the fields ended and the dark woods began, and she thrilled Naomi with scary stories of the mysterious creatures that lurked deep in the shadows of the forest.

She glanced up to see if Lauren would like to join, but she was still texting on her phone, so Liz turned back to the little storyteller beside her.

As they played, a butterfly fluttered past them and came to rest on the play structure nearby. Naomi put a hand on Liz's arm to still her, and, holding her breath, she watched it intently.

Its wings flickered open, the vibrant red and black pattern flashing in the sunlight, before it took flight again and landed, much to their surprise, on Liz's shoulder.

"Auntie Liz!" Naomi exclaimed in a hushed whisper. "It chose you!"

Liz laughed softly as she marveled at its beauty. The rich velvet wings, both fragile and bold, with an intricate, transcendent beauty that belied its fragility, and for a moment Liz thought of Rachel.

A moment later, it lifted into the sky, flying towards the sun. Liz shaded her eyes but lost sight of it in the sharp rays of the blinding light.

Laughing and blinking, they hugged each other and grinned, then Naomi jumped up and ran to her mother to tell her what had happened.

"And then it just sat on Auntie Liz's shoulder this close," Naomi exclaimed, putting her nose right up against her mothers.

Lauren laughed and pushed her back gently.

"Wow, that's pretty cool, isn't it? Butterflies are the best." She said as she hugged her little girl.

Naomi ran off with another game in mind, and soon she was engrossed in a fantasy about butterfly fairies who lived in the trees and promised to grant your wishes if only you wished hard enough.

Liz and Lauren watched her from their bench under the oak.

"Thank you, Lauren." said Liz, her eyes full of warmth and contentment. "It's been so long since we've been here that I'd forgotten all about this park. We used to come here all the time, and Naomi seems so happy to be back here again."

Lauren smiled, but her expression held the weight of dark clouds rolling across an otherwise clear sky.

As Liz looked at her, she could sense there was something she'd been waiting to say.

"Hey, you OK?" Liz asked. "You've been really quiet since we got here."

Lauren bit her lip.

"Liz. I need to talk to you about something."

Liz went cold. Deep down she had known this was coming, but hadn't wanted to admit it, even to herself.

Lauren took a deep breath and continued. "So, me and Gary were talking, and he asked me if I want to move in with him. Me and Naomi. Into his mum's house." Lauren's brow furrowed, and she squirmed a little. Looking at the ground, she said, "It's not perfect, but it means that we can save up a bit and then get our own place. And his mum said that she'll babysit when we're at work and pick Naomi up from school and stuff."

After a moment, Lauren looked up to meet Liz's gaze, her eyes both defensive and pleading.

She continued, "It's not that we're not happy living with you. Naomi loves you, and I don't know what I would have done without your help, but it was only ever meant to be temporary, yeah?"

Liz felt her heart crack and shatter. She was heartbroken, but not surprised. This was inevitable, after all.

"It's OK, Lauren," Liz said, putting her hand gently on Lauren's leg. "You're right, it was only ever meant to be a short-term solution." She inhaled deeply and asked, "So, when do you think you'll move out?"

Lauren smiled with relief, sat up, and began talking enthusiastically about the plans she and Gary had made.

Liz realized as she watched her young companion that this must have been a subject of conversation for quite some time. She also realized that Lauren had been holding back on having this conversation, hesitating in order to not cause Liz pain or distress. It was as if Liz was Lauren's mother and Lauren had been concerned about leaving and making her an 'empty nester.'

Suddenly Liz felt older than her years. She wanted to cry, but she couldn't find the justification for it. This is what should happen, after all. This was the natural course of events. Now Liz could go back to her life before she even knew about Lauren and Naomi.

But she wasn't that person anymore. And in that moment, she realized that she didn't know who she was, or what she wanted from life.

Liz smiled and nodded as Lauren discussed the logistics and challenges that came with moving into Gary's mum's house, all the while wondering where this left her.

After Lauren was spent with her plans, the excitement dropped from her face and was replaced by an expression of concern.

"Are you going to be OK, Liz?" she asked softly. "Are you going to stay in the house?"

Liz tried to smile.

"I'm not sure," she said with forced enthusiasm. "It won't be the same without you guys, and I don't need all that space if it's just me. The lease is up in a couple of months, so maybe I'll move back to the city? It'll be an easier commute for work."

Lauren's brow furrowed, and she said hesitantly, "I can pay something toward the rent for the next couple of months if you want?"

"No, it's fine, honestly. You'll have enough to think about setting up home with Gary. Don't worry about it. I've got it covered."

"Oh, OK. If you're sure," Lauren said with obvious relief. And then she added, "And you've gotta come over and spend time with us once we're settled in. Gary's mum said you're welcome anytime. She says you're a saint for what you've done for the two of us and everything."

Liz smiled and thanked Lauren for the invitation.

In silence, they sat and watched Naomi for a while as she built her sandcastles and wove her tales.

She felt the sorrow sinking into her heart. Lauren was building a life for herself, and Liz would have to do the same. But where would she go from here? What was next for her?

Smiling to herself, she wondered if Naomi's fairies would grant her a wish. If only she could find the right words to utter.

Then Lauren's phone buzzed, and she shouted over to the precious little storyteller.

"Alright then, time to go, Nay-Nay; it's almost dinnertime."

Naomi ran up, chattering and beaming, and reached out to

Liz.

Liz swept her up and balanced her on her hip, planting a kiss on her rosy cheek.

Naomi giggled and shouted, "Horsey ride back to the car!"

Liz smiled and complied, as always, and as the sun set behind the trees, they all headed for home.

6

Musso & Frank
Wednesday, May 6th - Los Angeles

Chrissy opened the front door of the restaurant and stepped inside, leaving the golden light of the California evening behind her. She blinked, her eyes adjusting to the shadowy, muted tones of the historic establishment, with its aromas of warm mahogany and wood smoke.

She had never visited Musso & Frank before, but she was well aware of its significance in the history of old Hollywood.

From the 1920s onwards, the stars of the silver screen would come here to dine, to gossip and to drink Manhattans as they signed studio contracts, and discuss the movies that would change the course of cinematic history.

Chrissy's breath was shallow in the dim light, as if she feared disturbing the enigmatic ghosts of these movie giants.

She half expected to see Humphrey Bogart sitting on a stool at the bar, a cigarette between his fingers, or Marilyn Monroe, laughing and chatting with Joe DiMaggio, her low cut dress sparkling as she sipped a glass of champagne.

She was nervous to meet her father, this stranger with

whom she shared nothing more than genetics, but in that moment she forgot her own discomfort and drifted away into the reveries of a glittering past.

"Welcome to Musso and Frank, ma'am. Do you have a reservation?" asked the concierge.

"Oh. Yes," said Chrissy, pulled back to the present. "I'm meeting someone for dinner. Joseph Graham?"

"Yes, ma'am," he nodded. "Mr Graham is at the bar. He asked that you be seated when you arrive, and he will join you momentarily. May I walk you to his booth?"

The concierge signaled for Chrissy to follow him, which she did, eyes wide, taking in the rich decor of this Hollywood shrine.

The wood-paneled walls gave the restaurant a heavy, luxurious feel, broken only at the low ceiling where a faded mural ran the length of the room. The Art déco light fixtures, obviously original, offered a warm glow, adding to the ambiance. This was an island out of time. A living piece of history.

Although it was early evening on a weekday, the place was a hive of activity. 'Industry types' sat opposite each other in the scarlet leather booths, devouring steaks and burgers while deep in conversation. Chrissy tried to catch snippets of their conversations as she walked past. Were they screenwriters? Or producers? Possibly discussing the next Hollywood blockbuster?

They stopped by a booth, and the waiter signaled for Chrissy to take a seat. She thanked him and slid in along the high-backed bench. The red leather of the booth was soft as silk and refreshingly cool.

With a nod, the concierge slipped away, replaced almost immediately by a waiter wearing a crisp red jacket with black lapels, who placed a bottle of water and some freshly baked bread in front of her. The smell of the bread curled towards her, making her hungry despite her nerves.

"Mr Graham will be with you momentarily," the waiter said, smiling warmly while pouring her a glass of water.

She thanked him and took a sip of the iced water, her mind still wandering through iconic scenes from 'Some Like it Hot' and 'Casablanca'.

"Ah. You must be Christina."

Chrissy jumped and looked up into the face of a tall, burly man with thick, silvery gray hair and an uncompromising manner. His face was square with a neatly trimmed beard and mustache, and he reminded her of a gentleman explorer, ready to set forth into the jungles of South America.

In one hand he held a heavy square glass filled with an amber liquid, a large ice cube clinked against the side of it as he flashed her a smile and held out the other hand to shake. His hand dwarfed hers, and after a swift, forceful shake, he took the seat opposite and waved for the waiter.

"Call me Joe. Did you order a drink yet?" he asked.

"No, but…"

"Tony, she'll have a martini, and I'll have another bourbon on the rocks."

"Actually, I think…"

"You've never been here, correct? Then you must try the martini. They're famous for it."

Chrissy watched as Tony strode off towards the bar. Apparently, the decision had been made for her.

"So," Joseph Graham said, turning to her. "Tell me about yourself."

Chrissy swallowed and looked at her hands. Where to begin? Why did this feel like an interview?

"Well," she started, "I'm married with two children. Josh is sixteen, and Jackie's thirteen."

"No, tell me about your writing," said Joe abruptly.

"Um, well, I recently finished writing my first novel. It's

loosely based on my close friends, and it's dedicated to someone very dear to us, that we lost unexpectedly."

"Hmm. What's the genre?"

"Well, um. Women's fiction?"

"Is that a question?"

"Sorry?" Chrissy was confused.

"You said it like it's a question. You should really know what genre you're writing in. It's pretty fundamental to any level of success in publishing. You're aware of that, yes?"

There was an awkward silence, relieved by the arrival of Tony and the drinks.

Chrissy took a sip to steady her nerves.

"I understand you write military and spy novels."

"Yes. Espionage and political thrillers. I've written several international bestsellers. Have you read any of my work?"

Chrissy's cheeks reddened as she shook her head.

"No. I haven't had the chance."

"Hmm," said Joe, draining his drink and waving at Tony for another.

Chrissy scrambled for something to say.

"I was wondering," she began, "why did you decide to contact me after all this time? How did you know I'd written a book?"

Joe spun his glass between his fingers before answering.

"I heard you were looking for an agent. The publishing world is surprisingly small, and I've been in this business for a long time. I was interested in what you might come up with, so I asked for a copy of your manuscript. There are some rudimentary mistakes that clearly show your inexperience, but there's some potential there. That's why I spoke to my people at the publishing house."

"And you're willing to mentor me?" Chrissy asked.

"That depends."

"On what?"

"On how committed you are. There's a difference between writing and becoming a writer. Most people are not cut out for it."

Chrissy sipped her drink, not sure what to say next.

She realized she should be indignant, mad even, that this man whom she had never met, who was her biological father but who had never shown any interest in her in the past, should now be 'interviewing' her for a position as his mentee. But she didn't feel anger, only a sense of awkward intrigue.

"Let's talk next steps," said Joe, breaking her train of thought. "I think it would be best if you come and stay with me in Scotland."

"What?" said Chrissy, totally lost. "Why Scotland? I thought you were American?"

Joe snorted with laughter.

"Yes, I am an American, born and raised in the Midwest and still a patriot through and through, but I call Scotland home now. I have a little place, well, a large place actually, in the Borders not far from Edinburgh. It's a hunting lodge with land where I fish and hunt deer and grouse, and write, and no one bothers me."

"It sounds wonderful."

"It is. And not many people get an invitation, so consider yourself lucky, young lady."

Tony placed another bourbon in front of him and swept away the empty glass.

"You should come next month, for at least a couple of weeks. May is beautiful in the Borders and I'm between projects right now, so we can focus on your work and on learning the craft."

Chrissy's mind raced.

"I'm not sure I could come for that long, or at such short notice. I have commitments here. My husband is a surgeon and I have to be here for the kids."

"I thought you said they were teenagers. Can't they take care of themselves? I certainly could at that age."

"Well, I could talk to Scott, my husband. Maybe we could work something out?"

"Attagirl. That's the stuff." Joe said, raising his glass to her and draining it. "We'll have some uninterrupted time to work, and then we'll see what kind of writer you really are, won't we?"

It sounded vaguely like a threat.

"I'm starving. Let's order," said Joe with aplomb.

As he worked his way through a wedge salad and a huge steak, accompanied by yet another bourbon, Joe regaled Chrissy with tales of his time in Vietnam.

She picked at her grilled trout and mixed vegetables, nerves stealing away her normally healthy appetite.

She wasn't sure what to think of this man. She had no connection to him, had never even thought to consider who her father might be. But here he was in front of her.

Her father.

And he was offering to help her become a successful author.

She nodded and smiled as she listened to his stories while trying to work through the logistics of how she was going to make this whole thing work. Could she really go to Scotland to learn from him? And if she decided not to go, would she regret the missed opportunity to advance her writing career?

Yes. She would go. She would jump into the unknown and see where this relationship would lead her.

7

Plans
Saturday, May 9th - Pasadena

Chrissy threw herself down on the living room sofa with a relieved sigh. She'd been on the go all day and she was ready for a break.

She'd got up early, as always, to walk Doogie, a ritual that provided a moment of calm in her otherwise hectic day.

The streets were deserted; the silence broken only by the rhythmic ticking of the yard sprinklers and the delicate birdsong from the oak trees above.

At the end of the road, she had stopped to admire the golden ridge of the San Gabriel mountains, and look down at the golf course below.

Thin wisps of mist still lay across the grass between the carefully placed trees, a delicate muslin shroud waiting to be pulled back by the sun, revealing the beauty of the manicured greens.

The damp air held the sweet scent of orange blossom and jasmine, and Chrissy breathed it in, grateful for the feeling of peace it brought.

When she opened the front door, the house was already

full of noise and energy.

Josh had a bad case of the jitters brought on by the imminent state championships he was competing in, and that he swore he wasn't ready for.

Jackie's gymnastics competitions were also ramping up, and the two of them were at each other's throats more than normal because of the stress of it all.

Chrissy had spent the rest of the day shuttling the kids from one destination to the next without a break.

As she turned the car around once again, she cranked up the a/c against the rising heat and sighed with exasperation. At least Josh would be able to drive himself around soon, if he could pass his driver's test, although Chrissy worried about him unsupervised behind the wheel, as he could be so easily distracted..

It was now past lunchtime and the various sports commitments were wrapping up for the day. Both kids had organized rides home, so Chrissy sat on the sofa and reached for her glass of wine as she hit Liz's number on her cell. She couldn't wait to catch up with her old friend.

"Hey girl!" answered Liz, "give me a second, OK?"

Liz stepped outside into the damp night air, pulling her sweater around her to guard against the chill. The weather in London had been blustery and rainy all day, although now the rain had finally stopped and the clouds were rolling away, allowing the stars to blink through against the night sky.

Normally, she would sit in the living room to take a call, but Naomi had been struggling to get to sleep at night ever since Lauren told her they were moving out, and Liz didn't want to disturb her any more than necessary. Plus, this way she could sneak a smoke. No harm now, after all, she thought with a sharp pang.

Chrissy's voice came across the line, light and bubbly, "It's so great to hear from you! It's been too long, I'm so sorry. It's been an insane couple of months."

"Same here," said Liz with a grimace.

"I have news!" said Chrissy excitedly. "It looks like I might have a publishing deal and a mentor!"

"That's fantastic! Tell me everything," Liz said, dragging on her cigarette, and she listened as Chrissy filled her in on recent events.

"Hang on a minute," said Liz, suspicion in her voice. "This famous author just happened to find out you'd written a novel? And then it turns out that he's your biological father, and he wants you to go to Scotland so he can 'mentor' you? That sounds kinda shady to me. No offense, Chrissy, but aren't you even a little wary about why he's suddenly coming out of the woodwork like this? What do you even know about this guy?"

Chrissy made a face.

"To be honest, it never really dawned on me to be curious about him until now," she said. "Mum and I were such a tight unit growing up that I could never imagine anyone else being a part of that. She didn't keep him a secret or anything. There just wasn't much to tell. She said she met him at the Glastonbury Festival in 1979 when she was in her twenties. She told me they danced and laughed and 'fell in love with each other's souls'."

"Bleh," said Liz, and wrinkled her nose in disgust.

"Anyway, the story goes that they parted as quickly as they met, and then Mum found out she was pregnant. She always knew I would be special because the name of the festival that year was 'The Year of the Child'. Apparently, he asked her to marry him, but she said no, and then they lost touch. That's all I've ever known, and that's all I've ever wanted to know, to be honest. I'd always thought of him as a shaggy-haired hippie type who was pretty insignificant in the grand scheme of things."

"Did you know he was an American?" Liz asked.

"Nope. I'd assumed he was English. But again, I never actually asked."

"How did he know you'd written a book?" asked Liz.

"I'm not sure," answered Chrissy, exasperated by all the questions. "Maybe he's been spying on me all this time. But even if he has, who cares? Now he's offering to help me, and he might be just what I need to become the writer I've always wanted to be."

Liz dragged on her cigarette, unconvinced.

"Anyway, what's new with you?" Chrissy asked, a little deflated, and ready to change the subject.

Liz heaved a heavy sigh before saying,

"Lauren and Naomi are moving out."

"No!" Chrissy exclaimed. "How come?"

Liz shrugged, then explained,

"Lauren got back together with an old boyfriend she was dating before she met Xander. They ran into each other at a party on New Year's Eve, and they've been pretty much inseparable ever since. He seems like a decent enough guy, but they're both so painfully young. Now they're talking about maybe getting married, and his mum has agreed to let Lauren and Naomi move into her house until they can get a place of their own."

"Oh, Liz. I'm so sorry. When are they moving?"

"In a couple of weeks." She dragged on the last of the cigarette and then stubbed it out. "I suppose it was only ever going to be a short-term solution, but I'm going to miss them so much."

"What are you going to do?" Chrissy asked, genuine concern in her voice.

Liz swallowed hard.

"I don't know. I suppose I'll get an apartment in the city. That way, I'll be closer to work."

Chrissy took a deep breath and blew it out.

"There must be something in the water. First Emily, and now you."

"What do you mean?" asked Liz.

"You know. Ed moving out."

"What?" said Liz, stunned.

"Oh shit. Didn't she tell you? She said she was going to call you and tell you. Ed moved out last weekend. He's renting an apartment. He said he needed 'space to think'."

"What the fuck does that mean?" Liz asked, shocked.

"I don't know. I knew things had been a bit rocky for them since they moved to the States, but I never imagined it was this bad. And Ed, of all people? I could never imagine him doing anything like that."

"Did they have a fight or something? How did it happen?"

"Honestly, I don't know. When Emily told me, I think she was still in shock. I've called her since, but she's been acting kinda cagey, and always says she's too busy to talk because of work. I'm actually a little concerned about her. I hope she's doing ok."

"I can't believe she didn't tell me," Liz said, a mixture of resentment and concern welling up in her.

"Well, like I said, she's been acting kinda weird about it. I suppose we all deal with stuff in our own way. I'm sure she'll reach out if she needs us. In the meantime, I'm going to give her some space. Plus, I'm going to be in Scotland for a couple of weeks, so I'll check in with her when I get back."

"So you're definitely going to go, are you? Even though this dude could turn out to be a complete nutter?"

Chrissy squirmed.

"I really want to. It could be amazing. But you're right, I am a little worried. He lives in the middle of nowhere, and I don't want to be all on my own with nothing but sheep and birds for miles. The countryside looks beautiful, and I've never been to Edinburgh so I'd love to go and look around, but his hunting lodge is very remote and I'm dreading being stuck there for two weeks if the two of us don't get on well."

"Actually, that sounds lovely," said Liz. "Just a book and a cup of tea, and no bastards hassling you to do stuff."

Chrissy suddenly sat bolt upright, her eyes wide.

"Oooh, Liz!"

"Nope. I know that voice, and whatever you're thinking, the answer is no."

"Liz, come with me! Come with me to Scotland!"

"Don't be ridiculous. I have a job, Chrissy. I can't just go swanning off to some hunting lodge in Nowheresville."

"But you deserve a vacation, and you haven't taken any time off in ages. It'll do you good to clear your head and take some time for yourself. You can read, and run, and we'll leave you alone to relax. And you can protect me if my estranged father turns out to be a machete wielding psychopath."

Liz snorted with amusement. It was an absurd idea, but at some level, she wanted this. Needed this.

"Hmm. I'll think about it. Just don't do the tiny clapping thing, OK?"

"Ok, I promise," Chrissy said, letting out a silent peel of air claps. "I'll call you next week to coordinate, yes?"

"Hmph," replied Liz in a non-committal tone, but she could already feel her spirits lifting.

8

Childcare
Friday, June 5th - Santa Monica

"I'm sorry, Ed, but I really can't get out of it," Emily said, trying not to let the irritation bleed into her voice. "I'm the lead on this project and they expect me to be in the meeting."

She was hot and stressed and already running late, and the traffic on the 405 was as awful as ever. She needed to get to the office, and the last thing she needed right now was another 'logistics' conversation with Ed.

It had been a month since he'd moved out and they were making it work, somehow, although it hadn't been easy. Emily was trying to give Ed the space he needed, but she hadn't fully appreciated just how much she'd relied on him over the last year to keep the house running and take care of the kids. Now they were both working, it was
a constant juggling act to manage school drop offs and pickups and extracurriculars, and Emily couldn't wait until Ed was ready to come home so their lives could get back to normal.

Ed's voice came across the speaker, curt and cold.

"I have commitments too, you know, Emily. You can't keep

doing this. It's not just me you're letting down, it's the kids as well."

"I am well aware of that, Ed," she snapped, "and I am trying my hardest here. There's no need to pile emotional blackmail on top of it all." She signaled to change lanes. "Fuck! Sorry, not you, Ed. This asshole won't let me get over, and I'm going to miss my exit."

Emily leaned on the horn and flicked the driver in the red Buick the finger.

"While I have you on the line," Ed said, "did you sign Philip's 'water safety' form for camp next week? He needs signatures from both parents before they'll let him swim."

"*Shit,*" thought Emily. "No, I meant to do it yesterday, but it slipped my mind. I'll do it tonight."

"He's asked you twice now and he'll be disappointed if he misses out."

"I know, I know. I'll do it tonight, ok?" she said, taking the exit off the freeway and joining the bumper to bumper Santa Monica traffic.

"Oh, and Sophie told me she doesn't want to do the theater arts camp next week," continued Ed. "She found out they'll be performing 'Peter Pan', and that girls are not allowed to try out to be a Lost Boy or Peter, they can only try out for mermaids or Indians, and she thinks it's sexist so she's boycotting. Can you talk to her? I'm getting nowhere."

"Oh, for Christ's sake," Emily said, feeling the sweat forming on her top lip even though the air was cranked as low as possible. "Fine, I'll talk to her, but she has to go. All the other camps will be booked up by now."

Emily weaved through the traffic, skipping through the traffic lights just before they turned red.

"Maybe she could do backstage?" said Ed, obviously thinking it through as he spoke. "I didn't think to suggest that, but that might work."

"Yeah, sounds great. Tell her to do that," Emily said as she pulled into a parking spot in the underground parking structure of the Apex building.

She flicked off the engine and grabbed her purse and briefcase. "So anyway, can you pick the kids up next Friday? I really can't miss the meeting," she said as half-walked, half-ran through the parking lot and hammered the elevator button.

Ed sighed, and Emily heard the exasperation in his voice.

"Fine," he said. "I'll pick them up from school, but you have to be at my place by 6pm to pick them up. I can't watch them any later than that because I have plans."

Emily was sorely tempted to say, "What plans could you possibly have on a Friday night that don't involve drinking a glass of cabernet sauvignon and watching the food channel," but instead she swallowed and said in a pleasant tone, "Thank you, Ed, I owe you one. And I'll try to make this the last time, I promise."

Taking a deep breath, she smoothed her hair, stepped into the elevator, and pressed the button for the top floor.

These last couple of months had been crazy, and she felt like she was holding everything together by a thread. Was Ed right? Was she letting the kids down? She loved being back at work, engaging her brain and working on complex problems, but was it to the detriment of her children?

She heard her mother's critical voice whispering to her, saying that she was being selfish, putting her own needs ahead of those of her family.

But they were here in California because of her, weren't they? And everyone loved it here. They had a new life because of what she'd achieved, and if she played her cards right, she could be in a senior management position before long. Working at Apex, she could earn enough money to put the kids through college and build a nice nest egg for herself and Ed's retirement. She was proud she was able to offer that to them, if only they could keep the train on the rails long enough.

As the elevator headed up towards the top floor, she thought of Ed and bit her lip.

She hadn't wanted to press him on the real reason for his moving out, and he hadn't offered any more explanation than 'needing time to think'.

Yes, if she was being honest with herself, their relationship had been strained as of late, but with three young kids and an international move, that was no surprise. She couldn't quite admit, even to herself, that things hadn't been right for a long time. It was never a bad relationship. They never fought, and they were always a good team, but there was something missing. Something intangible. She wondered if they should go to couple's therapy.

"Anyway, focus up," she said to herself, shaking her arms and taking a deep breath. "I am a strong, capable businesswoman, in charge of my own destiny. Watch out world, here I come!"

As the door opened, she lifted her head and took a commanding step into the hallway, only to find her heel stuck in the gap between the elevator and the sliding door.

Stumbling and cursing, her phone and briefcase flying in different directions, she did her best to regain her composure.

Gathering her belongings, she looked up, right into the face of Brody. Her heart sank as she saw the amused expression on his face.

"Morning," he said with a grin.

"Hi," she replied, her cheeks burning.

"I should have the maintenance guy check that elevator," he said, his eyes sparkling with humor.

"No, it was me. I was rushing."

"I see. How was San Fernando? You got time to give me a quick update?"

"Not really," thought Emily, but she smiled brightly and said, "Of course. Although I was due to meet with the finance team in fifteen minutes."

"They can wait," said Brody, smiling at her and holding open the door of the conference room so she could step through.

They sat in the leather chairs as Brody's assistant, Serena, delivered a mug of coffee for each of them.

"Thank you," Emily said to Serena, only to be met with an icy stare.

Serena reminded Emily of a Siamese cat; thin, painstakingly beautiful, and full of silent judgment.

Emily felt a little nervous at first. Talking with Brody always had that effect on her, but as she settled into the discussion, her nerves melted away. She knew this material intimately, and she felt confident that she had done a thorough job on this research.

She had prepared a PowerPoint presentation with graphics that elegantly compared the pros and cons of each manufacturing facility, and she flicked through it on her laptop.

She talked with enthusiasm about 'throughput' and 'capacity utilization', but each time she looked up, Brody's eyes were fixed upon her, rather than the slide deck she had stayed up all night putting together.

She concluded with, "I believe that if the plant in Valencia can show us a consistent OEE and they come in with a reasonable bid on the project, we should go with them. What do you think?"

Brody was silent. He looked at her closely, a slight smile curving the edge of his lips.

Emily's pulse quickened.

"Um," she stuttered, looking back at her screen and trying to control the color rising in her cheeks, "I can pull up the raw data vs. the metrics if you'd like? To give you a better comparison of the top bidders?"

She was flustered, but she wasn't sure why. She looked down at her hands, cursing herself for being so unprofessional.

A smile broke through on Brody's face and he leaned forward, putting his hand on Emily's arm. A jolt of electricity ran through her, and she swallowed hard.

"You've done amazing work on this, Emily. Thorough and comprehensive, just the quality of work I knew you'd bring to this project. We're lucky to have you as part of the team."

Emily blushed.

"Thank you," she said.

"Setting this aside for a moment, I wanted to talk to you about something else if that's ok? I understand that you've been having some challenges at home. Is that correct?"

Emily felt the color drain from her face.

"Um, yes. I mean, it's been hard, but we're getting there. I haven't let it affect my work, though," she said, fighting the stirrings of defensiveness.

"No, not at all. I wouldn't even have known if Carly in HR hadn't mentioned it. I understand that you and your husband have separated. Is that correct? And apologies if I'm overstepping the mark. Obviously, you don't have to share anything that you're not comfortable talking about."

Emily's head was spinning.

"It's just temporary," she said in a small voice.

Brody leaned in close, and she looked into his crystal clear, ocean blue eyes. She wanted to get lost in those eyes, to feel his arms around her, feel his body next to hers, his skin on her skin.

She swallowed hard and withdrew her arm. Her body was

prickling with energy and her breath was shallow.

"If you need anything, anything at all, then I'm here for you," he whispered, holding her gaze.

The door to the meeting room opened, and Emily snapped back into an upright position.

From the doorway, Serena cleared her throat and said,

"I'm sorry to interrupt, sir, but Kolleen would like to speak with you, if you're free?"

Brody turned and gave her one of his killer smiles.

"Of course, Serena. I'll be right there."

Then he turned back to Emily and said,

"Will you be at the company conference at the end of the month? I was hoping you could make it."

"Yes," said Emily, still trying to compose herself. "Ed is going to take the kids for an extra couple of days so I can come along. I'm looking forward to it," she smiled, trying to look nonchalant.

"Great! You been to Vegas before?"

"No, never."

"It should be fun, then," Brody said with a wink. "It's a crazy town, but I love it. There's nowhere else quite like it. It's where fortunes are made and dreams come true. I'm looking forward to showing you around, if you'll let me?"

"I'm sure you'll be too busy," Emily said, trying to control her breathing. "After all, you are the CEO of the company and everyone will want to spend time with you."

"I'll always have time for you, Emily," Brody said. "I should see what Kolleen wants, but let's catch up again soon, yes?" he said, running his fingers through his sun-kissed blonde hair before turning and heading towards the door.

Emily flushed as he left the room.

Had he really been flirting with her? Or had she just imagined it? Did he mean what he said about showing her around Las Vegas?

Now she was both excited and a little scared about this trip.

She was still a married woman, after all.

9

Edinburgh
Saturday, June 6th - Scotland

Liz smiled and waved a hand above her head as she saw Chrissy coming through the exit doors of the arrivals hall at Edinburgh airport.

Chrissy looked tired and harassed after her overnight flight from Los Angeles. She pushed a cart loaded with a large suitcase, a matching rolling case, and a purse wrapped around her shoulders.

When she caught sight of Liz, her weariness lifted, and she brightened, waving back enthusiastically.

Liz pulled her rolling case to the edge of the barriers and abandoned it so she could sweep Chrissy up in a huge bear hug.

"Hey you," she said finally, holding her at arm's length so she could look at her, "it's so good to see you."

"You too!" said Chrissy, beaming, before making a face of mild disgust. "I'm sorry. I'm sure I must smell like a dead skunk. I hate long-haul flights, and that was a long flight."

"I'll say it was," agreed Liz. "Did you manage to sleep at all? Wow, girl, you didn't pack light, did you? How long are you planning on staying?"

"In my defense, I'm not used to the cold anymore, so I need layers, lots and lots of layers," Chrissy said, smiling and shrugging.

Liz pursed her lips and raised an eyebrow, but the warmth in her eyes gave away how happy she was to see her old friend.

They walked through the terminal, following the signs for the car rentals.

"Were you waiting long?" Chrissy asked, looking concerned.

"No, not at all. The flight from Heathrow to Edinburgh was only an hour and a half, so I was waiting for about twenty minutes. Now let's find this car rental place and get into the city center."

They selected a car and, with some difficulty, crammed all their luggage into it. Both the trunk and the backseat were full to maximum capacity.

"I always forget how much smaller the cars are here," said Chrissy.

"That's because we have old, narrow roads built by the Romans, not those five-lane highways you're used to. Our cars are not small, they are appropriately sized for their surroundings. You've been away too long, young lady," Liz said in a feigned reproachful manner.

"I can't wait to see the Scottish countryside and Edinburgh city as well. It's supposed to be incredible," Chrissy said, the excitement of it all breaking through her weariness. "I'm glad we decided to spend some time in the city before driving out to Joe's hunting lodge. It seems silly not to take the chance to see Edinburgh, and Kallenford is only about an hour or so away after all. Thank you again for driving, Liz. I feel far more comfortable with you behind the wheel."

"Me too! I'm not sure either of us would survive your

driving," Liz agreed with a snort, as she punched in the directions to Edinburgh city center.

They chatted as they drove through the winding roads, Chrissy updating Liz on all the dramas back home in California, but as they reached the city outskirts, she grew quiet and her eyes widened.

Cars whizzed in all directions through the narrow streets, buses merging from the left narrowly missing fearless bicyclists who weaved between them like bees darting from flower to flower. The roundabouts and filter lanes made her dizzy and a little overwhelmed. It always took a day or two to re-acclimatize to the traffic in Britain, so different from the wide roads and freeways of Pasadena.

"You ok?" asked Liz.

"Yeah. I'm just really glad you're driving. This is crazy."

Liz chuckled as she maneuvered her way through the congested streets.

Chrissy checked the GPS on her phone and said, "According to this, we should be coming into 'Edinburgh New Town' right about now."

They looked about them at the rows and rows of tall, elegant sandstone townhouses towering above them. Guarded by ornate iron railings that separated them from the pedestrians on the pavement, the buildings rose to the sky, four, sometimes five stories high, with attic rooms protruding from their steeply sloping roofs. They were grand and imposing, standing to attention with a bristle of chimneys on each of their tiled roofs. They reminded Chrissy of the old brownstone homes in New York, except that these buildings were gray and etched with soot, like soldiers returning from the battlefield.

"This is 'new town'? Really? It doesn't look very new to me," Liz said.

Chrissy laughed and said, "Well, I googled it earlier and it said that this part of the city is Georgian and was built in the 1700s, as opposed to the 'old town' which is medieval. So technically, this is newer, I suppose?"

Chrissy swiveled her head, taking in the sights as they navigated their way towards the center of the city.

Her research had told her that Castle Rock, the craggy cliff face and seat of Edinburgh Castle, had been inhabited for over 3,000 years. The rugged, brooding hulk of this dormant volcano dominated the landscape, and set the tone for the medieval settlement that would eventually become Edinburgh.

The castle, constructed from Craigleith sandstone, showed none of the artistic beauty of other European fortifications. This was a fortress, first and foremost, a stronghold that made no pretensions to be otherwise.

The city itself grew from the castle, like a huge prehistoric sea monster with the castle as its head. The raised spine became known as the Royal Mile, snaking its way down the hill to the tip of its tail, the location of Holyrood House. The ribcage took the form of small alleyways known as 'closes' and 'wynds' that protruded off the Royal Mile in both directions before dropping to the valley below.

The people of Edinburgh had taken care to protect themselves from marauders by building walls to encase the city. With these walls, often twenty feet tall, and the natural barrier afforded by the Nor Loch, the city's safety should have been ensured. However, as Edinburgh grew, it became clear that the beast was trapped. As the population continued to grow, the city strained and fought against its self-imposed confinement. Trapped, it's only option was to build upwards, creating wooden tenement buildings often fifteen stories high, precarious and subject to regular devastating fires. Desperate for space, the inhabitants began to dig into the bedrock itself, creating a series of underground tunnels and vaults that were soon inhabited by the poor and destitute, hidden from the world above.

Even after the city burst through the walls and spilled into what would be known as 'Edinburgh New Town', the overcrowding was extreme, and with raw sewage pouring through the streets and into the Nor Loch, disease was rampant. It's no wonder the city became known as 'Auld Reekie'.

Chrissy looked up, her heart beating faster as they approached the Old Town and the streets began to narrow and slope upwards. They parked on a cobbled street and headed up the incline towards the castle, marveling at the Gothic architecture as they went.

They looked up in awe at the soot blackened monolithic sandstone buildings that towered over them, silent titans watching the bustling activity below.

Quaint, brightly colored curiosity shops filled the ground floors of the buildings on either side of the street, plying their merry trade to the steady stream of tourists. Lattice windows were stamped at regular intervals into the stone facades, some dark and impenetrable, others with lights flickering within, giving enticing glimpses of the everyday lives of the locals.

The melancholy drone of bagpipes drifted through the air. A deep vibration of the ancient wind instrument creating an eerie resonance that imbued the surrounding buildings with life, as if the buildings themselves were breathing.

Chrissy was captivated. Never before had she felt the pull of history as viscerally as this.

The dank, cramped alleyways running off the Royal Mile smelled faintly of barley and yeast and whispered to her as she walked past, hinting at the darker history of the city.

Gothic churches with pointed arches and flying buttresses, prickling with ornate decoration, added to the eerie feeling.

She could imagine the ramshackle tenement buildings of centuries past, confined by the city walls and forced to grow higher and higher, creaking and gasping for air against the stink of coal, and sewage, and fermentation.

The hair on the back of her neck stood up as she found herself believing in the old ghost stories.

"Hey Chrissy," said Liz, pulling her from her reverie. "This place is crazy, isn't it? It doesn't look real, and it's kinda creeping me out. Shall we grab some lunch and shake off this feeling? I've found a place that has good reviews."

Chrissy nodded in agreement, and they headed towards the top of the Royal Mile.

Walking up the cobbled street past taverns and store fronts overflowing with colorful tartans, Chrissy breathed in the eerie romance of it all.

The sight of the castle at the top of the hill was awe-inspiring. Standing straight out of the rough hewn volcanic rock, it seemed indomitable against wind or rain or foe.

As they approached the door to the restaurant, they felt a breath of cold, blustery wind, and the first spits of rain.

Stepping inside, they were met with a warm, modern ambiance and the smell of delicious food curling its way from the kitchen. Neither had realized just how hungry they were, and as they were escorted upstairs and shown to a window overlooking the castle, their mouths watered in anticipation.

They ordered a glass of white wine each and agreed to share the haggis balls as an appetizer.

"When in Rome," said Liz with a grin and a shrug.

They chatted and laughed together, happy to be back in each other's company.

"So, how are your kids doing?" prompted Liz.

Chrissy raised her eyes to heaven. "Well, Josh is settling in well at the new school. He's made loads of new friends and he is the star of the track team. But Jackie has been a bit of a handful."

"How so?"

"I don't know," said Chrissy, shaking her head in frustration. "She's just a moody teenager, I guess. She has a couple of friends, but no one close. Her grades are reasonable, but she could be doing much better. I don't know what to do. Scott and I keep trying to talk to her about it, but she just brushes us off."

"Teens are the worst," Liz said, making a face. "I can't even imagine how my mother didn't throttle me at that age. I was completely obnoxious."

They both laughed at the memory of all those years ago.

Chrissy leaned forward and asked, "How are you doing since Lauren and Naomi moved out? You feeling OK about it all?"

Liz's face dropped, and she shrugged. "I miss them. A lot. Which is no surprise, I suppose. When I look back on it, I realize I was a little naïve to think it could be a permanent thing, but I love that little girl so much. Lauren has been very good and said that I can come over and visit anytime, but it's not the same. My mum is finding it tough as well. She loved the feeling of playing Grandma. That was probably the only chance she'll have to experience it."

"You don't know that," said Chrissy. "You might still meet someone."

Liz snorted, "Girl, I'm forty-one years old. My eggs are literally shriveling as we speak. Plus, all the men out there are shits. I don't even want to date any of them, let alone procreate with them! Nope, I think that ship has sailed."

Chrissy put her hand on Liz's arm and squeezed.

"Anyway," Liz said, "here we are on an adventure in the wilds of Scotland. Are you looking forward to spending time with your wayward father?"

Chrissy grimaced. "I'm not sure. He's a fascinating guy,

but I'm a bit intimidated. I'm not sure I can live up to his expectations, whatever they are."

"Hey, girl, screw him," Liz said, looking combative. "You are perfect just the way you are, so don't let him try to change you, OK?"

Chrissy smiled. It was so good to have Liz fighting in her corner.

After a delicious meal of locally caught fish, they stepped back outside into the chill wind.

Pulling their jackets tightly around them and hunching their shoulders up to their ears, they headed back towards the car.

"Bloody hell, this is Scotland in the summer?" said Chrissy, incredulous, as she shivered. "If it is, then you can keep it!"

"Actually, I love this weather. It's kind of exhilarating, don't you think?" Liz said, her cheeks ruddy and her eyes sparkling.

Chrissy just wrinkled her nose and tucked her head deeper into the hood of her jacket.

They strode back to the car, leaving the ancient city behind them. The haunting sound of bagpipes floating faintly on the wind.

"OK," said Liz, shaking out her jacket and throwing it on top of the luggage in the backseat. "Ready or not, Kallenford, here we come!" She announced, as she turned on the engine and put the car into drive.

10

Kallenford
Saturday, June 6th - Scotland

The friends drove in comfortable silence through the lush, rolling countryside of the Scottish Borders. The weather had cleared, and the sun shone down from a clear blue sky scattered with white fluffy clouds.

Occasionally one of them would point out an ancient crumbling abbey, or a horse galloping through an adjacent field, but for the most part, they were content in each other's quiet company.

Chrissy felt relaxed and sleepy, the combined effects of wine and jet lag settling on her like a warm blanket. The countryside was idyllic and ancient, with gentle greens and browns washed across fields and trees as if painted in watercolors.

"It's beautiful, isn't it?" whispered Chrissy.

"Yes, it really is. I'm so glad I came with you," replied Liz.

Just as Chrissy was drifting off into a contented doze, Liz said, "It looks like we're coming into Kallenford now. Bloody hell, Chrissy, it's gorgeous."

The village looked like a film set; picture perfect, ancient, yet welcoming.

The streets were impossibly narrow, hardly wide enough for two cars to pass safely. On either side were thin pavements and then jostled up against them, ancient gray stone cottages with rambling roses climbing up their facades.

The cottages had brightly colored front doors with flower baskets and boot racks in the doorways, with the occasional umbrella propped jauntily against the door frames.

They rounded a bend as the road took on a soft incline.

They passed a pub called the 'Reiver's Rest', its original lattice window frames sagging like bleary eyes, as if the pub itself had partaken of one too many alcoholic beverages. It had an adjoining garden edged with nodding flowers and wooden tables and benches, where customers sat with pints in their hands.

Chrissy stared in wonder as she said, "These buildings must be at least five hundred years old."

Liz nodded in agreement.

They came to what must be the heart of the village, where the road encircled a well-tended village green with a stone war memorial at its center. Two children ran across the green, throwing a ball for their dog, their laughter ringing out.

Around the green were more ancient buildings, and as Liz drove the loop, they spied the local post office, butchers with a red and white striped awning, and what looked like either a coffee shop or a bakery.

Behind the roofs of these venerable old buildings, they could see the spire of a church.

"This can't be real," said Liz, incredulously. "I feel like I'm on the set of a murder mystery show or something. It's too damn perfect."

Chrissy laughed. "I agree. I've seen villages like this in the Cotswolds, but I've never actually stayed in one. We'll definitely need to walk over from the lodge one day and take a closer look."

"Sounds good to me," replied Liz.

"Ok. Enough sightseeing now," Chrissy said, with a businesslike air. "Let's get to the hunting lodge and settle in. Joe's instructions say that the lodge is on an unmarked track a little way behind Kallenford Castle. The castle grounds should be just past the edge of the village, although Joe said the entrance isn't signposted, so it's not easy to spot," said Chrissy.

They headed back to the main road, and as buildings gave way to thickets and hedgerows, Liz spotted a gap in the trees and made a hard right onto a narrow tarmac road. Flanked on either side by ancient oaks, they drove up the road until they reached an enormous set of entrance pillars supporting an imposing set of wrought-iron gates. The gates were topped with a family crest, and as Chrissy punched in the code provided by her father, they swung open slowly.

The friends looked at each other with raised eyebrows.

Driving through the expansive, manicured grounds, they rounded a bend, and their jaws dropped at the sight of the castle.

"Holy crap, Liz, this place is huge," Chrissy said, awed.

The sandstone castle rose above the grounds, solid and imposing with the formidable grace of a Georgian masterpiece. Solid and symmetrical with rectangular towers flanking a long central section, the fortress was given a romantic flair with crenelated battlements and dozens of pale turrets. Standing against the clear blue sky, the building seemed to revel in its magnificent grandeur.

Liz broke the silence with a question. "Where to now?"

Chrissy blinked and took a breath before looking down at her phone.

"Um. Ok, it says to follow the driveway to the left, past the main entrance, and then follow the road around to the back of the building. There we will see a dirt road leading off towards the forest. We need to keep going until we reach the old metal gate. It'll be open for us. Then we just go through it and down the lane until we get to the end. That's where the lodge is."

They headed around the edge of the castle, through a decrepit iron gate, and down the rough, unmade road.

Through clattering teeth, Liz said,

"This is going to destroy the car's suspension. I'm glad this is a rental and not my own."

The lane became impossibly narrow, with impenetrable brambles on either side that scratched at the car as they passed. But soon they came to a clearing, and there, in front of them, was the hunting lodge.

It was larger than Chrissy had imagined, maybe five or six bedrooms, she guessed. Built from the same rugged gray stone as the houses in the village, but more imposing and austere, with none of the warmth and welcome of the village cottages.

Standing in the open doorway waiting to greet them was Joe. He wore a heavy wine colored sweater, pants the color of moss, and dark brown rain boots. With his burly looks and silvery beard and mustache, he looked like a born hunter, ready to set out into the wilderness with his rifle at his side.

He raised a hand and stepped forward as Liz parked the car.

"Welcome to my humble abode," he said in his booming baritone voice, while bowing to them with a flourish of his hand.

The girls stepped out of the car and stretched their legs after the long journey.

There was an awkward moment when Chrissy wasn't sure whether to hug Joe or shake his hand, but decided a shake would be safer.

Joe turned to Liz and said, "I see. You're the chaperone, are you?"

"I suppose so," Liz replied, smiling politely while her eyes remained wary. She held out a hand to shake, which Joe took and pumped up and down vigorously.

"Well, come in, come in," he said, urging Chrissy to follow him.

"I'll get the bags then, shall I?" said Liz, raising an eyebrow as the other two disappeared inside the house.

She hauled the bags from the car and dumped them in the narrow hallway, then joined Chrissy and Joe as he led them through a low door frame into a large front room.

"This is my drawing room, and where I spend most of my time, especially when I'm writing," Joe explained.

The ceiling was low and the decor rich. Heavy wooden paneling covered the walls, and a thick red carpet the color of merlot absorbed their feet.

Dark brown leather chairs were positioned on either side of an ornate stone mantelpiece, and a welcoming fire burned in the hearth.

"This is lovely," Chrissy said, smiling at him.

"It's no castle, but I make do. What did you think of the big house?" Joe said, nodding in the direction of Kallenford Castle. "Impressive isn't it?"

"Extremely," replied Chrissy.

"It's been there since the 1700s and owned by the same family this whole time. Lord Kallenford is a pretty good guy. We go hunting together now and then when I have time."

After a quick tour of the rest of the house, Joe said, "Let me show you to your room so you can freshen up. It's a single room with two twin beds. I'm assuming that will work for you?"

Chrissy nodded, and they followed him up the narrow, creaking staircase, noting as they went the various oil paintings of grouse and pheasant that adorned the walls.

"I'll let Julia know that we'll be ready for tea in thirty minutes."

"Julia?" Chrissy asked.

"Julia is my housekeeper. She's invaluable. I'll see you in the drawing room in thirty minutes sharp. And you'll need to let Julia know what time you'll want dinner. I won't be joining you as I eat alone."

"Oh, ok." said Chrissy.

"Alternatively, you can walk down the hill to the pub. I've heard that the King's Head serves good food, although I've not eaten there myself. No need to when Julia is such an excellent cook."

In the somewhat cramped guest room they unpacked their possessions, trying to find space in the tiny closet for all their clothes.

"Your old man seems a bit curt, doesn't he?" said Liz.

"Yeah. I'm having mixed feelings about this, I have to admit. Is it weird that he won't eat with us? What's all that about?"

"Maybe he's a vampire."

Chrissy snorted and threw a pillow at Liz.

"He could be, though," she said with a wink. "I'd believe anything after spending the day in Edinburgh today."

Liz sat down on her bed and smiled.

"This is really fun. It's completely insane, but really fun, and I'm so glad I'm here. Thank you for inviting me, Chrissy."

Chrissy sat next to her, leaned in and hugged her tightly, feeling a warm glow permeate her whole body.

"I'm glad you're here, too. I don't think I could have done this without you."

"You definitely couldn't have done the driving part," Liz said, nudging her.

They grinned at each other and giggled, feeling like

teenagers again.

Chrissy stood up and stretched.

"Well, I'm gonna brave the antiquated plumbing and try to have a quick shower. What's the bet that I'll either be frozen or scalded to death, eh?"

"Let's hope the pipes aren't as old as the rest of the place," Liz said, grimacing.

They freshened up and headed downstairs for tea with their somewhat brusque host.

Upon arriving in the drawing room, they saw a young woman of no more than thirty bending over the coffee table, setting out a teapot, three cups, and a plate of biscuits. She had rich curly red hair piled in a messy bun on the top of her head, secured with a brightly colored silk scarf. She was thin and muscular, and wore jeans and a spaghetti strap top that showed two full sleeves of intricate tattoos on both her arms. Around her neck and on her wrists hung heavy silver jewelry.

She turned and smiled at them with kind eyes.

"Come on in. Welcome to Kallenford. It's a pleasure to meet you," she said in a lilting Scottish accent that sounded like bells in the breeze.

"Are you Julia?" asked Chrissy.

"Och aye, I am indeed," she said with a grin, obviously amused by Chrissy's confused expression. "Were you expecting a little old lady?"

Chrissy blushed and stuttered, but Julia laughed and brushed it away.

"I'm your father's housekeeper, for now, because it pays the bills, but I'm actually an artist at heart."

"Oh, that's wonderful," said Chrissy. "Do you paint? Or write?"

Julia waved a hand in the air. "Och, no, nothing like that. I make jewelry like this, see?" and she held out the piece around her neck.

"It's beautiful," said Chrissy. "I love the patterns. Is that Viking?"

"Close," said Julia, with an approving look. "It's based on Pictish stone carvings. The Picts were an ancient race that lived in the highlands of Scotland thousands of years ago. I'm a fan, as you can see," she said, holding out her arms to display the geometric patterns that wove their way from her fingers right up to her shoulder blades.

A booming voice came from the doorway, making Chrissy jump a little.

"Getting acquainted, are we?" said Joe. "Thank you Julia, that will be all for now. Ladies, let's sit," he said, and Chrissy and Liz complied.

"Now, let's hear all about this friend of yours, shall we, Chrissy?" Joe said, fixing his eyes on Liz. "Tell me about yourself, young lady."

Liz met his eyes, and with a cool expression, she gave a good account of herself while sharing as little personal information as possible. She still didn't trust this American author who had entranced her best friend, and she intended to keep her distance until she had a better grasp on the facts.

11

Pizza
Monday, June 8th - Pasadena

"Please, Mum. I really want to go," Philip begged as he followed Emily around the kitchen.

She was exhausted from another day of back-to-back meetings, and although she'd intended to go to the grocery store after she picked the kids up from camp she hadn't had the energy, so now she was trying to scrape together spaghetti bolognese from the meager supplies left in the fridge.

She grabbed the pasta sauce and dumped it into the skillet alongside the ground beef and onions.

"Well, Philip, if you knew you wanted to go, then you should have been more organized," she said, taking another sip of her wine. "And stop trailing around after me like a lost puppy. I'm trying to make dinner."

"But they only told us about it today. I know it's a pain, but please, Mom?"

She heard the desperation in his voice, and it filled her with equal measures of irritation and sympathy.

"Why do they need both our signatures, anyway?" She

asked, while stirring the sauce. "Normally, one parent is enough. It seems like a bit of overkill to me."

"I don't know," he said, leaning on the counter next to her. "They said something about you both being emergency contacts, but having different mailing addresses. They said it's 'standard procedure' to have both caregivers sign if they are taking us off camp grounds. I suppose it's a custody thing."

She saw the pain in his eyes as he dropped his gaze to the ground. "I told the lady in the camp office that I wasn't going to see Dad tonight, so I couldn't get him to sign, but she said that if I didn't hand in the form tomorrow, then I couldn't go on Wednesday."

Emily swore under her breath as the pasta water boiled over. She turned down the heat, took another sip of her wine, and asked,

"Where is this escape room, anyway?"

"It's in Glendale." Philip answered. "Please, Mom? All my friends from camp are going, and if I don't go, then I'll be the only one left behind."

Emily sighed with exasperation as she drained the pasta and reached into the cupboard for the bowls.

"Oh, for heaven's sake. Fine. Dinner is ready, so you guys can eat at least. Go and set the table while I serve up, then I'll drive over to your father's and get him to sign it. But you have to promise to watch the others while I'm out, and clear the dishes off the table when you're all finished. And don't just dump them in the sink either, put them in the dishwasher and turn it on, please. Don't let Sophie sneak any ice cream while I'm out. She's had enough sugar already today, and after dinner you can let Harry watch Transformers if he wants to - that should keep him out of trouble until I get back."

"Thank you, Mom! You're the best!" Philip said, throwing his arms around her neck in an uncharacteristically enthusiastic gesture.

Emily maintained her annoyed expression as she served up and then grabbed her phone and keys, but secretly her heart was full of love for her oldest boy. He had been so quiet and withdrawn since Ed moved out that it filled her with relief to see him happy and excited about something again.

Each of her children had reacted differently to the temporary separation; Philip acting silent and moody, Sophie flying into fits of rage at the slightest thing, and Harry becoming clingy at night, often crying himself to sleep under the covers. But this week they had seemed almost back to their old selves again. Emily hoped this meant they were adjusting to the new arrangement, at least until she could get the whole family back under the same roof again.

As she left the house, she looked back at her brood and said, "I'll be back in about 40 minutes. Don't burn down the house, OK?"

"We promise not to," Philip said, grinning. "Love you, Mum, and thank you," he said, as she pulled the door closed behind her.

She speed-dialed Ed as she drove through the Pasadena streets. It was 7pm already, so the rush hour had subsided and the roads were quiet.

Ed's cell went straight to voicemail, which was unusual, as he almost always answered.

"I hope he's home," thought Emily as she listened to his voicemail greeting. "Where else could he be on a Monday night? The gym, maybe?"

She hadn't thought to check with him before getting in the car. She'd just assumed that he'd be home.

At the beep she said, "Hi, Ed? Are you there? I'm sorry to bother you on a night when you don't have the kids, but Philip needs a form signed for a field trip they're going on. The camp only gave it to him today, and he needs it signed for tomorrow. Apparently we both need to sign it, which is a pain I know, so I'm heading over to your apartment now, if that's OK? I hope you're home? Call me if you're out, yes?"

She considered turning around and heading home, but she'd promised Philip, and she didn't want to let him down. Surely Ed was home. Maybe he had his phone switched off because he was still working on something for his new job?

"I hope this isn't going to be a wasted trip," she thought, the irritation rising in her again.

Fifteen minutes later, she parked up outside the large apartment complex, and, using the key fob Ed had given her, she buzzed herself through the side entrance gate.

She walked through the shared pool area, which was empty, but still smelled of chlorine and coconut sunscreen. A young man from the facilities department was rearranging the sun loungers and closing the umbrellas for the night, and he nodded to her as she passed.

Heading up in the elevator, she checked her phone again. Still no message from Ed.

"Well, I'm here now. I might as well see if he's home," she thought.

She walked down the nondescript hallway to his apartment door. His was the only door with a welcome mat outside and a potted plant stand to greet visitors. The rest of the complex had an elegant but impersonal feel to it, but Ed could make even the most sterile space feel like home.

She could hear faint music coming from inside. "Oh, good. He is home, after all," Emily thought to herself.

She rang the bell and waited, pulling the permission slip out of her purse.

After a minute or so, Ed opened the door.

He was wearing a white T-shirt and shorts and looked ruddy and glowing with damp, tousled hair, as if he'd just stepped out of the shower. His face was relaxed and content with a huge, beaming smile.

The smile vanished as soon as he saw Emily, replaced with wide eyes as the color drained from him.

"E.. Emily?" he managed to stutter.

"I'm so sorry to barge in on you on your night off" she said, quickly, "but Philip needs this permission slip signed for tomorrow for some field trip they're going on. He was very insistent, so I agreed to bring it over for you to sign. Here. Maybe you could drop it in to the summer camp office tomorrow morning?"

Ed just stared at her, taking the form in silence.

"Are you OK?" asked Emily. "You look a little pale"

Before he could answer, Emily heard a voice coming from the bathroom.

"Hey, is that the pizza delivery guy already? That was fast. Fantastic, I'm starving."

From the bathroom doorway stepped a glistening figure, wearing nothing but a towel around his waist.

It was Conner.

It took Emily a minute to recognize him out of context. The last time she had spoken to him was when he was fixing the decking at their house, and now here he was, virtually naked in Ed's apartment.

She looked from him to Ed, unable to process what she was seeing.

Conner's face went as white as Ed's as he looked from Emily to Ed with wild, panicky eyes.

For a moment, there was nothing but silence as the three of them stood, frozen in shock. Then Emily found her voice enough to say,

"I.. I have to go."

"Wait," said Ed. "Emily, I…"

"I can't.." she said in a strangled whisper and turned to walk down the hallway.

She swung sideways as if she was drunk, crashing into the wall and holding it to steady herself.

"Emily!" said Ed, alarm in his voice. "Are you OK? Here, let me help you."

He reached out to steady her, but she reeled away from him.

He grabbed her arm, the concern in his eyes turning to panic.

"Don't touch me," she hissed and wrenched her arm away from him.

"I'm so sorry," he stammered, "I never meant for you to... I was going to tell you. I promise."

"Don't talk to me, Ed," Emily said, her voice shaking. "I can't hear anything you have to say right now. I just need to leave."

"Can you drive?" Ed asked, standing between her and the elevator. "I think you're in shock, Emily. It might not be safe for you to drive right now."

"Leave me alone. Get out of my way," she said, the tears welling up, and refusing to let him see her cry.

She pushed past him and ran to the elevator. She pummeled the button, unable to turn around in case they were both there in the doorway, staring at her.

Her cheeks were burning, and her legs were like jello.

She just needed to get away.

Away from here.

The elevator doors opened, and she fell inside, punching the button to close the door.

The doors opened on the ground floor and she fell through them, steadying herself on the wall.

She staggered through the gate and to her car, fumbling to open the car door, barely able to see through the tears that streamed down her face.

She was shaking with rage, grief, and confusion. Drowning

in emotions.

Forcing herself to breathe deeply, she wiped away the tears and turned the car engine on.

She drove down the road and around the corner for fear that Ed would come out to check on her.

Switching off the engine, she sat in the darkness, weeping.

She replayed what had just happened, seeing every moment in vivid, agonizing detail.

Ed's face as he opened the door, the expression of deep contentment in his eyes that she hadn't seen for the longest time.

The horror of realization as he saw her face, as if she had shattered a perfect dream, turning it instantly into a nightmare.

Then she saw Conner. His tan muscular body sculpted by a life of physical labor, the moisture from the shower still glinting on his skin.

How could this be?

Her brain refused to allow her to reach the obvious conclusion.

Maybe Conner just came over after work? Maybe he was dirty from a construction project he'd been working on, and took a shower before they hung out as friends, eating pizza and watching the game? They were friends after all, weren't they?

"Oh, god," Emily thought, as the blackness opened up into a yawning abyss. *"The fishing trips."*

Now she was spinning, fighting to keep a grasp on reality.

Ed and Conner had been going on 'fishing trips' for months now, and she hadn't seen it. Hadn't realized what that had really meant.

How long had this been going on? Was this why Ed had needed 'space'? So Conner could come over to his place? So they could…

She was furious now. She wanted to claw and bite and scream. She had been abandoned, betrayed, and she felt so desperately lonely.

For a moment, she felt the sudden need for Ed's strong, familiar arms around her, protecting her as he always had. She had always relied on him to shelter her from the storms of life, and at that moment, she thought she might break into a million pieces at the heartbreak of it all.

She sat in the dark for a long time, but eventually she dried her eyes, knowing that her children were waiting for her at home.

She would have to go back to them as if everything was fine. As if none of this had happened.

She would have to be strong for them, even though her life had changed irreparably.

12

Anthems
Monday, June 8th - Kallenford

It was Monday afternoon, and after a delicious lunch prepared by the ever-patient Julia, Liz was more than happy to leave Chrissy and Joe to their creative convolutions.

Joe had made it perfectly clear to Liz that she was neither needed nor wanted during this 'mentoring' process, so she had taken the opportunity to explore the local countryside, and what better way to explore than to go for a run?

She donned her running clothes and shoes and stepped outside into the perfect Scottish summer day.

Taking a deep breath, she filled her lungs with the sweet, fresh air. It was so clean she could almost taste it, the hints of cut grass and honeysuckle cleansing her body and filling her heart with joy.

It was revitalizing to be out in the countryside again, and Liz felt alive for the first time in a long while.

She ran, slowly at first, down the dirt track beneath her feet, and the clear blue sky above her head.

She was out of the habit of running, and her lungs and calves protested at the exertion. It was surprising how out of shape she had become.

While living with Xander she had run almost every day and had completed a couple of half marathons with ease. But after moving in with Lauren and Naomi, the habit had slipped.

In some ways, she had become healthier during that time. She had quit smoking for one, and she'd curbed her swearing when Naomi began to copy her, but she'd picked up some bad habits, too. She had started to watch TV in the evenings, collapsing in a heap with a glass of wine, watching mind-numbing shows with Lauren until late at night.

She'd tried to eat healthily, to cook for the three of them and prepare balanced meals from fresh ingredients, but the constant treadmill of shopping and cooking had exhausted her, and they would regularly give in and order a Chinese takeout or a curry.

After grueling work days and busy weekends, there never seemed to be enough time to exercise, and when she did have the time, she was too exhausted to drag herself out of the house.

But now she was running again, and as her muscles loosened and her breathing fell into a rhythmic pattern, she felt the exhilaration of a soul set free from its ties and able to soar once more.

She hadn't realized just how much she'd missed it, and as she stopped to admire the strong flowing river in front of her, she lifted her face to the gentle warmth of the sun and felt a quiet bliss.

Running along the path that ran parallel with the river, she breathed in the damp air and the delicate hints of the wildflower meadows in the distance.

She stopped once more to watch a mother duck with her ducklings swimming towards the reeds at the side of the river. The mother duck looked so serious, contrasted by the tiny balls of golden fluff that swam furiously to keep up with her, their earnest expressions so endearing.

As the path split in two, she turned away from the river and into the meadows, running along a rough track between two fields of swaying green grass.

She headed for the tree line, and as she entered the oak forest, she was folded into the shaded, dappled light of the ancient oak trees.

Slowing to a walk to catch her breath, she thought she heard the faintest whisper of music coming from somewhere on her left.

Following it, like a hound that had caught a scent, she broke out of the trees onto a single track road that led towards an impossibly ancient and somewhat dilapidated stone building.

The sound was unmistakable now, a deafening cacophony that she recognized as 'Living on a Prayer' by Bon Jovi.

This banging rock anthem could not have been more incongruous against the archaic structure, and she couldn't help but approach.

A rusty corrugated metal door was propped open with a large tree stump, and as she came closer, Liz could smell coal smoke and something sharp and industrial that caught in her throat.

Covering her ears to keep out the ear-splitting music, she peeked in.

A blast of heat hit her, and she could see at the end of the room a huge forge filled with a glowing red hot fire. There was a man bent over an anvil, hammering what appeared to be a metal knife, its tip glowing red hot. As he brought the hammer down, bright sparks flew off and shimmered through the air.

The man wore a black t-shirt and jeans, with what looked like a heavy leather apron over them. He also wore a large set of ear protectors, and was singing his heart out to the Bon Jovi song.

He seemed to sense her presence in the doorway and stood upright, pulling off the ear protectors and raising an eyebrow as a smile grew across his face.

He was young, tall and broad shouldered, with grimy blonde hair. His face was smeared with ash, but his smile was perfect white, and his eyes sparkled with a combination of confidence and mischief.

He mouthed something to her.

She grimaced and signaled at her ears before covering them again.

He turned and switched off the deafening music. Turning back, he caught her eyes again and that smooth, easy smile reappeared as he looked at her.

Liz felt her pulse quicken. This guy was cute. Young, and probably trouble, but very, very cute.

"Hi there," he said, putting down the hammer and placing the knife in a bucket of water where it hissed like an angry cat.

His voice was deep and his accent sounded English rather than Scottish.

"Hi," she responded, kicking herself for feeling uncharacteristically flustered.

He grabbed a cloth and wiped his face and hands as he walked towards her. Then he held out a hand.

"I'm Andrew, and you are?"

She shook it, saying, "Liz. Sorry, I heard your music and, umm.."

Andrew chuckled and replied, "I'm not surprised you heard it. You a fan?"

"Um, yeah. I guess. Maybe not quite that loud, though."

Andrew grinned again as he wiped his neck.

"It gets loud in here, especially when I have the power

hammer going. Are you lost? Or does my reputation precede me?" he asked, mischief in his eyes.

"Sorry. You're working. I should probably go," Liz said, embarrassed.

"Not at all. I was just about to take a break, anyway. Would you like a cold drink? I have Coke, Sprite or water? Or you could join me for a beer if you'd like?"

"Oh. Um, yes. A beer would be lovely."

"Let's sit outside," he said. "This place is full of soot and iron filings, and I wouldn't want you to mess up your clothes."

Stepping outside, he pulled up a rusty-looking lawn chair for her to sit on.

"Give me one second, will you? I'll be right back."

He returned with two ice cold beer bottles.

He had shed the leather apron he'd been wearing, revealing the t-shirt underneath.

As they talked and sipped their beers, Liz took in his muscular arms and torso, and the relaxed way he swept his unruly mop of hair out of his eyes.

"So what brings you to our little village, Liz?" He asked, studying her.

"I came with a friend. We're staying at the hunting lodge with Joseph Graham. He's a writer, and he's mentoring my friend, Chrissy." Liz wasn't quite ready to share that Chrissy was in fact his daughter, and in any case, she didn't feel that this information was hers to share.

"Ah, the eccentric American writer, eh? He's quite a character, isn't he?" Andrew said, watching her closely.

"Yes, he seems to be," replied Liz tactfully. "Are you local yourself?" she asked, steering the conversation away from the subject of Joe.

"I am. I was born here, but I spent most of my childhood in England, hence the English accent, which you no doubt have already spotted."

Liz swallowed. Somehow she felt as if she were playing a game of chess, but she couldn't work out why.

"its beautiful countryside out here," she continued, "and Kallenford castle is stunning, isn't it?"

"It is indeed. Pretty old, I've heard," he said, his eyes sparkling. They were a soft bluish gray color, like the morning mist.

"The town seems lovely too. Chrissy and I have plans to go down and have a look around when we get the chance."

"What else do you plan to do with your time while you're here?" Andrew asked, leaning forward towards her. For a moment Liz caught the scent of his aftershave, and she felt the heat rise in her.

"Don't even think about it, Liz," she thought to herself. *"He's a kid. He can't be more than thirty at most. That's cradle snatching."*

"So, how long have you been a blacksmith?" she asked in a casual tone.

Andrew combed his fingers through his hair and swigged his beer, smiling to himself.

"About seven years," he replied, looking at her directly. "I started when I was twenty-eight." He paused, his eyes holding a mischievous and knowing expression.

Shit. Was she really that obvious? She must be losing her touch.

"I used to spend a lot of time around horses when I was younger," he continued. "I watched the farrier changing their shoes, and I asked him to show me how he made them. Once I'd felt the heat of the forge and seen the glow of hot metal, I was hooked."

"Do you make anything specific?" Liz asked.

"Most of my work is on commission for local folk. I make iron gates and bespoke fasteners. I've made some agricultural tools, too. I've even done some swords and shields for battle reenactments."

"What were you making when I came in?" Liz asked.

"It's a chef's knife. The blade is so sharp it can slice through raw meat like its butter."

"Can I see it?"

Andrew hesitated for a moment, then shrugged and stood up.

He walked back inside the forge, and a moment later, he came back with the knife.

Liz was taken aback.

"It's beautiful," she breathed. "The patterns on the blade look like oil on water. I didn't know you could do something like that with metal."

"Do you want to hold it?" Andrew asked quietly, his earlier bravado replaced with a quiet solemnity.

"Can I?"

"Just be very careful of the blade. It's extremely sharp."

Liz carefully took the knife and turned it in the light. It truly was a work of art.

"Thank you," she said, as she handed it back to him.

He returned it to the workshop, and when he came out again, he was back to his former charming self.

"Would you care for another beer?" he asked. "I'm not quite done for the day, so I can't just yet, but you're welcome to have another if you'd like? It's not wise for me to be working with large red hot metal poles if I don't have my wits about me."

"It looks like challenging work. Very physically demanding."

"It is. But I've never yet shied away from anything physical. In fact, I very much enjoy that kind of thing, if you know what I mean?" he said, with a glint in his eyes.

Liz felt her color rising. She handed back her empty bottle

and stood.

"Thanks, but I should go. I'm sorry I disturbed you. I should be getting back now, but it was a pleasure meeting you."

Andrew looked taken aback.

"I'm sorry, Liz. I shouldn't have said that. It was inappropriate, and I didn't mean to embarrass you. Please stay. I promise to behave from now on."

Liz brushed away the comment. "Oh, don't you worry, you'd have to work pretty hard to embarrass me. No, it's just that I said I'd be back by now, and I don't want Chrissy to worry."

"Well, in that case, I will say au revoir à la prochaine, mademoiselle," he said as he took her hand and kissed it.

He grinned with satisfaction as she tried not to look taken aback.

As she walked away, she heard the music crank back up to deafening levels. This time Andrew was rocking out to 'Take On Me' by A-ha.

Liz couldn't help but smile to herself as she began the long run home.

13

Locals
Wednesday, June 10th - Kallenford

The warmth of the Reiver's Rest was a welcome comfort as Liz and Chrissy stripped off their jackets and took a seat at a table near the bar. A cheery wood fire burned in the old stone fireplace, filling the pub with delicious aromas of woodsmoke and casting a warm glow over its patrons.

"It might be summer, but once the sun goes down, that wind is still pretty cold, isn't it?" said Chrissy.

"Sure, whatever you say, California girl," said Liz with a smirk.

The atmosphere in the pub was jovial and welcoming. Folks sat in groups, chatting and laughing as if this was home, which, for some of them, it pretty much was.

Faint music played in the background, and the occasional cheer could be heard from the group of old timers playing darts in the corner.

Sue, the landlady, stood behind the bar, pouring pints from the shiny brass beer taps and dishing out advice, her unmistakable laugh ringing out regularly, both throaty and raucous.

Chrissy and Liz had met her briefly the night before when they had walked into town in search of dinner. They had quickly learned that she prided herself on being the unofficial matriarch of the village, knowing everything that was going on there. There was no need for introductions, as she somehow already knew who they were and why they were here.

"I'm starving," Liz said. "What are you going to have?"

"I think I might have the haddock again," said Chrissy. "It was delicious last night."

"It's nice to give poor Julia a break. I feel so bad for her having to cook three meals a day for us as well as cooking for Joe, and she's refused to take any extra money to cover our costs."

"Yes, I agree. And the food here is delicious, so it's no hardship to come down to the village to eat dinner now and then."

Liz nodded in agreement.

"Well hello again, young lasses," Sue said, appearing at their side. "And what can I get for you tonight?" she asked, her round face ruddy and beaming.

The friends ordered two local ciders, the haddock, and the shepherd's pie, and with a quick nod, Sue vanished off to put their orders in with the kitchen.

A young barmaid delivered the ciders, and Chrissy and Liz toasted to friendship as they relaxed into the comfort of the pub, the fire crackling in the background.

"So," Chrissy said. "You disappeared again today, I noticed. Another 'run' was it?" she asked, raising an eyebrow suggestively. "Did your route take you past a certain blacksmith again, perchance?"

Liz swatted at her through the air.

"OK, I admit it," Liz said. "I may have stopped by again. But there's nothing else to do in this godforsaken place, and he's an interesting guy, so where's the crime?" she said, struggling to suppress a smile.

"Sure, whatever you say, girl," Chrissy said, her eyes sparkling. "So, what did you talk about this time?"

"Stop looking at me like that. There's nothing going on between us. He was just telling me about the local wildlife, the deer and the birds of prey."

Liz leaned forward and said, "Once when he was younger, he climbed to the top of a tree to look into an ospreys nest, but the mother bird saw him and dive bombed him, ripping at him with her claws and beak. He fell out of the tree and broke his arm, but he says it was worth it to see those tiny babies in their nest."

Chrissy smiled and nodded and sipped her cider.

Liz continued.

"He was telling me all about the history of the area as well. You know that this whole stretch of the country is known as 'the Borders' because it's the border between England and Scotland, and it used to be wild and virtually lawless. Andrew told me that back in medieval times, the border people paid little to no heed to who was on the throne of either England or Scotland, and instead they were a law unto themselves. Powerful clans formed warrior groups called the Border Reivers, and they would steal and plunder from anyone they chose. This went on for centuries, apparently,"

Liz took a sip of her cider then continued. "The Reivers were incredible horsemen and fearless fighters, and both the English and the Scots feared them. Isn't that fascinating?"

"Wow. That is pretty cool. So this Andrew is a bit of a history buff, is he?" Chrissy said, with a glimmer in her eye.

"He's a local boy. He was born here, remember? He loves everything about this area. Oh, and he told me that the family who live in Kallenford Castle are descended from one of those Reiver clans, and they were some of the worst of them.

He said that they're no more than cattle thieves and robber barons who gained the favor of the king when James came to the throne. It's funny how history works out that way, isn't it? Thieves become noblemen?"

"It is indeed," said Chrissy. "So, you going back there again tomorrow for another history lesson?"

Liz pulled a face.

"But honestly, though," Chrissy said, grinning like a schoolgirl. "You think he's cute, don't you?"

"Stop it. No. Well, yes, kind of. But he's a baby, Chrissy. He's six years younger than me, and he acts like a clown. He doesn't take anything seriously, and everything's a joke to him."

"He's just free spirited. There's nothing wrong with that. And there's definitely nothing wrong with it when it's wrapped in a package as delicious as he is," Chrissy said, wiggling her eyebrows up and down suggestively.

"Oh god, you are so immature. Now stop before I leave and never come back. Let's talk about something else. How are things going with your old man?"

Chrissy blew out a long breath.

"Hmm. It's still early days, so we'll have to wait and see. He's obviously very knowledgeable and I appreciate him taking the time to teach me, but to be honest, I feel like a fish out of water."

"Did he explain where he's been all these years? Or why he contacted you now?"

"I asked him this afternoon, and he quoted some philosopher called Lao Tzu, saying 'when the student is ready, the teacher will appear.'"

"What? What the hell is that supposed to mean?"

"I don't know. He also told me that, 'all I need in order to be a great writer is a beautiful fountain pen, a Moleskine notebook, and an old typewriter'. Then I just need to 'sit down at the typewriter and bleed.'"

"Ew! Gross."

"Apparently it's a Hemingway quote," Chrissy said, shrugging. "He is a big fan of Hemingway. And bourbon, it seems."

"He sounds like an ass," said Liz, frowning.

"Yeah, maybe, but he's a New York Times bestselling ass, so I'm just going to keep my mouth shut and try to learn what I can. He's been going through my manuscript making corrections until there's more red ink than black. He told me my writing is vapid and clichéd, but that it isn't altogether irretrievable."

"And that kind of feedback is 'helpful', is it?"

Chrissy took another sip of her cider. "The kicker was when he started talking about how to set up a 'writing space'. Joe has a whole ritual when he writes, involving silence and coffee and the positioning of notepads. He believes that to create great art, you need to create an atmosphere conducive to artistic expression. Only then will the words flow through you and onto the page."

"Is that what you do?" asked Liz.

"What?" Chrissy replied, taking another sip of cider.

"Well, you've already written a book, haven't you? Did you 'create an atmosphere conducive to artistic expression' when you were writing it?"

Chrissy snorted with laughter, almost choking on her cider. "God, no. If I waited for the 'right time' to write, then I'd never write anything. I use an app that syncs between my laptop and my cell phone and I write on that. In fact, I do a lot of my writing sitting in various parking lots while waiting for my kids to finish extracurriculars. I have to grab the opportunities when I can and be smart with my time. But also, and let's be clear on this, I've written a manuscript, not a book. I'm a long way off being a published author, you know?"

Liz shrugged.

"And does Joe know about these nefarious, app using, car sitting, writing habits?"

Chrissy made a face. "I couldn't bear to tell him. I worry he'd kick me out directly if he knew. That's going to remain our dirty little secret, OK?"

Liz was frowning, but as she was about to respond, Sue appeared at their side again.

"I see yer all done wi' yer dinners. Let me just take these plates out of yer way. Can I tempt you with dessert? Maybe a wee bit of sticky toffee puddin'?"

They both passed on dessert, but thanked her for the offer.

As she cleared away the dishes, Sue turned to Liz and said,

"A wee birdie tells me you've met our gentleman blacksmith, eh? He's quite a catch, isn't he?"

Liz raised her eyes to heaven.

"Nothing gets past you, does it, Sue?" said Chrissy.

Sue chuckled, "Oh no, deary. I'm the eyes and the ears of the village. I'm assuming he's told you who he is?"

Liz's brow furrowed.

"Maybe not then, eh? Well, not only is he our local blacksmith, and a very handsome one at that, but he's also the youngest son of our very own Earl of Kallenford. Ye've been conversin' wi' The Honorable Andrew Armstrong-Bell, although he hates it when anyone refers to him by his title. Oh yes, my dear, he's blue blood through and through."

Chrissy's jaw dropped as she stared at Liz.

Liz tried to speak, but words failed her.

Looking decidedly pleased with herself, Sue turned and headed back towards the kitchen, carrying the empty dishes.

"Oh. My. God, Liz," said Chrissy.

"Stop," said Liz quickly, holding up a hand. "Whatever

you are about to say, just stop right now or I will disown you."

Chrissy stifled a laugh.

"Well, that explains why he doesn't have a Scottish accent," said Chrissy, her eyes still wide with amazement. "Didn't he say he 'grew up in England'? Oh, Liz, he probably went to boarding school at Eton, or somewhere else equally fancy. How did you not register such a posh, upper class accent?"

"I don't know," Liz said, her head in her hands. "It didn't even occur to me. He just sounds like all the other guys I work with. I've been in the banking world for so long that I don't even hear the accent anymore. Oh God, I'm such an idiot," she said, kicking herself.

"So, he's the son of an Earl, big deal!" said Chrissy. "That doesn't have to change things between you, does it?"

Liz bit her lip. "I don't know. I feel like he wasn't honest with me. Why would he keep something like that a secret?"

"Did he, though? Really? Did it ever come up?"

"No, I guess not." Liz answered.

"So, maybe he wasn't withholding anything out of dishonesty. Maybe he was just worried about how you would react. Maybe he wanted you to see him for who he is; a blacksmith who loves nature and history."

"But all those stories he told me about the Border Reivers, and the villainous Armstrong-Bells who live in Kallenford Castle. That's his family he was talking about. I don't know, Chrissy. It all feels a bit weird."

"Do you think you'll see him again? That way you could talk about it."

"I'm not sure. I have to think about it."

Chrissy stretched and said, "Well, that's enough revelations for tonight. We should be getting home before it starts to rain again."

They paid the bill, including a healthy tip for Sue, and waved their goodbyes to her as they left. She was leaning on the bar, chatting with some locals and laughing in her distinctive deep, barreling way.

As they walked back on the forest trail towards the hunting lodge, using the flashlights on their phones to guide the way, Liz spied the lights of Kallenford Castle glinting through the trees.

She swallowed hard as she thought of Andrew.

Andrew the blacksmith. Andrew the birdwatcher and storyteller. But it seemed this wasn't the true Andrew at all.

He was, in fact, The Honorable Andrew Armstrong-Bell. The son of an Earl. An aristocrat of noble birth with a lineage that went back hundreds of years. His family lived in a frikken castle for Christ's sake. She thought she knew him, but it seems she didn't know him at all.

Her thoughts wandered back to the happy hours they'd spent together over the last couple of days, talking about history and politics, nature and humanity. It hurt her heart to think that they might not talk again like that.

She pictured him, sitting on that ridiculously old rickety deckchair, telling stories of valor and villainy, acting out the brave feats of the Reivers as she laughed, captivated by his effortless charm.

He would laugh along with her, the sound bubbling up from within him, unrestrained and joyous, filling his eyes with warmth and joy.

Those clear blue eyes, merry and adventurous but also sharply perceptive, seeing through any pretense and looking directly into her soul.

She found herself smiling, and she forced herself to stop.

Was this really a path she wanted to walk down?

On the other hand, what was she so afraid of?

The Andrew she knew was a local boy who fished in the

river and watched the deer grazing in the meadow. She could have a summer fling with this young, free-spirited blacksmith, couldn't she? It wouldn't mean anything after all.

Or would it?

"You OK back there?" Chrissy said from the path ahead. "Can you see where you're heading? It's dark ahead, so watch your footing and tread carefully, yes?"

Liz smiled to herself as she took a deep breath.

"I'll do my best," she said. "I'll definitely do my best."

14

Confessions
Thursday, June 11th - Pasadena

Emily parked her car in front of the Pasadena City Hall and sat with the engine off, staring up at the elegant white columns, stretching with unfaltering grace towards the brilliant azure blue sky.

The building glowed as if it were made of the richest marble, its carved archways and intricate ornamentation reminiscent of the Trevi fountain, as if Michelangelo himself had carved and shaped each sinuous curve and sharp, clean edge.

This building was a perfect symphony of civic pride and architectural beauty, and it represented in so many ways the beautiful 'city of roses' that had become Emily's home over the last year.

She felt the familiar stab in her chest. A mixture of grief and guilt and rage that had become a dark companion over the last week, sinking its icy blade into her heart every time she thought of Ed, or her children, or her life in Pasadena.

She took a deep breath and steeled herself. This had to be done, after all.

Stepping out of the air-conditioned car, she braced against the dry heat of a Californian June afternoon. The 'June gloom' of the morning had burnt off, revealing a vast expanse of sky, with colors as deep as the Cerulean Sea, and just as vast.

As Emily pushed open the door of the coffee shop, she could smell the warm, earthy smell of freshly baked bread. On any other day, it would have made her mouth water, but today she had no appetite.

She saw Ed sitting at a table in the corner. He stared into his coffee mug, head held low, with deep lines furrowing his forehead.

He looked up and met her eyes.

Another cold stab to the heart.

She walked over to the table and took a seat opposite her estranged husband.

"Hi," said Ed, his hands gripped around his coffee cup. "Thank you for agreeing to meet with me."

"I don't have long. I have a meeting in Santa Monica at 2pm that I can't be late for," replied Emily, her eyes cold.

"I, I just wanted a chance to explain. To clear the air a bit, and work out where we go from here."

Emily's lips were a thin line.

Ed cleared his throat. "Can I get you a coffee? Or something to eat? Have you eaten anything today?"

"No. Thank you. I'm fine. Now, you had something to say?"

Ed shifted in his seat and swallowed.

"Emily, I am so sorry about Monday night. I never meant for you to..." his voice trailed off. He took a deep breath and tried again. "It's new. This thing with Conner. I don't even know what it is yet, or if it has any future."

"It didn't look very new from where I was standing," Emily hissed back. "In fact, it looked like you knew each other pretty well."

"Look," Ed said, holding out a hand to stop her. "Let me start from the beginning, so at least you know the full story."

He shifted in his seat again, glancing at a woman carrying her coffee to an adjacent table.

"I swear to you that when Conner was working on the decking last year, we were nothing but friends. Yeah, we got on well, but just as buddies, nothing more. When he invited me for that first fishing trip to Big Bear, neither of us had any feelings for each other. We just had a great time drinking beers and hanging out. We talked and laughed and joked around. It was a lads' weekend, nothing more."

"So, when did it start?"

Ed rubbed his forehead and took a deep breath.

"During our trip in November, we went out fishing on the boat in the evening. The sun was going down over the mountains and the lake was beautiful, still like glass. We were listening to music and talking, but when Conner stood up and leaned over me to grab a beer, I felt something that scared me. I felt a surge of attraction. I couldn't understand it, but at the same time I couldn't shake the memory of it. When we went back to the cabin in March, I knew I needed to talk to him about how I was feeling. I was worried that he'd laugh at me, or worse, tell me that our friendship was over. But, as it turned out, he felt the same way."

"So, March?" Emily cut in, her voice sharp as a razor. "This has been going on since March?" She said, white hot anger rising in her.

"No. I swear," said Ed, his eyes wide as he shook his head. "I could never do that to you. I told Conner that I loved you and I didn't want to do anything to hurt you. I told him that nothing could happen between us because I'm a married man and that my family means everything to me."

Ed tightened his grip on his coffee cup and continued.

"I was so confused. That's when I realized I needed to

move out. I needed to understand what was happening. I swear to you, Emily, nothing happened until just a couple of weeks ago. Conner came over so we could talk. I got upset, and he comforted me, and, well, one thing led to another."
Ed's cheeks reddened as he bit his lip, brow furrowed.

Emily stared at him.

"So, you're gay?" she asked, incredulous. "I don't understand this. You don't just 'become' gay. You must have always known. Why didn't you ever say anything? How could you marry me if you knew you were gay?"

"Emily, honestly, I didn't know. That's the truth, I swear. I had no idea until I started having feelings for Conner. I married you because I loved you. I still love you, and I would do anything for you. You and the kids are my entire world."

"I'm not sure I can believe you, Ed. I don't know what I think anymore. It feels like my whole life has been a lie."

"Please, Emily," Ed said, reaching across the table towards her, tears in his eyes.

She whipped her hand away.

"No. I can't touch you right now. I can't do that."

A silence settled between them.

Ed gave a deep, shaky sigh.

"We'll need to tell the kids," he said.

Emily squeezed her eyes shut at the thought.

"What do you propose we tell them?" she asked, her voice cold and sharp.

Ed rubbed his forehead again.

"I don't know. I think it's safe to say that this separation is no longer temporary, but I don't think I'm ready to tell them about Conner yet."

"This is a total fucking shit show," Emily said, hurting at the thought of the conversations to come.

"We can do this, though," said Ed. "We can still parent our kids together, even if we're not together as a couple."

"We're going to have to, aren't we?" Emily said, venom in her voice.

"Are you OK? I'm so sorry to put you through all of this. It was never my intention. I never meant to hurt you," said Ed, tears welling in his eyes again.

"Well, you have, whether you meant to or not. I still don't understand any of this, and maybe I never will. But this is where we are, so we're just going to have to manage it the best we can."

"When do you want to tell the kids? Maybe I can come over at the weekend and we can all sit down together and talk about it?"

"Sure, why not? I'll bake a cake and we can all celebrate this new phase of our lives," Emily said, pursing her lips.

"Please don't be like that. I would never have chosen this, you must know that. But I can't help who I am, and it's not fair to any of us for me to keep lying about it."

"Sure. Whatever you say, Ed. I have to go. The traffic on the 110 is going to be awful at this time of day," she said, standing and pulling her purse off the back of her chair.

"Emily? I'm..." Ed dropped his eyes. "I'm sorry."

"So am I, Ed. So am I," she said, as she stood and headed out of the coffee shop towards her car.

As she reached for her keys, her cell phone rang. She fished it out of her purse and froze as she saw the caller ID.

It was her mother.

She stood still, the crisp heat prickling her arms and neck as she waited for the call to go to voicemail.

The ringing stopped, and a second or so later, the voicemail icon flashed up.

She inhaled deeply. Had she really been holding her breath?

She unlocked the car door and slid in, switching on the engine and blasting the a/c.

She stared at her phone, trying to blink away the tension headache that drummed at her temples.

Steeling herself, she hit the voicemail button. Her mother's voice sounded as crisp and unforgiving as the heat outside.

"Emily? Emily, are you there? I would like you to call me as soon as you get this message, please. I have been trying to reach you for two weeks now and your lack of response isn't just rude, it's getting concerning. I'm sure you are busy with your new job and what not, but I would appreciate it if you would do me the courtesy of returning my call. If I don't hear from you by the weekend, I will call Ed instead."

Emily sat, tears welling in her eyes. Her hands balled into fists, and she started pummeling the steering wheel, screaming out her rage and despair.

She looked up to see a concerned elderly gentleman looking at her through the windshield. He motioned for her to lower the window, but she shook her head, forced a smile, and mouthed that she was fine while doing a thumbs up.

He continued to walk past, still glancing at her anxiously as he headed to the pedestrian crossing.

Emily swallowed and tried to smooth her hair.

She hadn't told her mother what had happened with Ed, partly because she'd hoped it would blow over, and partly because she believed, deep down, that her mother would blame her for all of this. Maybe not to her face, after all her mother had never been one for direct confrontation, but she could picture her sitting across the dinner table from her father, suggesting that if Emily had been less demanding, had just been happy with her life in Surrey rather than dragging everyone to California, maybe none of this would have ever happened.

Of course, that was ridiculous, but how could she defend herself from 5,000 miles away?

For a moment, Emily wondered whether it was indeed

something she had done that had caused this. Had she known all along that Ed was gay?

No, that was crazy. After all, if he hadn't even known, there's no way she could have.

She swallowed again.

Should she call her mother back and pretend everything was normal? That nothing had changed? But then, at some point, she would have to come clean.

Maybe she could just ignore her until she called Ed instead. Then he could explain everything that had happened. This was all his doing after all.

She shut her eyes and clenched her jaw as she hit the 'call back' option.

It rang, and Emily could have cried from relief when it went to voicemail.

She put on her brightest, perkiest voice and said,

"Hi Mum. I just got your voicemail. I'm so sorry I missed you again. The summer has been so busy that I haven't had time to draw breath. We're all doing great here. The children are in summer camp and they're coming home grubby, happy and tired every afternoon. I'll send you some photos by email with all the things they've been up to.

My job is going well and I'm enjoying it a lot, and Ed is doing well, too." She cleared her throat. "Anyway, I should go now. It was lovely to hear your voice and we will definitely catch up soon. Love to Dad and speak soon, yes? Bye for now."

She hung up the call and slumped into her seat, exhausted. That should keep the wolf from the door for now, but she was going to have to deal with this sooner or later. Whether or not she was willing to admit it, her life would never be the same again.

15

Flowers
Friday, June 12th - Kallenford

Liz sat in an old wicker chair the garden, her legs covered with a woolen blanket as she read a dog-eared murder mystery she'd found on one of the many bookshelves in the lodge. She looked up at the sound of the front doorbell ringing. Closing the book, she listened.

Julia open the door and greet someone, then she appeared in the kitchen doorway that led out into the garden. She grinned, then stepped aside to let Andrew through. He was carrying a bouquet of wild flowers, and was scrubbed and shaved and wearing a light blue shirt.

"Hi," he said with a soft smile.

"Hi," Liz replied, putting the book on the table next to her.

Julia took her leave, briefly glancing at Liz, giving her a knowing look.

"May I join you?" Andrew asked.

"Sure," she replied, careful not to show any emotion.

"Is this seat taken?" he asked, nodding to the chair next to her, his blue eyes earnest.

"Not that I'm aware of," she replied, and then, before she

could stop herself, she said, "You look nice."

The hint of a smile appeared on his face.

"Thanks. I tried to make an effort. I brought these for you." He said, handing her the bouquet before taking a seat in the wicker chair.

"Thank you, they're lovely," she replied, breathing in the delicate fragrance.

Andrew looked at his hands, then said,

"I've missed you the last couple of days. Have you been busy?"

Liz stared at the bouquet so she could avoid his gaze.

"No, it's just... Sue at the River's Retreat told me who you are."

Andrew's brow furrowed in confusion, before realization tightened his jaw.

"I see," he said, his voice uncharacteristically cool. "So, she told you that my father is the Earl, but that has nothing to do with me, Liz. That doesn't change who I am."

"Why didn't you tell me?"

"Tell you what? There's nothing to tell," said Andrew, frustration seeping into his voice. "My family lives in a castle, so what? Nobody gets to choose their family, or where they come from, and I certainly don't believe it defines who you are. Wouldn't you agree?"

"I suppose," replied Liz. "So you live in Kallenford Castle, then?"

"God, no," he said, laughing. "I live in the old groundskeepers' cottage at the edge of the estate. It's falling down a bit, but it has running water and electricity, so it's just fine for me."

"Oh."

"Let me ask you something," he said, leaning forward and looking deep into her eyes. "Would it have mattered to you if my family had been dirt poor?"

"No," said Liz, as her breath quickened. *Why did he have to be so goddamn gorgeous?*

"Then I don't see why it matters who my family is. Did I misjudge you, Liz? I didn't think you would make assumptions about people so easily."

"Now, that's not fair," Liz countered.

"Isn't it?" He said, his eyes hard as steel.

Taking a deep breath, he exhaled and smiled at her. "Look, I'm sorry. This isn't how I wanted this to go. I only came to tell you I've missed our talks, and I wish you would come back tomorrow so we can talk some more. I enjoy spending time with you. I hope you can forgive me for my unfortunate heritage, and give me another chance?"

A smile broke through despite her defenses, and she said,

"I suppose you're right. You can't choose your family, so I will choose to overlook the fact that you own everything as far as the eye can see."

Andrew waved a dismissive hand in her direction. "I own nothing but a bashed up old motorbike and some threadbare clothes. It's my father that owns the rest of it, let's be clear."

"Whatever," Liz said, shaking her head and raising an eyebrow.

"Hey, now that we're friends again, do you want to go for a walk?" Andrew asked, holding out his hand.

"Sure, why not?" she replied. "Let me put these flowers in a vase and grab my sweater."

They wandered down the lane past the nodding cow parsley until they reached the edge of the river. There they stood in comfortable silence, watching the ducks bobbing under the water, busy collecting delicious morsels under the warm summer sun.

Andrew took Liz's hand and led her to a bend in the river. Her heart was thumping and her whole body tingled at his touch, but he was blissfully unaware, completely enthralled as he was, by the beauty of the surrounding nature.

He pointed out a hidden otter's den. Kneeling down, he whispered to her, "Look there, do you see it? She's had babies recently. If you crouch here for long enough, you'll see her going in and out. She'll care for them for an entire year before they're ready to venture out on their own."

Liz watched him as he identified different plant species along the riverbank and talked about the summers of his childhood catching trout and rowing an old wooden boat up and down this stretch of the river. His eyes shone with joy as he recounted his old adventures.

"See this old oak?" he asked, shading his eyes from the sun. "If you climb up about halfway, you can look right over the fields to the ruins of a pele tower. That was once the headquarters of the Armstrong-Bell clan. You want to see? Come here and I'll give you a boost up to the first branch."

As he laced his fingers together and signaled for her to climb, she put her hands on her hips and laughed.

"You are completely crazy if you think I'm going to climb a tree."

"Why not?"

"Who are you, Peter Pan? You know you have to grow up some time, don't you?"

"Never," he said, and winked at her. Her stomach contracted in response. She couldn't help but want him.

"You love it here, don't you?" She said, her heart full.

A deep, contented smile grew across his face. "Yes, I really do. It's home, but it's so much more than that.

"I love to watch the seasons change, everything moving together like the cogs of a huge invisible clock, so seamless and intricate, unaffected by the day-to-day worries of the human world.

In early spring, it's as if nature herself stretches, yawns and rubs her eyes as the snowdrops bow down to her. Then she shakes out her skirts and the daffodils raise their trumpets to herald the coming of a new year; the woodland floor blanketed with their golden glow. The chaffinch and the thrush begin to sing, and the ospreys come home to nest again.

"Then it's lambing season, and the rabbits have their kits, and if you sit still and quiet for long enough and look through the trees, you can see the new fawns wobbling about on their spindly legs. Then the days warm and lengthen and you can lie in the long grass with the warmth of the sun on your face, breathing in the honeysuckle as you listen to the bumblebees buzzing lazily from flower to flower.

"In the autumn, the leaves turn from soft green to flaming orange and gold, mirroring the warm crackling of the fires in the hearth. The stags stand tall in the early morning mist, pacing and pawing the ground, shaking their huge antlers, ready for rutting season. Then there's one last chance to wade out into the river and catch a shimmering trout before the fishing season comes to a close.

"In the winter, the ground is hard and everything is asleep. The sky is brooding with gray scudding clouds and the days are short and frosty. I love that time, though. It's a time for reflection. A time to turn inwards and breathe deeply after the excitement of the year. It's when our family gathers together for huge meals and glasses of whiskey, and to laugh and tell tales, before the cycle begins again."

Liz felt a lump in her throat.

"Well, Andrew, you are full of surprises, aren't you?" she said quietly. "It seems you are a blacksmith with the soul of a poet."

"Don't tease me," he replied, looking solemn.

"I'm not. Honestly. That was beautiful."

Andrew sighed, the shadow of a smile on his lips as he said.

"I'm very lucky to have so many wonderful memories here. I left to go to university, and I was away for a while, but I've always been drawn back here. It's where I'm at my happiest."

He combed his fingers through his hair as if to shake off the weight of the moment and looked at her, his eyes shimmering with adventure and merriment again. "Anyway. Where do you want to go next?" he asked. "You could borrow some waders and I'll teach you how to fly fish? Or we could take the horses out for a hack? Do you ride?"

"I have a better idea," replied Liz with a slow, suggestive smile. "This groundskeeper's cottage you mentioned earlier. It sounds like a death trap to me."

She stepped towards him, close enough to smell his warm, earthy aroma.

She traced a finger down his strong jawline as she continued. "I'm thinking that I should come and check it out, just to make sure you're not going to die in your bed from a gas leak, or have the roof cave in on you or something."

Andrew looked at her closely, his expression no longer that of a playful boy, and she felt the electricity build between them.

"You could be right," he said, taking her hand again. "It seems only wise to get a second opinion on the safety of the place, and I would value your advice. I wouldn't want to put myself at risk after all. It's just down the path there, if you can spare the time?" he nodded towards a break in the trees.

"Oh, I think it would be time well invested," Liz said, nodding sagely as her eyes met his. "It's for your safety after all," she said, and allowed him to lead her away from the river and through the forest.

They fell through the door of the cottage, pulling at each other's clothes, breathing in each other's scent.

He kissed her deeply before pulling off her sweater and

shirt in one movement. He laid gentle kisses from her earlobe down the side of her neck and across her shoulder blade whilst he slipped off her bra. She shivered, her knees almost buckling beneath her.

With no effort at all, he lifted her, kicking the front door closed behind him before carrying her to the bed. Slowly, he laid her down, pulling off her jeans as she writhed in anticipation. With his hands on either side of her head, he kissed her again, gently at first, then deeply, with a growing sense of urgency.

She ripped at his shirt, pulling it over his head, exposing the muscles of his arms and chest. Running her fingers down the contours of his body, she reached for his belt, but he caught her hand.

"What's the hurry?" he asked, his voice gravelly with arousal. "I'm in no rush. I've been dreaming about this ever since we met, and now I can't believe you're actually here with me. I want this moment to last forever."

He traced a line from her lips down to her breast and she exploded in a crescendo of delight.

"Jesus," she thought. *"What is he doing to me? I can't remember the last time I felt like this. In fact, I don't think I've ever felt like this."*

As he lifted her again and again to the brink of delight, allowing her to crash into the dark abyss of sweet ecstasy she lost all sense of time and place, and knew only the feeling of her body melding with his, moving with him and climaxing again and again.

They lay, exhausted and damp from sweat, neither wanting to break the silence as the sun set outside the cottage window.

"You good?" Andrew whispered as he touched her, making her skin tingle all over.

"Yes," she said, not wanting to say more.

"No regrets?" he asked, propping himself up on his elbow, his brow furrowed with concern.

"None," she said, running a finger across his soft lips.

"Will you stay a little longer?" He asked. "It's getting dark outside, so I'll walk you home if you'd prefer. I have a powerful flashlight and I'll make sure you get home safely, but I'd love it if you'd stay for a little while longer?"

He looked so earnest, so serious, that it made Liz want to kiss him.

"Yes, I'll stay. But only because you asked so nicely," she said, as she snuggled into the warmth of his chest.

She shut her eyes and breathed him in, listening to the owl hooting in the tree outside and floating in an ocean of contentment that enveloped them both.

"Watch out, Liz," she thought to herself. *"This is just a summer romance. You better not fall for him."*

But secretly, she knew it was already too late.

16

Butterflies
Friday, June 19th - Kallenford

Liz lay on her front, her head to one side, watching the trees slowly waving in the summer breeze outside the cottage window. Andrew lay next to her, propped up on one elbow, tracing shapes across her back with his fingers. It made her skin tingle deliciously, and she sighed with contentment.

He kissed her arm and said, "Can we just lie here all day? I don't want to be anywhere else, ever."

She smiled and rolled over to look at him.

She drew a finger lightly up his arm and across his biceps.

"You're asking for trouble, doing that. Now we have to stay here all day," he whispered, leaning in to kiss her, but she pushed him away playfully.

"No. No more of that. I've spent most of the last week in this bed, but now I have to go back to the lodge and pack."

"Go later. Stay here with me," he replied, and the fire in his eyes made her tighten and pulse, god he could turn her on with just one look.

"Stop it, you're incorrigible. No, I have to pack this afternoon. Our flights are early tomorrow morning and

Chrissy is already freaking out that I'm doing everything at the last moment. Plus, you said you had two projects you absolutely had to finish today. You can't let your customers down, and I'm not sure 'I've been too busy having sex' is a valid excuse for missing a deadline," she said, raising an eyebrow.

"Spoil sport," he said, play-swatting her as he reached for his shorts.

She watched as he pulled a white t-shirt over his arms and chest. He looked down at her.

"What?" He said.

"Just admiring the view," she replied with a suggestive smile.

"You're not making this easy for me," he said, leaning in to kiss her.

As he sat next to her on the bed, she ran her fingers over the thick cotton of his shirt.

"Why do you have these little holes everywhere? Do you have moths? It wouldn't surprise me in that old musty wardrobe of yours."

He chuckled. "Yes, I have moths. Tiny red-hot moths that fly around me while I'm working. They tend to eat holes in my shirts when they land on me."

"Oh, of course. I didn't think of that." Liz replied.

Just a week ago, they had made love for the first time, holding each other all night until the dawn rays shone through the window, casting soft patterns on their skin. Since then, she had spent every day sitting in the forge watching Andrew as he worked. It had been blisteringly hot and deafeningly loud, but also exhilarating, and she'd been fascinated to see how expertly he created beautiful shapes from otherwise unyielding pieces of metal.

She could see him now, standing by the forge, watching and waiting, moving the metal as it heated. The glowing reds, oranges and brilliant whites of alchemy, turning the hard steel into a material he could shape to his will. In the immense heat of the forge, the unyielding became pliable and compliant, its true nature exposed, its beauty brought forth by his expert hands.

At the right moment, he would transfer the bar from the forge to the anvil and, bringing all his strength to bear, he would swing the hammer down onto the glowing-red steel. Each impact would create a shower of bright sparks and her ears would ring with the clang as she watched him bend and shape the metal using pliers and tongs, blocks and swages, punches and chisels.

She had watched him create simple, practical items such as nails and horseshoes, but also stunning works of art like Damascus knives with exquisite patterns on a blade sharp enough to slice through paper with ease.

She smiled.

"What are you thinking about?" He asked quietly.

"I was just picturing you surrounded by all those tiny flying sparks. Not moths, but tiny butterflies. Creatures of transformation, hot as the sun, flying all about you, keeping you safe."

She looked at the ceiling and inhaled deeply. "I love butterflies. They have a special meaning for me."

"My mother loves butterflies as well," Andrew said. "Whenever she sees one, she quotes an old Irish blessing, 'May the wings of the butterfly kiss the sun, and find your shoulder to light on. To bring you luck, happiness and riches, today, tomorrow and beyond.'"

"That's beautiful," Liz whispered. "I lost a friend last year. Her name was Rachel. We were close when we were young, but we'd grown apart. She took her own life. It was heartbreaking. She loved butterflies and everything they symbolize; strength and fragility, and also breathtaking transformation. I always think of her when I see a butterfly now, and I hope that I'm making her proud.

"She brought us back together, you know? Me and Chrissy, and our friend Emily. We hadn't spoken in so long, but Rachel's memorial brought us back into each other's lives at just the right time. We all thought we were doing fine. Great, in fact. We'd each collected the necessary trappings of success; the high-powered career, the husbands and kids, all the things we were told we should strive for. But none of us were genuinely happy. Something needed to change in order to push us to risk everything we had and reach for something more. Something definitely changed for me. I lost Xander but gained Lauren and Naomi, and through them I found an ability to love that I didn't even realize was there." Liz smiled as she pictured Naomi's dear little face, then the smile faded as she bit her lip.

"And are you happy now?" asked Andrew.

Liz smiled at him. "I'm getting there. I'm realizing that this is a lifetime's journey, though."

As they sat in the stillness of the cottage, Andrew put an arm around her.

"I don't want you to go," he said quietly.

"I have to," she replied.

"Liz?" he said, turning to her, his eyes as dark and serious as an approaching storm, "I know it's only been a week, but I.. I think.."

"Stop," she said quickly, standing up and gathering her things. "This has been wonderful. Amazing. But Andrew, it needs to end here. We have very different lives, and it could never work between us. Don't spoil what we've had by thinking about what could be."

"I don't want to lose you," he said, reaching for her arm. "I've never felt like this before."

"It's only been a week. Let's not build this into something

it isn't," she said in a clipped tone.

"So, you don't feel the same way?"

"No, Andrew, I don't," she lied. "And now I need to leave."

He watched from the doorway as she walked down the path.

He hoped she would turn around, but she didn't.

She couldn't.

She didn't want him to see the tears running down her face.

"There you are, finally," said Chrissy, standing with her back to the bedroom door as she grappled with an overfilled suitcase that threatened to explode at any moment. "I thought I was going to have to come down to that cottage myself and drag you out of there. So," she said, in a gooey tone, "are the star-crossed lovers heartbroken to be separated?" She turned, the teasing grin dropping from her face in an instant as she saw Liz's tear-stained cheeks. "Oh god, Liz. Are you alright?"

"I will be," Liz replied, sitting heavily on the bed and taking a deep, shaky breath.

"Seriously, I'm so sorry to joke like that. I didn't realize you'd be so upset," Chrissy said, sitting next to her and putting an arm around her shoulder.

"I know. It's ridiculous, isn't it?" Liz said, wiping her face, while trying to shake off the feeling. "I'm acting like a bloody teenager. I need to grow up and move on."

"Oh, hun. I'm sorry you're hurting. Maybe this was more than just a silly summer romance, after all?"

Liz sat up straight, pulling herself away from Chrissy.

"No, you're wrong. Yes, it was fun and I'm going to miss him, but it was a week of fun and sex in the Scottish countryside, that's all, and I'm ready to go home and get back to my real life now."

Chrissy said nothing.

She watched as Liz began busying herself with packing; pulling all her clothes out of the tiny closet and throwing them on to the bed.

"Could you come back and visit?" Chrissy ventured.

"Just drop it, OK? I don't want to talk about it anymore," Liz snapped back.

"Do you really think there could be something in this? Something with a future?" Chrissy asked.

"For fuck's sake, Chrissy," Liz spat as she slammed her suitcase onto the bed. "Just leave it alone, please."

"But…"

"Of course, there's no future in this," Liz said, her voice breaking. "What kind of fucking future could there be? What? Do I leave my six-figure job to come and live here with Andrew in his tiny, unheated, leaky stone cottage? Then what? I get a job as a barmaid at the King's Head to make ends meet? No, thank you. We'd end up hating each other, and I would have lost everything I've ever worked for."

"I was just saying that maybe…"

"Maybe what, Chrissy," Liz said, whirling around holding a shampoo bottle that she looked as if she might throw. "Maybe what? Most of us don't live in a fucking fantasy world like you. Are you even aware of how lucky you are? You have an enormous house and a rich husband who dotes on you, and two amazing kids, and you're still not happy. Most people would kill for what you have, and yet you're still whining on about wanting more. Sometimes I think you're nothing more than a selfish little bitch!"

Chrissy stood up from the bed and walked over to Liz.

She wrapped her arms around her, and Liz, unable to hold back the emotion any longer, wept hard, deep, wracking sobs.

Her body shook as Chrissy held her.

Eventually her breathing slowed, and she sat back on the bed, spent.

"I'm sorry. That was a shitty thing to say," Liz said, quietly.

Chrissy smiled and put a hand on her knee. "It's OK. You reminded me a bit of Jackie. She always strikes out like a viper when she's hurting."

"Yes, but Jackie is a kid, and at my age I'm supposed to know better," Liz said, looking chagrined.

"To be fair, there is some truth in what you said. I see it. I'm not completely naïve. But right now, I'm more concerned about you and what we're going to do about this whole Andrew situation."

Liz shook her head and returned to her packing. "There's nothing that can be done. I suppose I just need to file it under 'maybe in another life' and leave it at that."

"Can I ask you something?" Chrissy said, her head on one side.

"What?"

"Do you love him?"

Liz continued to fold her sweaters. "Don't be silly," she said. "I can't love him. I've only known him for a week."

"But, do you?" Chrissy said, her eyes fixed on Liz.

Liz carefully folded one arm of the sweater over the other before saying, "I'm not going to answer that because I don't see that it matters either way. Things are the way they are, and we are going back home tomorrow. Back to reality."

"But if you feel this strongly and he does too, then shouldn't you do everything in your power to make it work?"

Liz placed the sweater in her suitcase and turned to Chrissy.

"What would you suggest I do? Can you think of a single

scenario where this works out and we all get our 'happily ever after'? I don't want to spoil what I had by wishing for more. Now, I love you, but you need to let this go, agreed?"

Chrissy nodded, but her eyes showed her pain. She wished she could give her oldest and best friend the fairytale ending she deserved, but Liz was right. Tomorrow, they would leave this Scottish country paradise behind them and head back to the real world.

17

Vegas
Thursday, July 2nd - Las Vegas

Emily waved down the barman.

"Can I get a glass of sparkling water, please? With a slice of lime in it?" She asked, raising her voice against the background music.

Further down the bar, a pack of young male Apex employees were downing tequila shots. Investors and Analysts with degrees and MBAs from all the most prestigious schools, they shouted and goaded each other on, the timbre of their voices unmistakably that of white, privileged, college jocks who had always had the best of everything.

"They take up so much space and energy in a room," thought Emily to herself, as she waited for her drink. *"Space they assume they are entitled to."*

"Hey, Emily," Zach shouted to her in a slurred tone. "Come join us." He beckoned to her, his wide, muscular frame swaying ever so slightly. He raised a shot glass in her direction. Salt, lime, and down it went. A cheer went up from the other guys as they clapped him on the back.

"Thanks, but I'm drinking vodka and soda," she shouted back, as the barman handed her a glass.

She raised it in the air towards them in salute and headed back to her table.

Kolleen greeted her as she sat back down.

"Those boys are going to be wasted if they keep going like that," she said, lifting her chin in the direction of Zach and his gang, who were ordering yet another round of tequila.

"I don't know how they haven't passed out already. There was so much wine over dinner, and so many toasts during the awards that I'm struggling to stay sober myself, and I'm pacing myself, unlike those goons."

"Yeah, but they pretty much drink for a living. They've been chugging down beer kegs ever since their frat days, and before that, no doubt. It'll catch up to them one day, though. You can't keep going like that forever."

"God, don't we sound old," Emily chuckled, and Kolleen made a face and nodded.

"What do you think of Vegas? This is your first time, yes?" Kolleen asked.

"It's insane," said Emily, sipping her water. "It's like another world. I mean, this place is incredible, but golden palm trees and huge sweeping staircases? Really? It's so opulent. I love Art déco, but I feel like I'm on the set of The Great Gatsby, which is appropriate, I suppose, given the extravagance of it all."

Kolleen laughed. "Yup, Vegas always takes it that extra mile. Brody loves it here, and the Wynn is his favorite place to stay. There are rumors he's friends with Steve Wynn himself. When they announced they were going to open a Delilah's right here at the Wynn, Brody was over the moon. He's a regular at the original Delilah's in West Hollywood, you know?"

Emily smiled and nodded, trying to look relaxed, but

secretly she was struggling with the feeling that she was completely out of her depth.

From the moment she stepped off the plane, she had felt wrong-footed. Walking out of the gate in the terminal, she had been taken aback by the rows of slot machines, flashing and whirring, while jangling tinny music played at volume. She had never imagined they would have slot machines right there in the airport next to the newspaper stands and the fast-food restaurants.

As she collected her bags from the carousel, she'd been jostled by men in dinner jackets, and others in Bermuda shorts. Everything seemed louder and more gaudy than she was used to, and the smell of weed and cigarette smoke was overpowering.

There had been a driver at arrivals holding a sign with her name on it, and as she sat in the back of the hulking black car she had strained to see through the tinted windows, craning her neck to look up at the buildings as they flashed past.

At that moment, she was glad she'd opted for a later flight. She wouldn't have wanted the other Apex employees to see her so wide eyed and enchanted with it all. She was like a country mouse in the city for the first time.

When she'd stepped into the foyer of the Wynn, her jaw had dropped. The cream-colored marble floors shone under the lights, and immense marble columns reached up to impossibly high vaulted ceilings. Rich carpets and heavy drapes softened the lines, creating an atmosphere of opulence that made Emily think of an ancient roman temple.

Rounding the corner, she found herself in a magical garden. Under the vaulted ceilings, avenues of trees glittered with fairy lights, while a sculptured carousel, its horses made entirely of tiny flowers, spun slowly as its organ music echoed softly up to the hotel floors above.

Walking through the casino towards the elevators,

everything seemed to glitter or spin or flash and she swallowed as the pervasive cigarette smoke caught in her throat. By the time she reached her room on the 36th floor, she was overwhelmed, drained and a little homesick.

But she had adapted and even come to appreciate the pulsing energy of this crazy town.

The conference had gone well, and Brody had been impressed with her ideas to increase productivity at the manufacturing plant. As they reached the final evening, she was confident and in control, and ready to let her hair down a little. She had purchased a long, emerald green dress to wear, and she'd been pleasantly surprised at how it had flattered her curves. Her world had been shaken to its very core over the last couple of weeks, but just like a phoenix, she was rising from the ashes.

"Can I buy you a drink?"

Emily started, pulled abruptly from her reverie. She looked up into the face of Brody, his deep blue eyes sparkling. He was wearing a baby blue cotton shirt open at the neck, with the sleeves rolled up to show his tanned, muscular arms. She spied the Rolex on his wrist, *"only the best for Brody,"* she thought to herself.

"Sorry, I was miles away," she said.

"I'm very glad you're not. I'd much prefer you to be right here, with me," he said, a soft smile on his lips.

"I think champagne is in order," he said. "Kolleen? Could you ask them to bring over a bottle of Dom Pérignon?"

Kolleen hesitated before heading to the bar.

"Oh, no. That's not necessary," said Emily, her eyes wide.

"Far from it. I'm celebrating, and who better to celebrate with, but the woman who's making my dreams a reality? You look incredible tonight, by the way."

"Thank you," said Emily, blushing. "In fact, as you're here, I wanted to talk to you about the new…"

"Not tonight," he stopped her. "Tonight is for celebrating."

"Actually, it's getting kinda late, and I wanted to get some sleep before the flight tomorrow," Emily said, swallowing.

"No problem. Can I at least walk you to your room?"

Emily felt a prickle as her senses became more heightened. She wasn't naïve, and she knew where this could lead.

"Sure," she found herself saying.

He took her hand as she stood, and her skin quivered deliciously.

As they walked towards the elevators, he talked about the architecture of the Wynn. He was both knowledgeable and appreciative when it came to the art and science of creating such a magnificent building.

As he pointed out the various features, Emily nodded and smiled, breathing slowly as she tried to stop her heart from thumping through her chest. Had she misread the situation, or was this really heading where she thought? No, it couldn't be. Brody wasn't interested in her in that way, was he?

As they reached the bank of elevators, he turned to her and said, "I'm staying in one of the tower suites. The views from there are quite spectacular. Would you like to see them?" he asked her, his eyes sharp and focused.

"I'd love to," she replied, shocked at her own boldness, her body tingling with equal measures of apprehension and desire.

As Brody held the elevator door open for her and she stepped inside, a whisper of guilt brushed the back of her neck. She was still a married woman, after all. But then, that hadn't stopped Ed, had it? He had fallen into bed with someone else with no regard for her or for their life together. If he could so easily toss aside their marriage, then why shouldn't she do the same? For as long as she could remember, she had put the needs of others before her own, until she had lost herself completely. Now it was her turn.

Now she got to choose what she wanted.

And she wanted Brody.

As the elevator whisked them up to the highest floors of the building, Brody stepped towards her, taking her face in his hands. His eyes burned into her, and she felt the heat rising from deep within her body.

Her breath was shallow, and her heart raced. She wanted to feel his skin on hers. To feel him inside her.

He leaned forward, slowly, and touched his lips to hers. An explosion of desire washed through her, making her shiver.

"I've been thinking about this for the longest time," said Brody in a whisper.

At the door of his suite, he swiped the plastic card against the pad and then stood aside, letting her walk through.

It was huge but tasteful, decorated in taupe and peach tones. A sofa, several chairs, and a coffee table stood in front of an expansive wrap-around window that overlooked the Vegas strip.

Emily walked to the window to take in the view. The scene below was both beautiful and gaudy, rainbow colored lights twinkling like a million fireflies trapped in a gauze of midnight blue satin.

"Vegas. There's no place like it," said Brody, standing behind her, his breath on her neck.

"It's not real, though," Emily whispered. "It's just a performance. An illusion."

"Isn't that true of life? Aren't we all just projecting our own carefully curated version of reality? All the world's a stage…"

"And all the men and women merely players," Emily murmured as she turned to face him.

"Life is what you make it, and right now, all I want is you, Emily."

His hand was on her back, pulling her towards him. His lips on hers, urgent and searching, his mouth hot and wet, he tasted of champagne.

His fingers found the zipper on the back of her dress and as it slipped from her shoulders and fell to the floor, she inhaled sharply.

Brody looked at her, taking in every curve of her body before saying, "You are stunning, Emily. Just incredible."

Breathing hard, she reached for him, pulling open his shirt and running her hands over his chest.

He pushed her up against the window, the cold glass making her naked skin shiver.

He grabbed her hands and held them above her head.

"I've got you now," he whispered. "You're mine."

"No, I'm not, and I never will be," said Emily, looking at him dead in the eye. "That's why you want me, isn't it?"

He pulled her to the bed, holding her down against the sheets, but she fought back, and climbed on top of him. Shaking with arousal, she felt a rush of power building inside her, a fire that could no longer be contained.

She straddled him, pinning him down when he tried to sit up.

"Now, I've got you," she whispered, her eyes flashing as she positioned herself over him.

"Fuck them. Fuck them all," she thought to herself, as she began to ride him. *"How dare they try to control me, dampen me down, and tell me who I am. I'm done with it. I'm rising from the fucking ashes and you'll see who I truly am. From now on, I'm going to take what I want, and be who I want, and no one will get in my way."*

As the sweet, wet, crescendo of pleasure rushed through her, she flung her arms out wide, reveling in the fiery explosion of her own delirious glory.

Collapsing next to Brody, she tried to catch her breath as the delicious aftershocks washed over her.

"I knew it," said Brody, quietly.

"What?"

"I knew that quiet country mouse act was bullshit. I called it from the start. I could see who you were the minute you walked into our offices."

"And who am I?" Emily said, turning to look at him.

"You're a fucking Alpha. Always have been, always will be."

"Yes I am," she said, smiling. "And don't you ever forget it."

18

Juggling
Thursday, July 16th - Pasadena

As Chrissy reached into the sink to grab another plate, she heard her cell phone ring. Pulling it out of her back pocket, she wedged it between her ear and her shoulder so she could continue to fill the dishwasher.

"Hi baby, you OK?" she asked.

"Hey mom," said Jackie, "I'm going to the mall with Genevieve after practice, so you don't have to pick me up from the gym. Her mom is going to drop us there, but can you pick me up at 6.30pm?"

"Which mall are you going to?"

"The Galleria."

Chrissy huffed in frustration. "Jackie, I can't be in Glendale at 6.30pm because your brother's track meet finishes at 5.30pm in Oxnard. Can Genevieve's mom drop you home?"

"No, because they're going straight out for dinner. Really, mom? I've said I can go now," Jackie replied with irritation in her voice.

"Well, I can't be in two places at the same time Jackie, so you need to check with me before you agree to things like this."

"Can't I just stay at the mall until you get there? How long will it take to get back from the track meet?"

"No, you're not hanging out at the mall on your own, and you know these track meets can run over. I'll just pick you up from the gym after practice, like we agreed."

"But, mom," whined Jackie. "That sucks. Can you at least wash my jeans before you leave so I can wear them tomorrow for Antonella's sleepover? I've got no clean clothes, and my laundry basket has been full for three days now."

Chrissy closed the dishwasher and headed towards Jackie's room.

"There's nothing to stop you putting your dirty clothes in the washing machine yourself, you know? Why can't anyone in this house do anything for themselves?"

"Thanks, mom. Love you. See you in a bit."

Chrissy maneuvered her daughter's overflowing laundry basket down the stairs and into the laundry room. She opened the lid of the washing machine and cursed. It was already filled with a load of laundry, and who knows how long it had been sitting there. She pulled out a t-shirt and sniffed it. Yuck. Damp and musty. It would all need to be washed again.

As she refilled the detergent and softener and pulled Jackie's jeans out of the basket to add them to the wash, her phone vibrated again.

"What now?" she cursed under her breath.

Grabbing the phone, she looked at the caller ID.

A moment of confusion, followed by a slam of guilt.

Shit.

It was Joe, and today was Tuesday. She looked at the time. 1pm.

Shit. Shit.

"Hi, Joe," she said into the phone.

"Hi. You ready? You said you would send over the new chapters before our call, but I checked my email and I haven't received them."

Chrissy grimaced.

"Um, yes. I'm so sorry, Joe. I totally forgot to put our call on my calendar. When we spoke last week, I was in the car and I was going to put it in as soon as I got home. But when I got inside I realized that Doogie had thrown up on the living room carpet, and by the time I'd cleaned it up our arrangement had totally slipped my mind."

"I see," said Joe with irritation. "Well, you can send them to me now and we can discuss them, unless you have some other canine emergency that needs to be dealt with?"

Chrissy put her hand to her forehead.

"Um, well, you see, I haven't actually had time to write anything this week. It's been crazy busy with the kids' activities. Jackie is in camp every day and Josh has track meets all over the place right now, so we're up at 5am most days so I can drive him to practice."

There was silence from the other end of the phone.

"Chrissy, I'm not sure how committed you are to your writing, and I'm not prepared to waste my time on someone who keeps prioritizing other things. Don't you have a nanny or someone who can drive them to these activities? How do you ever expect to become a serious writer when you're wasting all your time driving your kids around?"

"The kids are too old for a nanny, and I don't feel like I could justify hiring additional help until I'm earning some money from the writing."

"You're not going to earn anything from writing if you don't actually do any writing. That's how it works, Chrissy."

She dropped her shoulders and screwed up her face.

"I know, I know. I just need to manage my time better," she said.

"You need to start focusing on what really matters. On building your legacy. You will never become a successful writer if you spend all your time gossiping with other mothers at track meets, Chrissy. Come on, you're better than that."

"I know. I'm sorry. And I'm sorry for wasting your time today. I'm going to work on my new chapters this week and I'll have them to you by our next call, if that's OK?"

"Fine. But my patience with this whole business isn't going to last forever, understand?"

Joe hung up before she could respond.

Chrissy walked to the living room and slumped onto the couch. She put her head in her hands and rubbed her temples, trying to hold back the tension headache already forming behind her eyes.

He wasn't wrong, of course. Hemingway never wasted his time at ice cream socials, or school fundraisers, or gymnastics competitions.

But then, she didn't want to be Hemingway. She wanted to be herself.

Herself, but also a successful author. Were the two even compatible, she wondered?

And what did she know about being a famous author? She should listen to Joe's advice. He'd been there already, after all. He'd achieved what she could only dream of.

She thought back to the days she had spent in his drawing room in the hunting lodge in Kallenford, and her chest tightened.

On one particularly cold, blustery day, he'd set her a writing exercise designed to improve her ability to evoke 'internal struggle'. The setting; the Battle of the Somme, France, 1916. The protagonist; a seventeen-year-old boy from a poor Yorkshire village. The task; to describe his feelings as he went over the top. How he felt watching his fellow soldiers being mown down on either side of him as they ran towards the enemy lines.

In a moment she was back there, her pen hovering over the empty page of her Moleskine notebook. Her jaw clenched as she sat, trying to form the words, the oppressive silence broken only by the clink of the ice in Joe's whiskey glass, and the ticking of the clock on the mantelpiece.

She allowed her mind to fall into that awful scene. Hell on earth. The smell of open latrines and rotting bodies accosting her, the lingering gas stinging her lungs. She could see the fear in the eyes of the other young boys around her, lambs to the slaughter. As the call came to advance, she choked back the sickening mixture of anger and disillusionment that rose like bile in the boy's throat as he ran, stumbling, towards those deafening guns. All that blood. All that waste. Teenagers not much older than Josh. And her tears began to fall.

"What are you sniveling about?" Joe's voice came, harsh, like the crack of gunfire, making her jump.

"I don't think I can write about this," Chrissy whispered.

Joe slammed his whiskey glass down on the side table next to him.

"Would you rather write about sunsets and happy endings?" He snorted with contempt. "Anyone can write that drivel. It's worthless. Consumed one day and forgotten the next. Is that what you want? To write pointless nonsense? Or do you want to write something that matters? Do you want to be remembered?"

Chrissy bit her lip, looking towards the door, wishing she was brave enough to bolt through it. Instead, she sat stock still, her eyes fixed on the ground.

"Well?" Came Joe's voice, sharp as a razor. "I'm waiting for an answer."

"I don't want to write about war," said Chrissy in a small

voice.

"Why not?" demanded Joe. "War is the ultimate struggle. It reveals who you are and what you are made of. It gets to the very core of what it means to be human."

"I disagree," said Chrissy. "There's already enough pain and suffering in the world. I don't want to add to it. I want to offer something else with my writing."

"Oh, you do, do you?" said Joe, leaning back in his chair, his eyes boring into her. "And what is that, pray tell?"

Chrissy looked down again.

"I don't know, yet."

"No, you don't," said Joe, leaning forward, his eyes flashing, cold and hard as steel. "So, I would suggest that you stop telling me what you do and don't want to do, and do as I bloody well tell you!"

Chrissy shivered at the memory.

It had been a harrowing couple of weeks under Joe's tutelage, and she had found herself in tears on more than one occasion. Thankfully, Liz had been so engrossed with her budding romance with Andrew that she hadn't noticed.

It had been harder to keep it from Scott since she'd got home. She had tried to avoid talking about Joe because, however hard she tried, she could see her pain reflected in his eyes when she did.

Scott had suggested that maybe she find a different mentor, but she was determined to see this through. She was tough and she wouldn't let Joe break her. He was a talented writer, and despite the challenges, she would learn everything she could from him.

Joe's words came back to her again.

It was true. If she was going to become a successful author, she needed to dedicate more time to her writing. She needed to prioritize.

"How do I do it, though?" She thought to herself. "How do

I continue to be all things to all people and still have time for myself? Does something have to give? And if so, what do I give up?"

Suddenly Chrissy was exhausted.

Her phone rang again.

"Fucking hell. What now?" She reached for her phone in frustration, but was pleasantly surprised to see Emily's name on the screen.

"Hey, stranger! It's so good to hear from you!" Chrissy says with relief. "God, I could really do with some girl time right now."

"Me too," replied Emily. "You want to go for margaritas tomorrow night? I need to talk to you."

"Is everything OK?" Chrissy asked, concerned.

"Yes, and no. It's complicated. Basically, everything has gone to shit, but I think there's light at the end of the tunnel. I'm sorry, I should have called you earlier, but I'm ready to talk now, and we'll need several drinks to get through this, I promise you."

"Bloody hell. I can't wait to hear this," Chrissy replied, her eyes wide. "Text me the details and I'll be there."

Tucking her cell phone back into her pocket, Chrissy was determined to sit down and do some writing.

"But first I need to walk Doogie," she thought to herself. "He hasn't been out since before breakfast. And then I need to have a quick shower. It's an hour and a half to Oxnard, so I'll need to leave the house at 4pm, plus I promised to provide snacks for the team. Shit, I don't have any ice for the cooler, so I'll need to stop at the grocery store and get that on the way. And I haven't even thought about dinner yet."

Tick, tick, tick, Chrissy could feel her writing time being swallowed up. But what else could she do? She only had a finite amount of time, and what felt like a full plate of responsibilities.

"I'll write tomorrow," she promised herself, and grabbed Doogie's lead.

19

Margaritas
Friday, July 17th - Pasadena

"Wow, you look amazing!" said Chrissy as she hugged Emily. "Have you lost weight? California is obviously good for you. Let's get drinks and you can tell me everything that's been going on. It's been too long."

They ordered margaritas and found a table in the corner of the bar.

"Cheers!" said Chrissy. "Here's to a girls' night out with my fellow butterfly. About time too!"

They clinked their glasses, and each took a big swig.

"Ok, girl. Spill. I'm desperate to know what's going on with you!" Chrissy said, leaning forward with her chin in her hand.

Emily took a deep breath before taking another sip of her drink.

"Oh, my God. Where to start. Well, Ed and I are done. We're getting a divorce."

"What?" Chrissy looked stricken. "Shit, Emily, I'm so sorry. I had no idea."

"No, I know. I'm sorry, I should have called you, but I was

in denial. And I was kind of ashamed as well. Don't ask me why, it's stupid, I know. I suppose I just didn't want people to know that our marriage was in that much trouble. I genuinely thought it would all blow over, or that we'd be able to work it out."

"Could you go for couple's therapy or something? Maybe just talking it through would help?"

Emily raised an eyebrow. "Oh, we are way past that point."

"Why? What happened?"

Emily took another swig.

"As you know, Ed rented himself an apartment back in May so he could 'have some time to think.'" Emily said, doing air quotes and raising an eyebrow. "Since then we've been splitting childcare responsibilities and, in all fairness to him, he's been really flexible about stepping up when I've had meetings at work or when I'm running late. Originally, he said he needed 'time to think things over', so I gave him space. Then about a month ago, I had to go over to his apartment to get some stupid form signed for Philip. I tried to call ahead, but his cell phone was switched off. Anyway, I showed up at his door unannounced and… well…" Emily grimaced.

"What?" Chrissy said, her eyes wide.

"Let's just say he was not alone."

"Shit! So he's been having an affair? Is that the real reason he moved out? What a bastard! I'm surprised though, because Ed never struck me as the type. I guess you never know, eh?"

Emily took a deep breath and looked at her nails.

"He swears that the whole thing started after he moved out. I don't know for sure, but I'm inclined to believe him."

"Who is she? Do you know her?" Chrissy asked.

Emily cracked a bitter smile despite herself.

"Actually, I do. I do know…him."

Chrissy's brow furrowed for a moment, before realization and astonishment flooded her face.

"Ed's gay? But how?"

Emily snorted in both disbelief and amusement.

"You tell me, Chrissy. I'm as lost as you are." Emily's voice was cold and harsh. "He says he didn't even know himself. But how could you not know something like that?"

"Who? How? I'm so confused. Backup and tell me exactly what happened."

Emily drained her glass, then signaled to the barman for another round.

"The person in Ed's apartment was Conner. Conner was our contractor last year. He came out of the bathroom with a towel wrapped around his waist. We all just stared at each other before I left as quickly as I could. I was in shock for a couple of days. I mean, how do you process that kind of information? We told the kids a couple of weeks ago that the split was permanent, but we didn't tell them about Conner, or about Ed being gay. We're taking this step by step so we can try to minimize the trauma of it all."

"Oh god. How are they doing?" Chrissy said, the pain showing in her eyes.

Emily sighed and clenched her jaw.

"They're confused. And angry. It's understandable when your parents split up. At least it's not openly acrimonious. It could be worse, I guess."

"And how are you doing? You must be spinning from all of this."

Emily shrugged and gave a little smile.

"You know what? I'm doing ok. I'm more than ok, in fact," she said, her smile growing as she tilted her head to one side and gave Chrissy a knowing look.

"What? What the hell is going on? I'm completely lost," Chrissy said, throwing her hands up in surrender.

Emily laughed, her eyes sparkling and mischievous.

"Well, um. Something else happened. Something good."

Chrissy put her hand to her forehead and made a growling sound.

"I cannot keep up with this. Just tell me, Emily, for God's sake!"

Emily took a long sip of her newly arrived drink, then placed it back on the table.

"I'm sleeping with Brody."

Chrissy's eyes opened wide.

"What? Since when?"

Emily laughed, her face lit up with flirtatious fun.

"Since Vegas. I was a little drunk, I admit, but it was incredible, and we've not been able to keep our hands off each other since."

"I, I don't know what to say," said Chrissy. "I'm in shock with everything that's happened. Are you sure it's a good idea to be having a relationship with Brody? Isn't he your boss? Couldn't that get a little awkward?"

Emily shrugged her shoulders and downed her margarita.

"You know what? I don't care anymore. If I've learned anything from the last couple of months, it's that nothing is permanent, and everything can go to shit at a moment's notice. Why not have fun while you can, and not worry about what may or may not be?"

"Maybe," Chrissy said, her brow furrowed.

"Seriously, Chrissy, I'm exhausted from the constant treadmill of trying to meet everyone's expectations. I'm done. I've realized that there's no way to win. As women, it feels like we can never do enough, never be enough.

Society is always questioning us, criticizing us, and we can never measure up. Why aren't you married? If you're married, then why don't you have children? Why don't you have a career? Why do you have a career when you have children at home? Why aren't you more productive? Why are you so busy? Why aren't you thinner? Younger? Happier? It's a constant barrage of disapproval, battering at our self confidence and self worth, and often our worst critics are other women. Well, I'm tapping out of the bullshit. I'm not playing the game anymore. And I am going to champion every other woman out there who's trying her hardest to get it right. This poisonous culture needs to stop. We are enough."

A silence hung over them as Emily sat tall, her eyes sparkling.

Chrissy bit her lip before saying, "Holy shit, girl. I love this transformation. You're on fire, and you have an inner glow I've never seen before. It's like you're a totally different person."

Emily leaned in and raised an eyebrow before whispering,

"I feel different. I feel incredible. All the amazing sex helps, too. And let me tell you, the sex is mind-blowing. I'd forgotten what it feels like to want someone like that. To be completely consumed by the urge to rip his clothes off and screw right there on the desk. Seriously, I'm finding a side of me I didn't even know was there."

Chrissy covered her eyes and laughed, "Ew, stop! Enough. I can't take any more. My brain is overloading right now."

They laughed and ordered another round of drinks.

"Enough about me. How's everything with you?" Emily asked.

"Far less dramatic than you. I'm pleased to say," Chrissy replied. "Did I tell you that Liz and I went to Scotland together?"

"No, how lovely, though. Did you go on vacation?"

"Kind of. It's a long story, but it turned out that my biological father is a writer who lives in Scotland near Edinburgh and he invited me to visit."

"Your father? I didn't think you knew who your father was?"

"I didn't. But he knew about me, and when he found out I'd written a book, he got in contact with me. He offered to mentor me, to help me 'meet my full potential.'"

"Wow. Well, that's exciting."

"Yeah. I didn't want to go alone in case he turned out to be a nutcase, so I asked Liz to come with me. Lauren and Naomi moved out, so she was feeling a bit down. She needed to get away and reset, so she came with me."

"Oh, poor Liz. I feel awful that I haven't been in touch. I'll call her tomorrow and catch up with her properly."

"I know she'd like that."

"And? Was he?"

"Was who, what?"

"Your father. Was he a nutcase?"

Chrissy snorted with laughter. "Um, well, the jury is still out on that one. He's definitely eccentric, and he has some pretty rigid ideas on the 'craft of writing', but I'm learning a lot from him. Oh, and Liz met someone."

"Ooh, really? Who?"

"His name is Andrew, and he's a blacksmith. Well, kind of."

"How can you be 'kind of' a blacksmith?"

Chrissy grinned. "What I mean is that he is a blacksmith, but he's also the son of the Earl of Kallenford. His family live in a massive castle and they've lived there since the 17th century. He's basically a Lord."

"Holy shit!" Emily laughed. "Liz really knows how to pick 'em, doesn't she?"

Chrissy giggled and swatted at her through the air.

"Stop it. She was horrified when she found out who his family are. It almost derailed the whole thing. She claims it's over, but I'm not so sure. She's constantly talking to him on the phone, and my dad has invited her up to Kallenford in a couple of weeks for Andrew's surprise birthday party."

"Are they friends? Your dad and this new man of Liz's?"

"Not at all. My father has a pretty low opinion of the Armstrong-Bell family. He says they're a bunch of antiquated snobs who have no business lording it over the rest of the county. I've tried to explain to him that Andrew is nothing like the rest of his family, but he disagrees."

"Why was he handing out invitations to Andrew's birthday party if he's not friends with him?"

"I think he was just acting as an intermediary between some of Andrew's friends and Liz. Maybe he's an old romantic, after all?"

"I'm glad to hear that Liz has found someone. She deserves so much better than that awful Xander guy. I'm sorry to hear that Lauren and Naomi moved out, but I suppose it was never going to be permanent. It's a shame, though, because Liz loved that little girl."

"Yeah. Liz gave notice on the house they were renting and she's moving into a new apartment in a couple of weeks. She says that she's still on good terms with Lauren, and that she can see Naomi whenever she wants, but it won't be the same. I think Liz's mum is pretty cut up about it, too. She kinda enjoyed having a granddaughter to fuss over."

They both sighed, thinking of poor old Liz.

"How are your kids doing, by the way?" Asked Emily. "They're getting so grown up."

"Huh," huffed Chrissy. "Not grown up enough to do their own laundry, or cook for themselves, or do anything useful, it seems. Yesterday, Jackie called to me from the living room, and said 'Mom, I think the dog ate half a lizard.'"

"Ew! Half a lizard? That's very specific."

"Yeah, that's what I thought. When I asked for clarification, she said, 'it must have just been half, because the other half is lying here on the couch.'"

Emily grimaced, then guffawed, almost choking on her margarita.

The friends shared funny stories of their kids' various antics, as they ordered some appetizers from the bar. It was lovely to be back in each other's company and feel the camaraderie they had both needed more than they had realized. As the evening wore on and they shared their hopes and concerns for their children, Chrissy said,

"I just hope they can find friends as good as you and Liz, then I know they'll be alright."

"I agree," said Emily, smiling at Chrissy with love in her eyes.

20

Surprise
Friday, August 14th - Kallenford

"Hey, kid. You're late," said Joe as he opened the taxi door for Liz.

"I know. I'm sorry. The traffic getting out of Edinburgh was awful."

The taxi driver opened the trunk, pulled out Liz's overnight bag, and placed it on the driveway for her. Joe was already through the front door of the hunting lodge, so Liz thanked the driver and pulled the roller-case across the pebbled driveway. She scowled at Joe's back as she went. She was all for 'Women's Lib', but a little help wouldn't hurt.

"I know we're running late, but I might need to change before we head out. I'm worried I'm a little underdressed," she said.

"No need, kid. You look great as you are. You'll fit right in," said Joe, obviously keen to get going.

"Are you sure it'll be ok for me to stay at Andrew's place tonight? I mean, he still doesn't even know I'm coming, and I don't want to impose."

"What are you talking about, 'impose'? You guys are a

thing, aren't you? He should be more than happy to see you."

A smile flickered across Joe's face, and it gave Liz a moment of concern. Deep down, she began to question if this had been a good idea after all. Had she allowed her romantic fantasies to get the better of her? Before she could think any more of it, Joe said,

"Ok. Time to head out."

Joe bundled her into the car, and as they drove down the lane, she wished that she'd worn something more formal. It was only a small gathering at the Reiver's Rest, but it was a birthday party after all, so maybe something more elegant than her jeans and a green turtleneck sweater would have been more appropriate.

Liz looked up as the car came to a stop. She found herself looking up at the grand archways that formed the front entrance porchway of Kallenford Castle.

Confused, she turned to look at Joe. There was that grin again.

"Oh, yeah. I forgot to say. They switched the venue to the castle instead. But as you're such a lady, you won't mind adapting, will you? You're dating the Earl's son after all, so these are 'your people' now."

Liz went pale and began to protest, but the passenger door opened and a gentleman's voice said,

"Madam? Can I help you?"

"She's here for his lordship's birthday party. I'm not staying, I'm just the chauffeur," Joe said, his eyes full of cold mirth. "Go on then, Cinderella, it's time for the ball."

In a daze, Liz stepped out of the car. She followed the young man up the stone steps and through the massive, ornate front doors.

She couldn't quite process what was happening. As she stood in the imposing entrance hall, she stared at the paneled walls covered with portraits in heavy, gilded frames, her gaze drifting up the grand wooden staircase to the impossibly high, vaulted ceiling.

A waiter offered her a glass of champagne from a silver tray, and she shook her head almost imperceptibly.

With a quizzical look he said, "Madam, everyone's gathered in the drawing room. Can I show you the way? Madam? Are you OK?"

"I am, yes. Thank you for asking. Could you call me a taxi? I think there has been some sort of misunderstanding."

"As you wish," he said, nodding and turning to walk away.

At that moment, two young women came into the entrance hall, laughing and shouting, the sound of their voices echoing around them. They held champagne flutes, and it was clear from their behavior this was not their first glass.

The shorter of the two women, wearing an elegant, off the shoulder navy blue dress, squinted at Liz.

"Oh my gosh, well hello there! And you are?" she said, looking Liz up and down.

Liz steeled herself. There was no running now. She would have to face this situation head on. She lifted her chin and smiled warmly, holding out her hand to shake.

"Hi, I'm Liz. It's a pleasure to meet you."

"Fiona Stewart, and the pleasure is all mine." A cool smile turned to an expression of realization as she exclaimed, "Oh, wait a second, you're Liz. Andrew's Liz! You're practically famous around here. Andrew can't stop talking about you. But I didn't know you were coming to the party. What an absolutely wonderful surprise."

"It looks as though Liz was unaware of the dress code," said Fiona's companion, a tall, willowy woman with eyes as cold as steel. "Or are you just dropping by on your way to the shops?"

"Oh stop, Lili. She looks superb. Now, Liz, come on in and

meet everyone."

Fiona grabbed Liz by the arm and swirled her into the drawing room.

Liz did her best to keep up with the introductions, but Fiona was both excited and somewhat inebriated, so it was like being pulled along by a tornado.

"And there is Andrew himself," gushed Fiona. "Did he know you were coming tonight? Oh, he'll just die if not. How absolutely delicious!" Fiona was so gleeful that Liz couldn't help but smile.

Liz's heart jumped as she saw him. He stood by the stone fireplace, leaning on the mantle, drinking a glass of whiskey and talking with an older couple. She guessed they must be his parents, as the family resemblance was uncanny.

"For someone who claims to only be a blacksmith, he sure looks comfortable in these surroundings," she thought to herself.

He wore a kilt of rich greens and blues with a faint red stripe running through it. A white buttoned shirt and a blue blazer accentuated his wide, strong shoulders. As she watched him, he laughed, his characteristic carefree laugh, and she could feel the light and warmth radiate from him. God, she could watch him forever.

As if sensing her presence, he looked up, straight into her eyes.

For a moment, cold trepidation crept into her heart. Here she was, uninvited amongst his closest friends and family. Whatever expression crossed his face in this moment would tell her all she needed to know about how he really felt about her.

Much to her relief, his face lit up with amazement and joy.

"Liz!" He called, and, offering a quick apology to his parents, he strode towards her.

To her shock, he lifted her off her feet and spun her around, planting a kiss on her mouth.

"What on earth are you doing here? Did someone invite you? This is by far the best surprise of the evening."

Liz could only shake her head and shrug. This was not the time or place to go into Joe's scheming.

"Here, come with me. I want you to meet my parents. They're going to love you. You're staying for the whole evening, yes? And staying at my place tonight?"

"If that's ok?" said Liz, trying to seem happy and relaxed as she cringed inside. This was not how she thought this evening was going to go. "Wait," she said, stopping dead and tugging on Andrew's hand. "What do I do when you introduce me? Do I curtsey or something?"

Andrew let out a huge, rolling laugh, then hugged her and said, "No, don't be a ninny. They're not royalty, they're just like anyone else. My mother's name is Katherine and my father's name is Charles. Just shake their hands and say hi."

Andrew led the way, with Liz trailing behind.

"Mother? Father? May I introduce you to my girlfriend, Liz? Liz, this is Charles and Elizabeth."

Liz felt the color rising in her cheeks as she held out her hand to shake and said, "It's a pleasure to meet you both."

Later that night, they lay in bed together, beads of sweat glistening on their bodies as they listened to each other's breathing.

"I can't tell you how happy I am that you came tonight."

"Not as happy as I am," said Liz, raising her eyebrows and grinning suggestively at him.

"That's not what I meant, and you know it," he said, pushing her playfully. "Seriously though, I'm so glad you got to meet everyone."

"I still wish I'd had time to prepare before walking into the lion's den as it were. I can't believe Joe set me up like that. Why would he do that? He must have found out about the party from the folks in town and decided it was a perfect opportunity to humiliate me. That's a pretty shitty thing to do, and completely unprovoked."

"He's a nasty piece of work. I've always thought so. His plan backfired though, because everyone thought you were wonderful."

"Hmmm, I'm not so sure. I think there were some mixed feelings," Liz replied, pursing her lips.

"How so?"

"I loved your parents and your brother, James. They were so warm and welcoming, despite me being dressed like a damn farmhand. But there were a couple of party guests that didn't take so kindly to my arrival."

"Who?" Andrew asked, pushing himself up on an elbow, his brow furrowed.

"It's nothing. Now I sound like I'm telling tales, and we're too old for that."

Andrew's jaw set, and his eyes went dark.

"Don't tell me," he said, "Let me guess. Bloody Lili and Fiona, right? Those two are like Tweedle Dum and Tweedle Dee."

Liz smirked despite herself as Andrew continued.

"Fiona's my cousin and she's harmless, just a little immature. But Lili is something else entirely. She only has two modes; gushing or catty, and I find her truly obnoxious. I was foolish enough to date her briefly while we were at college together, and ever since then she's been convinced we'll get married and live happily ever after. I pity the man who ends up with her. She's pure vindictive poison."

"Wow. Don't hold back. Tell me what you really think of her," Liz said, pushing him playfully.

His eyes softened, and his shoulders relaxed.

"I'm sorry if she made you feel uncomfortable. She's nothing but a snob, and I'm embarrassed to be associated with her."

"Not at all. And don't worry about me, I've been in far more contentious situations. I can hold my own against catty women."

"Yes, you can. You're amazing," Andrew said, kissing her neck, sending shivers of pleasure down her arms and across her breasts.

"Before I forget, we're all going grouse shooting tomorrow to celebrate 'The Glorious Twelfth'. I can ask Alice to lend you some appropriate clothing if you want to come? She always packs extras. It's a lot of fun, I promise."

"No, thank you for the invitation, but I think I'll pass. You know, for someone who claims to despise this whole aristocratic lifestyle, you seem pretty comfortable with it to me. Wearing kilts and shooting grouse, what's next? Foxes and hounds? Carriages at midnight."

Andrew huffed. "The kilt was my mother's idea. Father appreciates it when we pull out the old Armstrong-Bell tartan for special occasions, so I said I'd wear it. And the shooting is entirely optional. You're right though, I have a better idea for tomorrow."

"What?"

"It's a surprise," said Andrew, leaning in to kiss her, and soon they were making love once more.

21

Picnic
Saturday, August 15th - Kallenford

"Where are we going?" Liz said, as Andrew opened the passenger door of his car and signaled for Liz to get in.

"I told you, it's a surprise."

Liz folded her arms and raised her chin in feigned defiance.

"I'm not getting into that car until you tell me where we're going."

"God, woman, you really are the worst," he said, chuckling. "Ok, fine. I'm taking you for a picnic. Maggie's packed us some sandwiches, sliced fruit and champagne. It's in the trunk. Can we go now?"

Liz raised an eyebrow before grinning and stepping into the car.

They drove through the narrow country lanes, past timeworn churches and neat village squares, until they reached what looked like a field and a tiny airstrip.

There was a small aircraft parked on the tarmac, and as Andrew pulled the car up and switched off the engine, a man stepped out from the cockpit and waved.

Liz looked at Andrew.

"What's going on? I thought we were going for a picnic?"

"We are. Just not here. Come on," he said, stepping out of the car before taking her hand and leading her towards the plane.

"Morning Sir," said the older gentleman, tipping his cap to Andrew. "She's all ready for you. Pre-flight checks completed and flight plan logged."

"Thank you, Bill. And thank you for doing all of this at such short notice."

"No problem at all, Sir. Let me get the picnic supplies for you."

Liz turned to Andrew, her eyes wide.

"We're going up in that?"

"Yup,"

"And you're going to fly it?"

Andrew laughed. "Don't look so alarmed. I'm a qualified pilot, so you're perfectly safe. This is my father's plane. We store it at Fife Airport and Bill here flies it down for us whenever we want to take her out. Now, shall we?" he asked, opening the passenger seat door and bowing deeply.

Liz hesitated for a minute, but then she took Andrew's hand and stepped up into the tiny aircraft.

Once Liz was situated, Andrew swung himself into the pilot's seat and pulled on the headphones. He turned the key and the propeller whirred to life.

"What kind of plane is this?" Liz asked, looking around her.

The instrument panel contained the usual plethora of incomprehensible dials, gauges and switches, and both the panel and interior of the doors had a wooden trim that was buffed to a shine. The seats were cramped, but upholstered in warm beige leather that was soft to the touch. "It feels more like I'm sitting in my dad's old Ford sedan than a private aircraft."

"This here is a Cessna 177 Cardinal," Andrew said, lovingly patting the top of the instrument panel. "She was built in the 1970s, but my dad's had her for years and keeps her in topnotch condition. She flies like a beauty. Do you want to listen to air traffic control? I have another set of headphones if you want, or you can just admire the view."

"I think I'll just keep my eyes shut tight until we get there if that's alright."

Andrew chuckled and taxied the plane into position.

She watched him flick switches and pull levers as he spoke through the mic on his headphones.

"Limpitlaw traffic? This is Golf, Charlie, Echo, Tango, Mike, taking off zero four, departing to the East."

As they sped down the runway and lifted into the air, Liz clung on for dear life. Andrew laughed and patted her leg.

However, her terror was soon replaced with awe as they flew through the delicate, skittering, wispy clouds and she gasped at the views stretched out below her.

Undulating fields of velvet green studded with thickets of dark, ancient trees. Tiny villages nestled amongst immaculate golden quilts of farmland. Church spires and well-tended gardens, and the ever present river, powerful and sinuous, winding its way through the countryside, shimmering in the sunlight as they passed overhead.

"I didn't think Scotland could be any more beautiful, but from up here it looks like another world," she whispered.

Andrew smiled, his eyes bright.

"That's the River Tweed. It runs all the way to the ocean. Do you see the ruined abbey down there? It dates back to the 12th century."

Liz craned her neck to see.

They flew across towns and villages, rivers and forests, until they reached the town of Berwick-Upon-Tweed and the coastline.

"Keep an eye out below," said Andrew, "and you might be able to see the smoke plume of 'The Flying Scotsman'. I was captivated by that old locomotive when I was a child, and I would beg my mother to let me ride it every summer."

Liz looked down eagerly, scanning the bridges and railway lines for the iconic train. She smiled as she remembered one of her favorite books as a child, 'The Railway Children', and she pictured the three young children, hanging over a fence by the railway tracks, waving at the kind gentleman as he passed on his way to London. Sadly, the old steam train was nowhere to be seen.

Bidding farewell to the patchwork of fields below, they headed out over the North Sea, Liz shading her eyes against the glimmering of the sun on the water.

"Where are we going?" she asked.

"There's an old RAF museum just up the coast at Montrose. It was Britain's first military air station. There are some fascinating aircraft there, and there's a great ghost story the guides are always keen to tell new visitors. I thought it would be a fun place for a picnic?" Andrew said, looking hopeful.

Liz smiled. "That sounds great, and I'm always up for a good ghost story over lunch."

They flew along the coastline, tracing the edges of the white sandy beaches and peninsulas. Liz settled into a comfortable silence, her nose pressed up against the passenger window as she watched the movement of the waves below.

As Andrew began to descend, Liz gripped the seat again.

"I like being up here, and I like being down there, the getting up and down bit? Not so much. Are you going to land on the beach? We seem awfully low."

Andrew laughed as he banked and brought the aircraft

down smoothly onto the landing strip.

After wandering around the museum, and indulging the guide who was both willing and eager to thrill them with the tale of the resident ghost, they set up the picnic on a bench with a view of the ocean.

Andrew popped the champagne cork and poured the bubbles into each of their glasses. They clinked and toasted to birthday surprises. As they sipped their drinks and looked out over the water, Andrew sighed with contentment.

"It's been wonderful to spend time with you, Liz. Can you come back again soon?"

Liz dropped her eyes, and her smile faded.

"Andrew, look, this has been an incredible day. One that I'll never forget, in fact. But I still don't see a future for us. You live in two parallel worlds, neither of which are compatible with mine."

"That's not true," Andrew said, his brow furrowed. "I am who I am. It's simple."

"It's not simple, and I think you're a little naïve if you think it is. Yes, you love your work as a blacksmith, but you're not the 'break-away black sheep' that you imagine yourself to be. However much you claim to have thrown off your heritage, you still step back into that life regularly, and with comfort. I mean, you still live on the grounds of the estate, for Christ's sake. You haven't even really left home."

Andrew's eyes darkened.

"So, you're saying that I have to abandon my family and the place I love or I'm a fraud? I think that's a little harsh, Liz."

"I'm not saying that. I don't think you should have to walk away from everything, but you also don't get to claim that you've rejected your background of privilege, and then casually make use of it whenever it suits you."

"That's unfair."

"Is it, though?" Liz raised her eyebrows. "So, calling your 'plane chauffeur' to fly your private aircraft over to the family castle just so you can show off to your girlfriend? That's something any blacksmith can do, is it?"

"Fucking hell, Liz," Andrew said, standing abruptly. "I'm sorry I offended your delicate sensibilities. I was just trying to do something nice for you, but now I see it was a waste of time. I'm not 'showing off', I'm sharing my life with you, every aspect of it. Yes, I have different facets of my life, but none of them are any more or less legitimate than the other."

Liz felt a weight in her stomach and she winced.

"God, I'm so sorry. I didn't mean that. It came out all wrong. All I meant is that... I can't see a way forward for us. This weekend scared me a bit, because I realized I don't fit into either of your lives, neither the blacksmith nor the Lord. Both are so far removed from my life in London."

Andrew softened.

"Look, Liz. I don't know how we're going to make this work, but what I do know is that I love you, and I want to be with you."

"What?"

"I love you."

Liz felt as if she were falling, and she grabbed the table for balance.

Andrew sat down next to her and put his hand over hers. "Is that so shocking? That I love you?"

"But it's only been a couple of months," Liz stammered.

"So?" he said, looking into her eyes. "I think I loved you the first day you stepped into the forge. You had a presence about you, an aura of strength and independence, but also curiosity and warmth. I knew right then and there that I didn't want you to leave, and as I've grown to know you better, that feeling has only intensified. I don't want to lose you, not now or ever. Let's not tie ourselves into knots trying to plan for what might be. Let's just take one day at a time. We'll work it out. I know we will."

Liz kept her eyes on the ground as she fought back the tears.

"I'm sorry for what I said. I made it seem like you were a spoiled brat. That's totally unfair and untrue. This has been wonderful. You've gone to so much trouble, and I spoiled it with my own stupid paranoia."

Andrew squeezed her hand.

"It's ok. Admittedly, this weekend has been a lot, and I know you were thrown into that party unexpectedly. For some reason, you seem to think you don't fit in with my family, but I don't believe that's true at all. Anyway, that kind of formal gathering is so rare that you don't need to worry about it. Plus, I get to fly under the radar most of the time. It's the perks of being the younger brother, I suppose. It's not so bad being 'the spare'," he said, and winked.

Standing, Andrew began to pack up the leftovers. Then he leaned towards Liz, his eyes warm and clear.

"Are we done fighting? Can I kiss you now?"

Liz stood and kissed him on the lips. Softly at first, then deeply.

She couldn't say it out loud. She wasn't as brave as him.

Not yet, anyway.

And she was grateful he hadn't expected her to reciprocate.

But she felt it in her heart, as solid and unbreakable and timeless as the steel he molded in his forge, and it both excited and scared her.

22

Gossip
Wednesday, August 26th - Santa Monica

Emily stared through the window of the meeting room into the courtyard outside. The leaves on the trees fluttered in the stifling breeze, crisp as ancient paper. Even here by the ocean, the dry Southern California air had parched the landscape, leaching the rich green shades of Spring and replacing them with arid browns and golds.

Her attention snapped back into the room as she heard Brody's voice, a sharp edge in his tone, addressing one of his analysts.

"Marc, can you take that as an action, please? I'd like to hear back from them by Friday at the latest." He flipped his notepad shut and stood. "Ok, that's all for now, folks. Let's break for lunch."

Everyone began to pack up their possessions as Serena swept the discarded papers off the meeting room desk, sorted them into a neat pile, and slid them into the recycling bin.

As they headed out of the meeting room Brody turned to Emily, touched her arm and said, "Good job on that future measures piece, very insightful. I'm going to have Marc add it into the deck for the investors' pitch next week."

"Thanks," she said. "Actually, I've been meaning to talk to you about the investors' meeting. I still don't have it on my calendar, and I'd love to be there to provide more color around the manufacturing Q&A standards. Could you ask Serena to add me to the invitation? I've asked her a couple of times already, but the message doesn't seem to be getting through."

"Yeah, let's talk about it later. I'm starving. You wanna grab lunch?"

"I can't. I have too much to get through, so I'm going to eat at my desk again."

"All work and no play, girl," he said. Then, dropping his voice, "And talking of playing, you coming over tonight?"

"I can't tonight. I have the kids, remember?"

Brody shrugged.

"How about Friday, then?" he asked.

"Or you could come to my place?" Emily suggested. "Ed has the kids for the weekend, so we'll have the place to ourselves. I can cook if you'd like?"

"Yeah, maybe," he replied.

Emily sat at her desk, scrolling through her emails. The work kept piling up, and however carefully she managed her time, there just never seemed to be enough hours in the day. She could do with staying late tonight and working through the figures for the proposal, but it was her night with the kids.

She stood up and stretched, making a face as she moved her head from side to side. Her neck and shoulders were pulled tight as a cord, and she wished she had time to get a massage to release some of the stress.

"I'll pee, then I'll eat, then I'll work." She thought to herself and headed towards the restroom.

Sitting on the toilet, she scrolled through Facebook on her phone. Not a good use of time, but a welcome and needed break.

She scrolled through photos posted by friends back in England; local football matches in the rain, and the annual village fete, complete with the traditional tombola and raffle. Nothing had changed since she left. Everything was still exactly as it was when they had lived there.

Then she came to Chrissy's photos of Edinburgh and Kallenford. She'd forgotten how beautiful the Scottish countryside was, with its winding roads and ancient hedgerows. The rolling fields and soft muted colors were a balm to her soul.

She smiled at a photograph of Liz draped over the shoulders of a handsome, strapping man with warm, playful eyes. This must be Andrew, the new love interest that Chrissy had told her about. Liz looked so different. Softer. Happy and content.

The countryside looked idyllic, and Emily had a pang of jealousy, thinking how nice it would be to just watch the sheep grazing and hear the babble of a nearby stream. She needed a vacation, she realized.

Just then, the main door of the restroom opened, followed by two voices, gossiping and laughing.

"Seriously, though, it's so obvious, and I think it's kinda unprofessional if you ask me."

Emily recognized Serena's voice. She was answered by another; Ava from reception.

"I know, right? And I don't even see it. I mean, she's so much older than him, and she has kids and everything."

"Isn't she married?"

"I heard her husband left her. No surprise there. Maybe she's trying to relive her youth? She'll have to reach back pretty far to do that, though."

The giggling resumed.

"O.M.G, girl, I love that color of lipstick on you. Do you have eyelash extensions? Your eyelashes are so long!"

"No, silly. You're too adorable for saying so, though."

Emily was frozen. Should she step out of the cubicle, or wait for them to finish reapplying their makeup and leave? This was ridiculous. It was like being back at school, hiding from the popular girls.

The gossiping continued.

"Gina told me it started at the conference in Vegas. She said she saw Brody and her heading up to his room. Apparently, she was wobbling all over the place because she was so drunk."

"No way. What a hoe. And now she's the golden girl, and all her ideas are 'insightful' and whatever. We'll see how long it lasts until he gets sick of her, just like the last one."

As realization dawned on Emily, a white hot anger overtook her and she burst out of the cubicle.

The girls turned from the mirror, their eyes opening wide.

"Oh, I'm sorry," spat Emily. "Did I interrupt your bitching session? If I were you, I would watch what you say in the future. As you know, I am on 'good terms' with the boss, and if you continue to drag my name through the dirt, you might find yourselves out of a job."

She stormed to the restroom door, shoving it open so hard that it slammed on the wall outside. As she left, Serena and Ava looked at each other, smirked, and giggled once more.

Emily, breathing hard, her whole body taught, pushed through the fire door at the end of the corridor and stepped into the staircase. She didn't know where else to go, and she couldn't let anyone see her like this.

She held back the urge to punch the wall, instead she crumpled onto the top step, and began to cry, angry, bitter tears.

She sat in silence, leaning up against the wall, too ashamed to go back into the office.

Was that really what people had been saying behind her back? She hated those skinny, air-headed bitches. How dare they talk about her like that?

She ran the whole evil conversation through again. She had not been drunk in Vegas. Not so drunk that she was stumbling, anyway. Fuckers making up lies about her. But at the same time, she swallowed and grimaced, feeling the specter of guilt and shame hanging over her. Had it really been that obvious? If so, then they had a point about it being somewhat unprofessional. Then again, Brody owned the whole damn company, so he could do what he liked. And it wasn't any of their bloody business, anyway.

She jumped as the fire door opened. It was Kolleen, and as she came to sit beside her, Emily wiped the tears from her face.

"You ok?" asked Kolleen quietly.

"Yeah. Well, kind of. How did you know I was here?"

"I heard Ava telling Gina what happened. I figured you'd bolt for the nearest quiet spot, and no one ever uses these staircases. This is where I would come if I needed to be alone. Do you need to be alone? I'll go if you want?"

"No. Stay. I could use a friend right now," Emily said, the tears welling up in her eyes again. "Did you hear what they were saying about me?"

Kolleen nodded.

"Bitches gonna bitch, though." Kolleen said, shrugging. "It's just office gossip. Don't let them get to you."

"I don't want people to think I'm getting recognition because... well, because, me and Brody... you know? I'm working my butt off, and I'm good at my job. That's why I'm doing well and getting promoted."

Kolleen ran her fingers through her hair and looked at

Emily. She hesitated, then said,

"But you must have known this might happen? You start sleeping with the boss, and people are going to talk."

Emily put her head in her hands and said,

"I didn't think it was that obvious."

Kolleen snorted a laugh.

"Um. Yeah. It's pretty obvious."

She sucked in a deep breath and blew it out before biting her lip and saying,

"I was worried this might happen. That's why I tried to hold back the tide. But Brody had you in his sights from the get go, and you were oblivious. I feel partly responsible for this whole thing."

"What do you mean?"

Kolleen lowered her head, looking at Emily from under an arched eyebrow.

"Remember our first face-to-face meeting when you flew over from England to meet us all? You were practically giddy around him. He saw your talent and ability, even when you couldn't, but he also saw how attracted you were to him. We could all see it. I tried to get in between you guys, but it felt like a losing battle. At the party in Vegas, he sent me off to get some champagne, and when I got back, the two of you were gone. Now, I'm not telling you what to do, Emily. You're a grown woman who can make her own decisions. I'm just saying that you should be careful."

Emily took a deep breath, wiped the mascara from under her eyes, and straightened her top. Tucking her hair behind her ear, she stood and turned to Kolleen.

"With all due respect, Kolleen, I think you're wrong. Maybe that's how you see it, but I see it quite differently. Brody and I are equal in this relationship. I don't believe it was ever his intention for us to become involved. In fact, I think it grew out of a mutual respect for each other's talents and abilities. I'm sorry that our relationship appears to be putting people's noses out of joint, but you're right, 'bitches gonna bitch' so I will rise above it. And I'd appreciate it if you didn't share your 'theories' about our relationship with anyone else."

Emily turned to leave.

"Hey, now," said Kolleen. "Don't swipe at me. I've only ever been on your side."

"That's not what it sounds like to me," said Emily in an icy tone. "You make it sound like I'm some sort of inexperienced, wide-eyed, immature girl who fell prey to a devious manipulator. I think you've been watching too many bad movies, Kolleen. This is real life, and I know exactly who I am and what I'm doing, so let me assuage your guilt on that front."

Kolleen opened her mouth to respond, but before she could, Emily pushed through the fire exit door, allowing it to slam behind her.

She stormed down the corridor and into the restroom.

Hiding in a stall, she rocked back and forth, a hand over her mouth to stop the sound of silent tears.

What had she done?

Was Kolleen right?

No.

No, she wouldn't be derailed like this. She would not buy into this funhouse of mirrors, this distorted truth. Kolleen meant well, but she'd read this situation wrong. Emily had this under control, and she wouldn't let a couple of office airheads and a well-meaning but misguided friend threaten everything she'd worked for.

She had a budding career, and both the ear and the respect of the owner of the business. They could gossip and fret all they liked, but she was flying high and nothing was going to stop her soaring towards success.

23

Gabriella
Friday, August 28th - Pasadena

"Hi, Gabriella, yes, this is Chrissy. It's a pleasure to talk to you."

Chrissy shut her eyes and tried to calm her breathing. Her heart was thumping in her chest.

"Thank you for making the time to speak with me, Chrissy," Gabriella's voice replied, crisp and warm. It reminded Chrissy of biting into an autumn apple just picked from the tree. "I'm sorry it's taken me a while to come back to you. I've been swamped."

"No problem at all," said Chrissy, sitting down on the couch, then standing again. "I have to admit that I was surprised to get your email. I submitted the query letter so long ago that I had assumed you weren't interested."

"We've had quite a backlog, but I'm glad to hear that you haven't signed with an agent yet. I wanted to talk to you a little more about your work and your plans for the future. I like your style. It's fresh and honest, and, with the help of the right editor, I can see a lot of potential."

"That's great to hear," said Chrissy, trying to keep her

voice level and calm.

"You mentioned in your email that you've been working with a mentor? How is that going?"

The smile dropped from Chrissy's face and she bit her lip.

"It's been, um, how do I put this? Very intense. But I feel like I'm learning a lot."

"Who is it, if I might ask?"

"Um. It's Joseph Graham. The writer? I'm not sure if you've heard of him?"

There was a pause before Gabriella said,

"The Joseph Graham? Interesting. Can I ask how you know him?"

"Actually, he's my father."

"Really?"

"Yes. We've been estranged for most of my life, but he reached out after hearing that I'd written a book and offered to mentor me."

There was another pause.

"I see. Well, I won't hold it against you. Let's talk through your novel, shall we? And then we'll see where we go from there."

As they discussed Chrissy's novel, her nerves fell away, and she became engrossed in the story once more.

After an in-depth discussion about imagery, dialogue and pacing, Gabriela turned to more practical matters. She explained how the editorial process would work, and which publishing houses and imprints she would approach. She talked Chrissy through how she would prepare to submit the manuscript, and what the timelines would be, and finally they discussed comparative titles and reader markets.

At the end of the discussion, Gabriella said,

"It's been a pleasure talking with you, Chrissy, and I would be very interested in representing you. I'll send the contract over. Please take your time to think about it, and hopefully we can start working together soon."

"Thank you for your time, Gabriella. I'll let you know my decision, shortly," said Chrissy, before saying goodbye.

As soon as the phone disconnected Chrissy screamed and jumped up and down, causing Doogie to fly into hysterics, barking and spinning, not quite knowing what was going on, but keen to join in, nevertheless.

"Sorry, baby," she said, sitting on the couch and stroking his head, trying to soothe him as she shook with excitement.

He jumped up next to her on the couch and tried to lick her face. She pushed him away gently, and he looked at her with a mixture of confusion and concern, his head tilted to one side, tongue lolling, with one ear flopping over his face.

Her heart filled with love as she hugged him.

Then it dawned on her.

She had an agent.

All they had to do was to sign the contract, and it was done.

This put her one step closer to becoming a published author.

Her dream was becoming a reality!

Was it too early to have a celebratory drink she wondered?

Yes. Sadly, it was. School run and extracurriculars first, then drinking.

Just then, her phone lit up with a message.

You free for a chat?

Chrissy hit the call button.
"Hey, Liz. Great timing! I have amazing news."
"Fantastic. What is it?"
"I think I've found an agent to rep me!"
"I don't know what that means. In fact, it sounds quite painful, but if you're happy, then I'm happy."

Chrissy laughed.

"It stands for 'literary agent'. A literary agent represents you in front of publishing houses. They're kind of like an acting agent who gets you gigs in movies and on TV, you know? Anyway, now I can work with her to get my book ready to submit to publishers. It's a huge step."

"Well done. I'm so proud of you. You're going to be a famous author. I just know it."

"The agent said something odd, though," Chrissy said as she walked into the kitchen. She needed to rinse the breakfast dishes and load them into the dishwasher.

"What?"

"She asked me who my mentor was, and when I told her it was Joe, she sounded kinda weird."

"Weird, how?"

"She obviously recognized the name. She asked me how I knew him, and when I said I was his daughter, she said she 'wouldn't hold it against me'."

"Ha!" Liz barked with amusement. "I'm sorry to say it Chrissy, but I think your old man is a monumental asshole, and it seems I'm not the only one who holds that opinion."

Chrissy's brow furrowed.

"That's a bit harsh, don't you think? Yes, he drinks too much, and he can be a little curt, but he's an incredible author with a history of success, and he's not a bad guy, I don't think."

Liz was silent, and Chrissy could feel the tension in the air.

"What?" she said.

Liz swallowed.

"So, something happened and I think you should know about it."

"What?" Chrissy said with alarm.

"You know Andrew's 'casual surprise birthday party at the pub' that Joe invited me to? Well, it wasn't any of those things."

"What do you mean?"

Liz sighed and shifted her weight. She wanted a cigarette, but she'd been trying to quit.

"Joe set me up. There was a surprise party alright, but I wasn't invited. It was for close friends and family only, and it was a formal event. Then I rock up in my jeans and sweater looking like a farmhand, while they're all dressed in suits and kilts and evening gowns."

Chrissy leaned on the kitchen counter, ignoring Doogie, who was jumping up and down at her side.

"Why would he do that?" She asked in disbelief.

"Honestly, Chrissy, I don't know. Andrew and I think he must have overheard about the party in the village, and decided it was the perfect opportunity to humiliate me."

"But I don't understand. What have you ever done to him to deserve something so awful?"

"Nothing that I'm aware of. Absolutely nothing. Like I said, he's a monumental asshole."

"Did you speak to him about it? Demand an explanation?"

"No, Andrew said not to give him the satisfaction of knowing that he'd riled me. Apparently there's no love lost between Joseph Graham and the Armstrong-Bell family, either. Andrew told me that when Joe first moved into the hunting lodge, he made an absolute menace of himself, constantly pushing to be invited to shooting parties and private events at the castle. He was determined to embed himself within the family, and when they finally conceded and invited him to the annual ball, he got drunk and insulted their guests. He's not been welcome since, of course. I think he's got a real chip on his shoulder, and maybe in his mind I'm guilty by association?"

"Oh, god, Liz. That's awful. I'm so sorry."

"It's not your fault. You can't help your genetics. My father isn't exactly a pillar of society either, remember? But from the sound of things, Joe is pissing people off everywhere he goes."

Chrissy felt torn between her loyalty to Joe and her long founded love for Liz. How could he do this to her friend? And why? It didn't make any sense.

"I gotta go," she said to Liz. "I need to walk the dog before I pick the kids up from school."

"I'm sorry, Chrissy. I didn't want to tell you, because I would never intentionally jeopardize your relationship with your dad. It turned out not to be a problem after all. Andrew's family were very gracious and welcoming, so it was fine, but I thought you should know. I'm just worried about you. If he can be that callous for no reason at all, I don't know how much I trust him. Just watch yourself, yes?"

"I will. And thank you for telling me. Speak to you soon, yes?"

"Definitely," said Liz, and they both rang off.

Chrissy and Doogie walked along the road to where the verge dropped off steeply.

As Doogie sat at her heels, she looked over the golf course towards the Rose Bowl Stadium, and away to the mountains beyond.

She considered what Liz had told her about her father.

She'd only known the man for a few months, but he had taken her under his wing and dedicated his time to helping her reach her goals. How could he be so generous at one moment, and so spiteful the next?

Then she thought about what Gabriella had said. Why would she dislike him? Surely he had a good reputation in the literary world, if nothing else.

Chrissy felt a knot in her stomach.

As they turned for home, she thought back to her time at the hunting lodge, sitting in the dimly lit drawing room, trying to please the constantly incensed Joe.

She remembered one particularly savage rant, his eyes flashing like hot embers, his whiskey spilling over the rim of his glass as he gesticulated.

"They destroyed my talent with their greed," he spat. "They never understood. I didn't give a shit if people 'liked' my work. I wrote for myself, the smartest audience in the world, and the only one that ever mattered to me. If others read my books and understood my message, then so be it. But those publishers, the bastards. As the sales grew, so did their hunger. They clawed at me, trying to suckle from the teats of my creativity. They sucked me dry. They were ravenous. They hoarded the awards and accolades like they were precious fucking treasure. It made me sick."

He leaned towards her, his face contorted with such rage that Chrissy held her breath.

"They tried to inveigle me into writing some derivative trash to please the masses. They wanted me to churn out slop to be chewed, consumed and shit out without a second thought. Most people are illiterate, you know?" he said, waving his glass towards the window, the whiskey sloshing over the edge once more. "But far worse than their ignorance is the fact that they don't care. They sit there growing fat, feeding their bodies and minds with trash, never questioning, never pushing back. Passive lumps of meat for the carnivores of the corporate world to feed on.

No!" he shouted, making Chrissy jump. "I will not have my genius stymied by the bovine nature of the mass populous."

Doogie barked, making Chrissy's heart leap in her chest, pulling her back to reality.

She realized with alarm that she was standing in the middle of the road.

She didn't know how long she'd been standing there, but

her breath was ragged and she had a pounding headache.

She walked briskly to the sidewalk and ruffled Doogie's ears as she tried to regain her composure.

All the pleasure of her earlier conversation with Gabriella had been erased, and she felt drained and shaken. Maybe Scott was right? Maybe Joe wasn't the best mentor for her, after all?

She sucked in a deep breath and steadied herself as they started for home.

Things were good. She was entering a new chapter of her life. She had a literary agent, and she was on her way to becoming a published author.

A smile formed on her lips as she opened the front door and unclipped Doogie's leash from his collar.

She would call Joe and let him know about Gabriella, then they could discuss their plans going forward. Maybe now that she was ready to submit to publishers, he would step back from the mentorship? After all, this was what they had been working towards, wasn't it? Maybe he would even use his contacts to help Gabriella get in front of some of the bigger publishing houses? He had retired as a writer, but her star was now on the rise, and Chrissy couldn't wait to tell Joe the good news.

24

Gold
Saturday, August 29th - London

"You look so beautiful tonight," said Andrew, reaching across the table to take Liz's hand.

The soft glow of the candlelight lit her face, and the flickering flame reflected glints of gold in her diamond earrings.

"It's lovely to get dressed up, and this place is gorgeous," Liz said. "Thank you. This is such a treat."

Andrew had suggested they go for dinner, and to Liz's surprise, he had booked a table at an upmarket restaurant in a fashionable part of London.

When he'd arrived at her apartment to pick her up, he'd raised his eyebrows and whistled at the slinky steel blue dress she was wearing, and they almost hadn't made it out of her apartment.

"Down, boy. You'll have to wait until later," she'd teased, as he stroked a hand down the dress and tried to pull her towards the bedroom. "I'm hungry, aren't you?" she'd said, and he'd looked at her with an expression that made her tingle all over.

"Oh, I'm hungry alright," he'd growled, "and I've spotted a dainty morsel that will do just perfectly." He grinned and began to stalk her from across the room. She'd laughed, then squealed as he pretended to bite her, before threatening to beat him off with her evening purse.

"If you carry on like this, you're going to mess up my hair, and then we'll be going nowhere."

"Suits me," Andrew said with a shrug, his eyes full of mischief and desire. "I can't help it. You bring out the animal in me," he said, before throwing back his head and howling.

Liz raised her eyes to heaven and said, "you're crazy. Well, fetch your collar and leash and let's go to dinner, shall we?"

They arrived at the restaurant a little early, so they sat at the bar enjoying a cocktail before the meal.

They chatted easily, and as Andrew told her all about the goings-on in Kallenford, Liz felt the warm, familiar glow returning. The special glow she felt when she was with Andrew. A feeling she missed so much when they were apart.

The hostess came over to show them to their table, and Liz noticed several men watching her as she walked past. Andrew wasn't wrong. This dress really did make an impact.

Andrew ordered champagne with the appetizers, and the meal itself was outstanding, the wine pairings perfectly complimenting the exquisite food.

Now they nibbled on the last mouthfuls of dessert, neither of them willing to let this moment come to an end.

Andrew put down his fork and looked at Liz. His eyes held an intensity she hadn't seen before, and it made her skin tingle with expectation.

"I have something for you," he said, his voice low.

He reached into the inside pocket of his jacket and pulled out a small velvet box.

Liz's eyes widened, and she felt her heart start to race.

Andrew laughed at her expression. "Don't worry. It's not a ring. I know you're not ready for that. Not yet, anyway."

He turned the box to face her and opened it.

Inside was a golden necklace, a thin gold chain with a pendant in the center, shaped like a butterfly. It was incredibly delicate, and it seemed to glow in the candlelight.

Liz gasped, lost for words.

"Do you like it?" asked Andrew, his voice small and nervous. "I made it for you."

Liz looked up into his eyes.

"You made this?" she whispered.

"I did. Turn it over. There's an inscription." He said, his eyes shining.

She lifted the delicate golden butterfly from its velvet resting place and turned it over in her hand.

On the back was a tiny inscription, barely visible. It read,

Kiss the Sun

Andrew watched her intently as her eyes filled with tears.

"It's from the Irish blessing, remember?" he said. "'May the wings of the butterfly kiss the sun, and find your shoulder to light on. To bring you luck, happiness and riches, today, tomorrow and beyond.' You are my sun, Liz. You illuminate my life."

Liz's hands were shaking. She looked from the necklace to Andrew and back again.

"I've never seen anything so beautiful," she whispered, her voice catching in her throat. "It's so vibrant, it's almost glowing."

Andrew smiled.

"It's 24 karat gold. That's why the color is so rich. I'd never worked with gold before, and I'd never made a piece of jewelry, but Julia introduced me to an incredibly talented goldsmith in Edinburgh, and she helped me make it for you. She had to be patient because a clumsy oaf like me is used to bashing rods of steel, not working with intricate molds. But we got there, and it was worth it. You are worth it."

"Thank you," Liz said, her eyes filled with tears. "It's beautiful."

Gently, Andrew took the necklace from her. He stood, and, walking around to her side of the table, he fastened it around her neck. He kissed her softly behind her ear, and she felt as if she might float away.

She held the butterfly between her fingers and thought of Rachel and of Chrissy and Emily. She thought of lying next to Andrew in his tiny cottage, and how blissful it was to be with him. How, when she was in his arms, she felt complete.

In the taxi, they talked quietly, intertwining their fingers, as Andrew told her all about what he had learned from working with gold. She listened to his soft voice, melodic and comforting, as the wheels of the taxi swooshed through puddles, and the lights of London reflected in the ripples across the city streets, the colors running into each other like a painting left out in the rain.

When they reached Liz's apartment, they lost themselves in each other, their bodies becoming one, moving together in symphony.

Lying next to each other, sated and happy, Liz ran her fingers through Andrew's hair. Then she traced her fingers across the lines of her golden butterfly necklace, and, half asleep, she dreamed of the molten gold, shaped by Andrew's careful, dexterous hands.

Turning, she looked deep into his soft blue eyes and felt utterly content.

He smiled and sat up.

"I have another surprise for you," he said.

Liz laughed and said, "What now?"

Andrew's eyes sparkled.

"When I was in Edinburgh, I met up with an old university buddy of mine. He owns a financial consulting firm in the city, and business is booming. He told me he's been considering expanding into new areas of consulting, Human Resources in particular. I was telling him all about you and your headhunting firm, and he said that if you were interested, then he'd love to talk to you about heading up a talent acquisition and restructuring division. They've had it slated for a while now, but they can't find the right person to run it."

"In the city? Like, London?"

"No, Edinburgh." Andrew was alive with enthusiasm, his eyes shining at the thought of it. "It would be perfect, Liz. You've been saying that you want to get out of headhunting, and this would play to your strengths. Plus, it's only an hour away, so we could live together. I've been wracking my brains to think of a way we could spend more time together, and this is it!"

Liz's jaw tightened as she tried to suppress the irritation growing in her.

"And you're proposing that we live together in the cottage? The shoebox sized, leaky, structurally questionable cottage? Where the hell would I put all my stuff?"

Andrew's brow furrowed.

"There are bigger properties on the estate," he said. "We could make it work. Come on, Liz, shouldn't we give it a shot?"

Liz swung her legs off the bed and stood up. She pulled a long t-shirt over her head.

"No, Andrew, we shouldn't 'give it a shot'"

She headed for the kitchen as he followed.

"Why not? Why are you being so combative all of a sudden?"

Her body tensed as she turned to him, her eyes dark.

"You're asking me to give up everything. My career, my friends, my connections and my family, to move to Scotland. And why? So we can 'hang out' some more? No, Andrew. That's not how it works. I know you've always had everything you've ever wanted, but I'm not a playmate who's willing to change her life on a whim to suit you."

Andrew looked shaken.

"But I want to be with you. I want us to have a life together. Don't you want that?" he said in a small, deflated voice.

Liz reached into the fridge and grabbed the orange juice. With her back still facing him, she took a long, slow swig. She didn't want him to see the frustration on her face, the tears welling in her eyes. She breathed deeply.

"Liz?" he asked.

She turned and met his gaze.

"Andrew, I told you this would happen. We're back here again. Yes, of course I want to be with you, for Christ's sake. I've never felt like this about anyone before. Isn't it obvious that I…"

She bit her tongue and put her hand to her forehead, turning away from him again. She'd almost said it out loud, and that would be the worst thing she could do right now.

"We're from different worlds," she said. "We're making it work, but if we push too hard in any one direction, the whole thing is going to come tumbling down. Can't you see that?"

Andrew sat down heavily on the couch, his head in his hands.

"Is what we have really so fragile?" he said in a low, broken voice. "Because, to me, it's the only thing that matters."

Liz went to him. She sat next to him and wrapped an arm around his shoulders. Her heart broke to see him so crumpled and despondent.

"Maybe we should never have started this," she whispered.

He looked up, fear in his eyes.

"No, don't say that. We'll find a way. There has to be a way to make this work. I love you, and I can't lose you." He wrapped his arms around her and held her tight.

"I love you, Liz," he whispered.

"I love you, too," she thought to herself.

25

Grades
Tuesday, September 1st - Pasadena

Scott could hear the bass thud of 'Imagine Dragons' before he even opened the front door.

"That's not good," he thought to himself, and braced for the inevitably furious Chrissy.

"Hey babe, you ok?" He bellowed over the music.

The volume was lowered, and Chrissy stepped out of the kitchen holding a large glass of Chardonnay.

"I'm done, Scott. Seriously," she said, holding a hand in the air as if she were directing traffic. "I've had it. Screw Josh. And Joe. And everyone. I'm sick of it all. I'm gonna move to a cabin on a tiny island in Fiji and leave all this bullshit behind me."

"Sounds lovely. Can I come?" He asked, as he planted a kiss on her cheek, then headed into the kitchen to grab a beer. He was going to need it.

He patted Doogie on the head, and Doogie gave him a pitiful look. "I know dude," he whispered to his canine buddy, "it'll be ok, though, I promise." Doogie whined and, with a final glower, snuck under the kitchen table to lie down with his head on his paws.

Scott slid himself onto one of the barstools and said,

"Right. Start from the beginning and tell me everything. Should I order takeout?"

"Yes. I can't even think about cooking right now," said Chrissy.

Scott ordered Mexican as Chrissy, still striding around the kitchen, broke down her shitty day blow by blow.

"Ok, so at drop off at the high school this morning, I was about to swing out of the exit when Josh's counselor, Miss Patel, waves me down. She asked me if I had a moment to talk. I said yes, of course, and pulled into a parking spot. She said that she was going to email me today anyway, but that it was better to talk in person."

Chrissy drained her glass and refilled it as she spoke.

"It seems that Josh hasn't been submitting his homework assignments, and now he's failing math and chemistry. She basically said that if he doesn't get his shit together, he's going to get kicked out of his honors and AP classes, too. She told me that socially he's doing great, he's popular with the other kids and all the teachers say he's respectful and charming, but the work just isn't getting done."

Scott frowned and said,

"Hmm. That's worrying. I haven't been tracking his grades because he's normally so on top of this stuff."

"I know," replied Chrissy. "I felt like such an idiot just staring at her. I couldn't believe what she was saying. I don't understand it though, he's always been so conscientious. Maybe it's the change of school? Or is the workload too much? His track team commitments have increased. Maybe he's feeling overwhelmed? But this is his junior year, and he doesn't have the luxury of messing this up. I've tried to talk to him about college applications, but he just brushes me off. I'm worried about his attitude, Scott. He's not going to get into a good college if he keeps acting like this."

"Hmm. I'll talk to him tonight about it all. Did you talk to him about it at pickup?" Scott asked.

"Yes, and he just grunted at me. I told him I was shocked and disappointed, and that he needed to get it sorted out, and he just said, 'Whatever, mom.' Jackie and him started arguing, and it escalated into a huge fight."

Chrissy took another big swig of wine and continued.

"When we got home, they both stormed out of the car. Josh grabbed his bike and headed off down the road, saying that he was going to Caleb's house to study. Jackie was furious and yelled at me that I was 'blind and couldn't even see what was going on under my own nose,' and then she ran upstairs. She's locked her door and refuses to come out. I'm exhausted and done with both of them. When did parenting become a blood sport? Teenagers are the worst!"

Scott nodded in agreement.

"Do you want me to talk to her?"

"Maybe. Jeez, what a mess. Oh, and that's only the half of it."

Scott slugged his beer before saying,

"Yeah, you said on the phone that you and Joe had some kind of disagreement?"

"That's one way to put it," Chrissy said, shaking her head and blowing out hard. "I was so excited to tell him about my call with Gabriella. I thought he'd be excited for me. She's a fantastic agent, and we seem to get on really well, but when I told him I was considering signing with her, he was so scathing. He said that she's small time, and that she doesn't know anything or anyone. He said she's nothing more than a wannabe, using my name and my connection with him to further her own ends, and that I'd be wasting my time and my talents on someone like her."

The fiery energy drained from Chrissy and she sat down

heavily on one of the kitchen chairs.

"I told him she'd looked over some of my more recent work, the stuff I've been working on with Joe, and she said it felt 'muddled'. Like I'd lost my authentic writing voice. He said that was bullshit, and it proved his point completely. He said I was 'evolving' from a mediocre writer to a great one, and that she couldn't see that. I don't know, Scott, he's always so convincing when you're talking to him, but afterwards I'm never sure what to think or feel."

Chrissy looked up at Scott, her eyes filled with hurt and confusion.

"I don't know where I'm going with this anymore," she said. "It's stopped being fun, and now it's just draining."

Scott stood and walked to her. He wrapped her in a bear hug and held her tightly.

"Scott? Do you think I'm cut out to be a writer? Or should I quit before I get in too deep?"

He looked into her eyes and said, "I think you're already an amazing writer. But then, I also think you could do pretty much anything you put your mind to."

"Oh, and then," she continued, "because I was kinda pissed at him anyway, I asked him why the hell he did that to Liz. It was a shitty thing to do, to set her up to be humiliated like that."

Scott's eyes darkened at the memory.

"Did he have an explanation?" He asked, a hard edge in his voice.

"Nope," Chrissy said with an exaggerated shrug. "He said that the Armstrong-Bell family are too big for their britches, and they need to be brought down a peg or two."

Scott clenched his teeth and shook his head.

"Chrissy, I know he's your father, and I don't want to get in the way of you building a relationship with him, but I think Joseph Graham is a nasty piece of work."

"Funny you should say that. Liz said the same. And even Gabriella made it clear that she's not a fan."

Scott held out his hands in agreement.

"I don't like the way he treats you," Scott said, "nor anyone else, for that matter. And when it comes to your writing, I'm not sure if he's more of a hindrance than a help."

Chrissy looked at her hands and made a face. Scott had a point.

"But he is a bestselling author. Or he was once, at least. He won awards. He might not be a particularly nice person, but he still holds the respect of a lot of people in the industry."

Scott said nothing, but his face was hard as flint.

Chrissy sighed and said, "I was thinking of asking Trish what more she knows about him? I feel like I've spent all this time with him, both in person and over the phone, and I still know virtually nothing about his life. I've tried to ask questions, to get to know him better, but he just shuts me down. I know he was some sort of war hero that served in the navy in Vietnam and Afghanistan, but almost everything I know I've read on the dust jacket of his books. Maybe if I knew him better, I could understand where he's coming from?"

Scott shrugged.

"Or maybe he's just an asshole. You're always looking for the best in people," he said, shaking his head with both frustration and love in his eyes.

He kissed her, soft and long, then said, "The food should be here soon. In the meantime, I'm going to go and see my other ferocious girl. I'll call if I need reinforcements, or a medic."

Chrissy chuckled as he headed up the stairs to Jackie's room. She loved that girl, but boy was she a handful. Scott had a way with her, though, and he could always pour oil on her troubled waters.

Sitting down on the couch, she ruffled Doogie's ears and drained the last of her wine. She could hear voices from upstairs, but the tone sounded peaceable, so she breathed a deep sigh and allowed the tension to release from her body.

In the relative silence of the living room, she ran through the events of the day.

What were they going to do about their wayward son?

Should she accept Gabriella's offer of representation? And how would she handle the inevitable backlash from her mercurial father if she did?

Would it be better just to part ways with the infamous Joseph Graham, or should she push for a closer relationship? After all, she'd spent most of her life not knowing anything about him. It seemed like such a wasted opportunity not to get to know this man who had fathered her.

So many decisions.

So many paths in the road, and no clear direction in sight.

26

Paradise
Saturday, September 5th - Marina del Rey

Emily parked, as instructed, in the guest parking lot of the yacht club. As she walked towards the clubhouse, she tried not to let her jaw drop. The cars in the member parking lot looked like something from a photo shoot on Rodeo Drive. Maseratis, Bugattis, Lamborghinis; holy shit, she'd be rubbing shoulders with millionaires today, and she swallowed hard, trying to look rich and sophisticated, and not gawp or trip over and fall on her face.

She texted Brody.

'I'm here. Where should I meet you?'

A text pinged back:

"Walk down past the swimming pool and around the outdoor bar, then walk to your right. I'll be at the end of the dock."

Feeling noticeably underdressed and with her eyes glued to her phone, she walked past the slim, tan patrons of the yacht club as they lounged by the bar, sipping their cosmopolitans in their casual Armani outfits.

Brody greeted her with a huge smile and a hug. He looked

at home in these surroundings with his aviator sunglasses and a white polo shirt over his honey colored skin.

Taking her hand, he led her down the dock to his yacht.

She gasped when she saw it. A brilliant white beauty of a sailboat with a huge central section supported by two parallel hulls. Its sleek, streamlined body was both elegant and powerful, with masts that soared into the sky above.

"Oh my god, Brody, it's huge!" Emily whispered in awe.

"That's what all the girls say," he said with a wink, as he jumped on board and held out a hand to help her up.

"But… I can't sail this," she protested. "I've only ever sailed a tiny boat before, nothing this size."

He laughed and said,

"Don't worry. I'll lead you through everything, step by step. It'll be fun, I promise."

Emily hesitated for a second, then reached for Brody's hand, allowing him to help her on board.

True, she had never sailed a boat this size before, but this year had been a year of firsts, so, why not? she thought to herself.

She frowned for a second as she saw the name on the hull.

This was 'New Horizons', the catamaran Brody had offered to take her out on just over a year ago. She had said no at the time, not wanting to be disloyal to Ed. How much her reality had changed since then, eh? Now she was sleeping with Brody, and Ed was sleeping with Conner. She swallowed at the thought and took a breath.

Brody started the engine, and they cruised out of the marina.

Emily settled herself on the bow, stretching out like a cat in a sunbeam. She shut her eyes and basked in the heat of the sun as the yacht rocked gently through the waves. The combination of the warmth of the deck and the rhythmic movement of the sailboat offered a welcome meditation, lulling her into a deep state of relaxation.

"This is paradise," she thought to herself.

Just as she was drifting off to sleep, Brody came up onto the main deck and shouted,

"Hey girl! You ready for some sailing?"

She groaned. "God, you're so loud. I was just starting to relax. Can't we just motor all the way to Catalina? It's been a really long week, and I don't want to haul sails around for the next four hours."

"No way!" Brody shouted back, busying himself with ropes and sails. "It's all part of the fun. Plus, we can have margaritas and watch the sun go down when we get there knowing that we've worked for it."

"I've already worked for it. I pulled another sixty-hour week this week, and I am beat."

"Come on, sexy, let's work those biceps." Brody said, bouncing down the length of the deck to unfurl the sails.

Emily groaned and shut her eyes for a moment, then, resigned to her fate, she stood up, stretched, and said,

"OK, Captain. Tell me what to do."

"Fantastic. First, grab me a beer. There's one in the fridge in the bar downstairs. Then I'll show you how this baby moves."

Emily sighed and headed down the stairs into the main cabin.

The word 'opulent' did not even begin to describe the interior of the yacht. White leather chairs were offset by black and chrome fixtures, and there were two staircases heading off the main salon to the bedrooms below.

Returning with the beer, she handed it to Brody, saying, "how many bedrooms does this boat have?"

"Five. And it's not a 'boat', it's a yacht," he said, taking the beer with one hand and pulling him to her with the other. He kissed her neck, and then her collarbone, and she shivered with pleasure.

She pushed him away. "Hey, Captain. We're going to crash into a reef or something if you don't concentrate."

"Not many reefs out here. But there's definitely something sizable appearing in the area of my shorts right now."

She swatted at him and shook her head while grinning.

"You ready to pull the sails up?" He asked, securing the beer bottle, his eyes bright with excitement and anticipation.

"You know that I have no idea what I'm doing, right?"

"Don't worry, I'll teach you," he said, looking into her eyes while he ran his hands down her torso to her lower back. "Turn around," he said, softly.

She turned, the heat rising in her.

He slipped his hands forward until they were on her stomach.

"You see that metal thing there? That's a winch. That's what we're going to use to pull in the sheets."

"Do what in the sheets?" Emily whispered, still breathing hard.

Brody laughed. "The sheets are what we call all these ropes. The ropes are connected to the sails. We use the ropes to pull the sails in and out. That's what makes the ship go forward. Got it?"

"Oh," said Emily, trying to collect herself.

"Let me show you how to load them."

Brody demonstrated and Emily watched, secretly wishing she could either just sit on the sundeck, or tempt Brody downstairs and explore the sheets in the bedroom instead.

Despite her initial reluctance, his exuberance began to rub off on her. As the huge white sails rose and the wind caught and snapped them tight, she felt the exhilaration of being at one with the ocean.

The energy of the sleek catamaran shifted from languid relaxation to focused speed and purpose, and as the wind whipped her hair and sea spray filled the air around her, she felt alive and joyous.

They sped through the waves, cutting through the surf with power and grace. When the sail began to buffet, the noise was almost deafening, and she could hardly hear Brody's voice as he yelled an explanation to her.

"The wind's moving. That's what's making the sail luff," he yelled across the deck. "We need to tighten up the mainsail."

The wind dropped a little, and they settled into a hypnotic rhythm.

"I could get used to this," thought Emily as she watched the horizon rise and fall. The sun glinted off the water, and it was as if they were the only two people in the world.

"Hey, Emily," Brody shouted, his hair wild with salt water and his cheeks ruddy from the sun. "Can you ease the sheet a little?"

"What?" she said, hoping that he wouldn't repeat the request.

"Can you let the mainsail out a bit? Do you remember how to do it? With the winch?"

Emily cringed. "Not really, no. Can't you do it?"

"You got this girl. I have faith in you," he replied and winked at her with those stunningly blue eyes.

She stood up and walked to the winch.

"OK. Press this button to release," she thought to herself.

"Not too fast, though," he said, but too late. The rope spun and tangled itself on the winch.

"Fuck it," swore Brody, slamming down the rope he was coiling, his face like thunder. "Really, Emily? I said slowly."

Emily was indignant. "I told you I didn't know what I was doing! I'm sorry if I messed it up, but you're acting like I'm an experienced sailor, and I'm not."

He shot her a disdainful look. "Maybe I overestimated

your abilities to pick things up quickly."

She felt the anger and embarrassment boil in her like hot lava.

"Shit," he said. "It's jammed. I'll need a rolling hitch to pull it off."

He looked around him and cursed again.

"Emily, go down to the closet by the master bathroom door and get me a thin rope. Like this one but thinner," he said.

She thought about arguing, but decided it wouldn't help the situation.

Heading down into the main salon, she passed the drinks bar and headed down the stairs to the master bathroom. Rummaging in the closet, she found a thin rope hung over a hook at the back. As she was about to turn, she saw an old photo on one of the shelves.

It was a photo of Brody, much younger than he was now, only a teenager, she guessed, with his arm draped around a stunning blonde. They were sitting on the deck of a beautiful old sailboat, their legs dangling off the edge of the deck. He was young, sun kissed and glowing, with floppy, sun bleached hair. He seemed so gloriously happy and content in that moment that Emily smiled along with him.

"I wonder who she is?" Emily thought to herself. *"Maybe a girlfriend? Or a cousin?"* She tried to remember if Brody had mentioned having a sister.

She jumped as he yelled impatiently from the deck.

"What the hell are you doing down there? Get up here. I need that rope."

She grabbed the photo and, along with the rope, headed up the stairs to the deck.

Brody unraveled the sheet for the mainsail and was starting to return to his jovial self when she produced the photograph.

"Who's this? You guys look so young," Emily said,

laughing.

Brody's face went ashen, and he snatched the photograph from her.

"Where did you get this?" He demanded.

"It was in the closet. I saw it when I was getting the rope," she replied, taken aback. "Sorry. I didn't mean to upset you," she said, faltering. "You both looked so happy and I... I just wanted to know who she was."

Brody hesitated, and Emily half expected him to say it was none of her business. He was controlling his breathing. She knew what he looked like when he was trying to hold back his anger.

He took a deep breath and said, "She's an old girlfriend. Her name was Eden. Is Eden. We lost touch, though. It's ancient history."

"It's not that ancient if you still have her picture with you," Emily said gently. "It's OK, Brody. We both have our past. I mean, I'm still technically married, for God's sake," she said, shaking her head in disbelief. "Just because we've had feelings for other people in the past doesn't mean this isn't real now. We just have to be honest with each other, agreed?"

Brody nodded, and with a blank expression he turned to coil and hang the main sheet.

Catalina was everything it had promised to be; both beautiful and romantic, and as the afternoon turned to evening they ate oysters on the deck of an expensive restaurant and watched the sky turn to fire red, then to soft peach, as the glittering ocean drew a dark veil across her waves.

Emily tried to move the conversation along, but she could

sense the distance between herself and Brody. He was civil, but he had lost his usual warmth and buoyancy, and he answered her questions with monosyllabic responses.

He claimed he was exhausted. That the craziness of the week had caught up with him. But his eyes were cool and his jaw tight and angular.

Later, they'd walked back down the jetty under the stars and made love on the yacht as the waves rocked to and fro below them. But Brody's love making had a hard edge to it, and afterward, instead of putting his arm around her and pulling her to his chest, he'd turned his back and fallen asleep.

As Emily lay in the dark, feeling the sailboat move beneath her, she wondered what she had said or done to trigger this change. But deep down, she knew it could only be one thing.

Eden.

27

Prospects
Saturday, September 19th - London

"Where are you taking me?" Asked Liz, as they headed up the steps of St James's Park tube station and out into the bright sunlight of a crisp autumn day.

Andrew had been giddy all morning, like a schoolboy desperate to share a secret. They had met for lunch at Liz's favorite tapas restaurant not far from the Tate Modern.

While sharing small plates of baby squid, meatballs and chorizo, Liz had told Andrew all about her new partners, and the significant contract she'd just landed. He nodded and grinned like a Cheshire Cat, and eventually her curiosity got the better of her. Although she'd tried to bribe, cajole, and finally threaten the information out of him, he would not tell her what he had in store for the day.

Now here they were, walking through Westminster, squeezing their way past tourists and locals alike, everyone muffled up in hats and scarves against the chilly autumn breeze.

Liz loved this time of year, when the leaves turned gold and orange and ochre, falling to the ground to form a carpet of color that lined the city's streets and pavements. The air was brisk but refreshing, and there was nothing better than to be in London, with its eclectic mishmash of architecture, all crammed into winding roads and alleyways. There was noise and movement everywhere you turned, delivery men squeezing their trucks down impossibly narrow streets, hollering to each other in jovial thick London accents, and the buzz of energy surrounding you.

Andrew took Liz's hand as they walked past a series of grimy red brick Victorian buildings, more suited for gas lamps and carriages than modern day cars. As they walked, Liz thought of the awe-inspiring Westminster Abbey, not far from where they were, with its looming gothic spires, and ornate gray building hewn from stone, and it dawned on Liz just how similar this area of London was to Edinburgh.

"No wonder Andrew likes it here," she thought to herself.

Walking down a wide stretch of pavement, they stopped outside a row of red brick townhomes. Four stories tall with the telltale Georgian flourish of gabled roofs and dormer windows, they were neat and well kept, with flower boxes in the windows, and the occasional bicycle chained to the wrought-iron fence that separated the buildings from the street.

Andrew looked at Liz, his eyes shining.

"What?" she asked him. She was starting to lose her patience with this game.

"What do you think?" Andrew asked.

"About what?" She said, trying to read his face.

He bowed to her and flourished his arm as he did so, saying, "M'lady, welcome to my new home."

Liz stared at him, bemused.

Andrew laughed and said, "Do you want to come in and have a look around?"

"OK, what the hell are you talking about, Andrew? Have

you completely lost your mind?"

"No, I don't believe I have," he said with a grin. "Let's go inside and I'll explain everything."

He walked towards a wrought-iron gate that stood under an arch separating two of the buildings. Unlocking it, he stood aside and ushered Liz into a beautiful courtyard filled with rose bushes, manicured topiary, and a fountain surrounded by cream stone columns.

Walking up to one of several front doors that surrounded the courtyard, Andrew unlocked the deadbolt and stood back, allowing Liz to step over the threshold and into the immaculate ground-floor apartment.

It was simple and classic, with chic modern touches, a far cry from the ramshackle cottage back in Kallenford.

"What do you think?" asked Andrew, proudly. "It's small, but the heating works without having to bash the boiler, there's hot water all the time, and the roof doesn't look like it might cave in at any moment. Far more sophisticated than my old hovel, no?"

"It's... lovely," said Liz, "but I still don't understand..." her voice trailed off. She couldn't comprehend what was happening.

"Here," said Andrew in a soothing tone, "come with me to the kitchen. I don't have everything I need quite yet, but I do have a kettle, so let's have a cup of tea and I'll explain."

Cups of tea in hand, they sat in the small living room that overlooked the courtyard.

Andrew let out a long breath and began.

"I thought long and hard about what you said last time I was here, and you were right. I wanted it all. I wanted you, and I wanted my old life as well, plus all the perks that come with being the son of an earl. I've done some growing up over the last couple of weeks, and I realized that if I wanted to be with you, I'd need to make some major changes in my life. So I have. I spoke to an old school friend who works in banking, specifically in private wealth management, here in London, and he pulled some strings and got me a job. I'm moving to London. Permanently. This is just a short-term rental, but once I'm settled at the firm, I'll look for something more permanent. Unless, maybe, we want to find somewhere together, eventually? I'm not in any rush, though. Whenever you're ready, I'm here."

Liz was dumbfounded.

"I don't... You can't..." she stammered.

"Oh, yes I can," Andrew cut in. "When I said you were the most important thing in my life, I meant it, Liz. And I realized I needed to show you through my actions, not just my words."

Liz smiled, but her heart felt uneasy. This was a big transition, and she couldn't quite picture her soot-smeared blacksmith working in the city as a banker.

"When do you start?" she asked.

"Monday."

"This coming Monday?" she said, incredulously.

"Yup. I'm not hanging around," Andrew said, smiling. "And I know what you're thinking. It's a huge change, and it is. I'm not denying that, but I'm ready for it."

Liz looked down at her mug of tea.

"What does your family think about all of this?"

Andrew laughed, and said, "Well, to be honest, they were pretty taken aback when I told them. But my brother congratulated me, and said it was high time I got a 'proper job', and although I know my parents will miss me, they understand my reasoning, and they want me to be happy."

Liz bit her lip.

Andrew could sense her hesitation, so he said, "Do you want to see the rest of the apartment?"

"Sure."

Andrew walked her around the compact living quarters. The kitchen was furnished with all new appliances, but wasn't quite big enough to fit a table to sit at. The master bedroom had thick cream carpets and a large bed with matching dresser, and a small but functional en-suite off to the side. The second bedroom was barely large enough to fit a dresser and a couch, and the guest bathroom was tiny, with just a toilet, a sink, and a narrow shower.

"It's nice," said Liz. "It's quite small, though."

"I know, but it's only going to be me here, and you, whenever you want to stay over, of course."

"Is there anywhere to sit outside in the evening?" Liz asked.

"Sadly not," Andrew replied, making a face. "The courtyard is technically a 'shared garden,' but the letting agent said it's not really the done thing to sit outside, because it faces into everyone's living room windows."

"But won't you miss your outdoor space? That's where you go to relax and unwind."

"I know," Andrew said, shrugging. "But I imagine I'll be far too busy to worry about that. And anyway, we're so close to all the bars and restaurants that if we want to go out, I'm sure we can find somewhere lovely to sit and relax," he said with a beaming smile.

Liz's brow furrowed.

"You don't seem very enthusiastic about any of this," said Andrew, looking both dispirited and concerned. "Did I overstep the mark? I don't want you to feel pressured by this. That was never my intention."

"No, it's not that," said Liz. "It's just that… you were so happy in Kallenford. It was your home… and this…"

"This is different," said Andrew. "It's a new phase of my life, and I'm excited about it. I promise everything will be fantastic. Now stop looking so worried and let's have some champagne to celebrate!"

He went to the fridge and took out a bottle of champagne. Popping the cork and pouring them each a glass, he proposed a toast. "To a new life, and new prospects."

Liz smiled and shrugged in resignation.

"Ok, if this is honestly what you want, then I applaud you and wish you all the best. To you, Andrew. And to happiness."

They drank, and he lent forward to kiss her.

As he looked into her eyes with so much love and enthusiasm, she felt the stirring of excitement. Maybe this could work after all? Maybe they could be together and be happy? Maybe it was time for her to finally say those three little words she'd been holding back so long.

28

Past
Sunday, September 20th - Pasadena

"Ugh, it's still insanely hot out there," Chrissy said, falling through the front door and unclipping Doogie's leash from his collar.

The air conditioning felt delicious on her sweaty skin and she chided herself as both she and the dog headed straight to the kitchen to get a much needed drink of water. She should know better than to try to do a long walk after midday at this time of year in Pasadena. September might be Fall in other parts of the country, but Southern California clung to the summer like a kid to a candy bar, and everyone was forced to tolerate the heat far longer than many would choose to.

"Chrissy? Is that you?" Scott called from the family room.

"Yes, we did the long loop around the golf course and now we're both melting," Chrissy said, smiling down at the panting but jovial Doogie.

Scott came into the kitchen, his eyes heavy and serious.

"Chrissy, can we sit down for a minute? I need to talk to you."

"Sure," she replied, cold alarm running through her.

He walked into the living room, and she followed him. Sitting next to him, she grabbed a coaster for her glass of water and placed it on the coffee table.

Scott looked at her, then rubbed his jaw and took a deep breath.

"What is it?" Chrissy asked, feeling her heart beating faster. Her skin was cold now, the heat of the sun forgotten.

"I have a confession to make," he said, looking into her eyes. "I did something I probably shouldn't have done, but I'm hoping that you'll understand and forgive me."

"What the hell is going on, Scott? You're scaring me."

"It's about Joe."

"What is it?"

Scott ran his fingers through his hair and breathed deeply.

"That guy has been pissing me off from the minute you met him at the bar downtown, Musso & Frank was it called? He was rude and condescending to you then, and he hasn't changed since. I didn't want to get in the way of you getting to know him, Chrissy. He's your father, after all, and you have so much lost time to make up for. But he's been nothing but a jerk since the get-go."

Chrissy shrugged. "Agreed. So what did you do?"

"I contacted an old college friend from USC. We studied medicine together until he dropped out to become a journalist. Now he's one of the senior editors at the New York Times and doing very well for himself. Well, I got in touch with him, and asked him if he would do some digging on Joe. Nothing illegal, of course, just some investigative work. He can find information that I never could, and he said he'd see what he could do. It'd been weeks, so I figured it must have slipped his mind. But then he sent me a load of files last night."

"I see. And what was in these files of his?" Chrissy asked, feeling both indignant and nervous.

"Let's just say it made for some interesting reading." Scott said, looking stern. "Mr Joseph Graham positions himself as a war hero, but he's far from it."

"But he served in Vietnam and Afghanistan. He won medals."

"No. He didn't. It seems he enlisted in the Naval Academy at nineteen, but only served three years before being discharged because of an injury. He spent most of his twenties as a 'war correspondent' in Vietnam and Afghanistan, but in fact, most of that time was spent in bars, shooting the shit with military men and getting arrested for being drunk and disorderly. The enlisted men loved him because he was a natural born storyteller and could amuse the troops for hours with his tales, but he was also well known as a troublemaker and general layabout."

"So all those tales of heroism?"

"Either someone else's, or complete fiction."

"Shit."

"Yeah. I printed everything out. Everything that Evan found. Do you want to read it?"

Chrissy nodded, not able to speak.

"I'll get you a coffee if you want? Or something stronger if you need it?"

"Coffee's fine. Thank you." Chrissy said, quietly.

As she flipped through the pages, she saw her father's life unfold before her.

He had published a couple of short stories in the late 70s when he was in his mid twenties. Standard 'war hero' stuff in the style of Hemingway.

It was noted that he had visited England in 1979 to do research for his first full-length novel.

"That's when he met Trish," thought Chrissy. *"That's when I was conceived."* Although there was no mention of it in the paperwork. *"Why would there be, I suppose,"* she thought to

herself, and felt a small stab of pain.

Scott padded into the living room, quietly placing the coffee down in front of her, before heading back into the kitchen.

She continued sifting through the papers.

Joe had studied writing in New York. He had married a fellow writing student in 1982 when he turned thirty, although they quickly separated and divorced a year later.

At aged thirty-two he published his first novel, which immediately met with critical acclaim. He was awarded literary prizes and speaking engagements, and later, funding to complete further novels.

Between 1986 and 1999, he wrote seven more novels, all bestsellers, and he became a household name. It seemed his star was rising, and, accompanied by a frenzy of media coverage, he married an up-and-coming movie starlet.

Then it all fell apart.

The writing stopped, the drinking increased exponentially, and the starlet filed for divorce.

Joseph Graham went from being a talented author to a mercurial, temperamental, over-sensitive drunk. He harassed journalists, agents, and publishers alike, constantly reminding them of his talent, and how he was being disrespected.

He was often combative, and after throwing a mug of hot coffee at the editor of his publishing house, his contract was terminated.

In 2002, he sold his property in New York and disappeared, only to be found later, living in a hunting lodge in a small village in Scotland.

"Kallenford," Chrissy thought to herself.

Having ostracized everyone that had ever supported him, the publishing community now considered him to be a joke and a pariah.

The name 'Joseph Graham' had become synonymous with self-destruction. He was a parable. He was the Icarus of the publishing world, flying so high, then flaming out, burned by the sun of his own ego, before plunging into the depths of anonymity.

Chrissy sat back and took a deep breath, trying to process her feelings about what she had read.

Scott had been watching from the kitchen and seeing her set down the papers, he padded back into the living room and sat down next to her.

They sat in silence for a while before Chrissy turned to him and said.

"I think I want to call Trish."

Scott frowned. "Really?"

"Yes. I don't know why, but I want to talk to her about this."

"OK, whatever you want, baby." He put his arm around her and squeezed. "Was I wrong to do this? I never meant to hurt you. I just wanted you to have all the facts. I want you to know the truth, then you can decide what you want to do with that information."

She looked into his eyes and felt the love well up inside her. This man was her rock. Her protector through life's storms. He was strong, and sensitive, and supportive, and she didn't know what she would do without him.

"No, you did the right thing. I needed to know this. Now I'm going to call my mum."

Scott stood and left the room as Chrissy dialed Trish's number.

The phone connected, and she heard Trish's muffled voice saying,

"Hey, Chrissy. Hang on a sec."

The line became clearer and Trish said, "Hi! I wasn't expecting your call. Is everything OK?"

"Yes. Well, kind of. Actually, no. Do you have a second?"

"Of course! Hang on. I'm fixing the electrics on the narrowboat. Let me just get rid of all this wiring and I'll be with you."

Chrissy rolled her eyes.

"OK. I'm all yours. What's up?"

"Where to start," thought Chrissy. "So, you know that I went to see Joe earlier this year so he could help me with my writing?"

"Yes," said Trish, her voice guarded.

"Well, he's been mentoring me ever since, but it's been... um...how do I put it...rocky."

"Hmmm."

"Let's just say that Scott has never been a fan of Joe's, and he finally snapped and asked a friend to do some digging on Joe's background."

"And?"

"It seems that he's not been altogether honest with me, or with anyone."

"Yup, that sounds like your father."

"I'm trying to decide what to do with this information, how to feel about it. Did you know about his military days? About his wives? And his drinking?"

Trish sighed.

"Chrissy, your father is a complicated soul, and he always has been. But there's more to him than you might think. As a young man, he was passionate and incredibly talented, but also deeply troubled. I fell in love with that passion. The poet inside him. But I also knew that he could never be a father. He just didn't have the capacity for it. He's not a bad man, although his behavior is often unacceptable. He is who he is, though, no more, no less. That's why I decided it was best to raise you on my own. Now you know his past, you need to make up your own mind about what kind of relationship you want with him. But don't expect him to change for you. He won't and he can't. That's just the way it is."

Chrissy sighed.

"Thanks, mum."

"You're welcome hun. And if you want to talk some more, then let's catch up next week. I have to go now before I electrocute myself. Live voltage and water are a terrible combination, if you know what I mean?" Trish said with a laugh.

"Take care of yourself, mum, and try not to blow anything up."

"I'll try," said Trish in a sing-song voice, and then she hung up the phone.

Scott sat by Chrissy again and slipped his hand onto hers.

"What's the plan?" He asked.

"I have no idea," replied Chrissy.

29

Truths
Tuesday, September 22nd - Pasadena

Chrissy took a deep breath, held it for a moment, and steeled herself before dialing Joe's number.

After a couple of rings, the phone connected, and Joe answered.

"I haven't got long, kid. This is an unscheduled call, and I have things I need to get done today that don't involve talking to you."

"I know it's unscheduled, I'm.." She stopped herself from apologizing. She wasn't going to apologize anymore. She was done being intimidated by him, and she was ready for this conversation. "I need to speak to you about Gabriella."

"This, again?" Joe spat. "For God's sake, how many times do I have to tell you that this is the wrong direction? What the hell does that twenty-something year old know about publishing? I was writing bestsellers before she was even born. She's taking you for a fool, kid. And the way you're acting, maybe she's right!"

Chrissy felt a sense of calm come over her. Gone were her days of being flustered and intimidated by him. Now she could see him for what he was. A bully.

"Joe," she said in an even tone. "I want to thank you for everything you've done for me, but I think it's time for us to part ways. I feel like my time would be better served elsewhere now."

The silence stretched, taught as a ligament, before Joe exploded.

"What the hell does that mean?" he roared. "How dare you speak to me like that? You are nothing without me. You have a glimmer of talent, and that is being generous. That talent needs to be nurtured into a flame, but without me it will sputter out, and you'll be like all those other pathetic wannabes who never made it as a writer. Is that what you want?"

Chrissy breathed again.

"I appreciate your feedback, Joe, but I have to disagree. I no longer believe that my success is reliant upon your help. In fact, according to Gabriella, my writing is better without your help. She also told me that she contacted the publishing house you said you had such a close relationship with, the one you used to get in touch with me in the first place? It seems you don't have the sway you implied. There is one individual there who still idolizes you and would do anything to help you, but everyone else holds a different opinion, it seems."

"That's bullshit. This woman is taking you for a fool," Joe hissed down the phone. "Are you actually going to swallow all the lies she's feeding you?"

Chrissy's eyes narrowed.

"That's the funny thing, isn't it? At first, you want to believe what you're being told, especially when you assume that someone has your best interests at heart."

"What do you mean?" Said Joe, his voice less certain now.

"Hmmm, now let me see. When I came to visit you in

Kallenford and I asked you why you reached out to me after all those years, you quoted Lao Tzu, remember? You said that 'when the student is ready, the teacher will appear.' Do you remember that, Joe?"

"Yes, of course, now what the hell does that…"

"I've thought about that quote a lot recently, and you know what's interesting? What you shared with me isn't the entire quote. The full quote is, 'when the student is ready, the teacher will appear, and when the student is truly ready, the teacher will disappear.' So, you were only telling a part of the story. A half truth."

Chrissy waited a beat before continuing.

"And then, when I researched a little further, you know what I found out? It seems this isn't a quote from Lao Tzu at all. In fact, it's of Theosophical origin. It's amazing what you can uncover with a little research, isn't it, Joe? So many lies passed off as truths, so many half truths that tell only part of the story."

There was silence for a moment before Joe replied, his voice as threatening as a cornered beast.

"What are you getting at, Chrissy? Stop patronizing me with this smoke and mirror routine. If you have something to say, then just say it."

For a moment, Chrissy's confidence faltered. She was walking down a dark path here. Was she ready to accept the consequences of standing up to a man like Joseph Graham? He might be a belligerent old drunk, but he still had some sway in the literary world.

She braced herself and continued.

"I recently found out some information about your life that has made me question whether I want to be mentored by you."

"How dare you dig into my past? What gives you the right to snoop around in things that don't concern you?"

"I'm sorry, Joe, but when you decided to come back into my life unannounced, you opened the door for me to want to know more about you. You are my biological father, after all."

There was a snort from Joe, and Chrissy could hear the chink of ice against crystal, him draining a glass of bourbon, she presumed.

She continued.

"I'm not going to judge you for the decisions you've made, or how you've led your life. Who am I to pass judgment on anyone, after all? I just think it might be time for us to go our separate ways, at least professionally. I don't want us to part on bad terms, Joe, and I promise I won't pry into your past anymore, but I will be working

with Gabriella going forward. We have a connection. She gets me, and she understands where I want to take my writing career. I feel like she's better equipped to help me become a stronger writer using my own voice, not just a version of yours."

Joe mumbled something under his breath, his words slurring slightly.

"I'm sorry? I missed that," Chrissy said.

"I said you will never get published," spat Joe. "I'll see to it that no publishing house will ever touch you. I know how this industry works, and how to ensure a budding authors' reputation goes up in flames. I'll save you the inevitable embarrassment and scar tissue that comes from trying to swim with the sharks, when you are so obviously incapable. Your arrogance will be your undoing. And I won't stop there. I'll destroy your reputation to the point where even your husband and children will start to question who you really are."

An icy fear ran through Chrissy, quickly followed by a burning anger.

"How dare you threaten me? Who the hell do you think

you are? You're barely capable of lifting a pen anymore, let alone destroying anyone's reputation. You are nothing more than a washed up, has-been drunk who is terrified of obscurity. You would rather be hated than forgotten, and you can't stand that you've done this to yourself. You're a bitter old man who doesn't deserve a family, and I'm glad that Trish kept you away from us as I was growing up. You are poison, for yourself, and for anyone who gets close to you. Don't ever come anywhere near me or my family again."

Chrissy slammed the phone down, breathing hard, her head exploding with rage.

She grabbed the coffee mug sitting next to her on the kitchen counter and threw it onto the tiled floor. It smashed into a million pieces, and as ceramic shards flew everywhere, poor Doogie fled under the table, his eyes wide with fear.

"Oh God, oh shit. I'm sorry baby," she said, reaching for him, her heart breaking at his terrified expression.

She sat on the carpet in the living room, rocking and hugging her shaggy dog, as deep sobs wracked her body.

At first she cried with fury, and the hot bile of bitterness, but as the adrenaline dissipated, she felt the hollowness of loss.

The loss of what could have been. A mourning for something she never knew she wanted, but that she had always looked for. She mourned the father that Joe could have been; a passionate, creative guide, who adored her, and tended and nurtured her gift for storytelling. Someone to laugh with, to share ideas with, to lean on. But Trish had been right, Joe was none of those things, and never had been, and to wish for the truth to be different was to chase a dream.

Wiping her eyes, she returned to the kitchen and reached for the dustpan and brush. She began to clean up the broken pieces scattered across the floor.

That was the end of it, then. The end of her relationship

with her father, a man she had known only briefly and who had, in such a short period, changed the way she thought of both her writing and herself.

30

Damon
Wednesday, September 23rd - Pasadena

Emily made a face, her fingers clamping down hard on the steering wheel as Ed's name came up on the call waiting.

"What now?" She thought to herself, her jaw clenching.

"Brody?" she said, interrupting his latest rant about the 'damn manufacturing regulations'. "Can I call you back in a second? I have a call waiting." She kept her tone intentionally light as she pulled the wheel towards the right and slid over into the next lane. The 110 was its usual rush hour nightmare, and all the weaving in the world wouldn't fix that, however much she tried.

"Is it that QA guy?" he asked. She could hear him sifting through the papers on his desk. "Can you ask him to send over the latest production forecast? I've been waiting on those numbers all day."

Emily grimaced. "No, it's not him. It's my...um... husband."

She still hadn't quite worked out what to call Ed. 'Husband?' 'Ex?' 'Co-parenting affiliate?' It was too exhausting to even try to put it into words.

"Seriously?" Brody said, in a tone dripping with contempt. "Why is he calling you? It's not even 2pm yet. What the hell could be going on that he can't sort it out by himself? Whatever, Emily," he said, "Go deal with the latest drama, but I need those numbers tonight, understand?"

"Sure. No problem. I'll see you tomorrow." Emily replied in a clipped tone.

He rang off, and she banged the steering wheel in frustration.

"Really, Ed?"

Why did he insist on calling her at the most inopportune moments? Didn't he realize that this could seriously undermine her credibility? Whatever may or may not be going on with her and Brody privately, she was determined to keep her business reputation intact, and these constant interruptions weren't helping.

"What?" she snapped, as Ed's call connected. "You know I'm still working, right?"

"Where are you?"

"What do you mean, 'where am I'? I'm in the car."

"How far away are you?"

"From where, Ed. For God's sake, what is it you need? I'm extremely busy, and it's your night to take the kids."

"I'm sorry to disturb you," he said, his voice cold, "but you need to come over to the apartment. Something's happened, and we need to deal with it together."

"What?" she asked, her burning frustration dampened by a trickle of alarm.

There was a pause, then Ed said, "Philip got into a fight at school."

"What? Are you sure? He's never done anything like that before."

"I know. The nurse called me to come and pick him up. He won't tell me what happened, but he's got an ugly bruise on his left eye, a cut on his right eyebrow, and his bottom lip is cut and swollen."

Emily hit her brakes as the cars in front of her suddenly slowed to a stop. "Shit! Sorry. I almost rear-ended someone. These drivers are a bunch of fucking idiots."

There was silence from the other end of the line.

"Fine," she said. "I'll be there in twenty minutes," and punched the 'end call' button.

Sitting in the stationary traffic, she gripped the steering wheel, shook it violently, and fought the urge to cry.

"FUCK!" she yelled, bringing her fist down hard on the wheel.

"FUCK, FUCK, FUCK!" she screamed, pummeling the air, the burst of adrenaline from her near miss making her jittery and ragged.

"WHAT?" She gesticulated at the guy in the car next to her, who was looking at her with alarm.

Facing forward, she blew out hard, trying to regain her composure, trying not to let Brody infiltrate her thoughts.

She could see him sitting at his sleek desk in the huge corner office of the Apex building, the Santa Monica skyline visible behind him through the floor to ceiling windows. She pictured his face, his tan, millennial face, explaining earnestly to some doey-eyed intern that Emily was 'doing her best', but that 'working moms just can't hack it in this business.'

She could slap him. Slap that sanctimonious, perfectly white smile clean off his face.

Then she thought of her boy, Philip.

Her first baby.

Her son.

That tiny miracle she and Ed fought so hard for, waited so long for, that they'd almost given up.

When he was born, he was so small. Holding him for the first time, she'd caught her breath, worried that the slightest movement might shatter him. His skin, pale and flawless, his fingernails minute yet impeccably manicured. He was perfect in every way, and her heart exploded with love.

That tiny baby was now taller than her, and the delicate, elf-like features of his childhood were thickening and strengthening, giving him a distinctive jaw line, exactly like Ed's. In fact, he had begun to so closely resemble his father that the only telltale sign he was Emily's son was his hair, which had remained an unabashed coppery red.

She wondered what on earth could have happened to result in him fighting another student? Was he being bullied, and they didn't know it? What had she and Ed missed while they'd been distracted with their own problems?

The all too familiar feeling of guilt seeped into her heart, covering everything with its black sticky ooze.

She tried to run through the conversations they'd had recently. His grades were fine. He had friends that he hung out with at weekends, and online in the evenings occasionally. He was too young for girlfriends, so it couldn't be that.

Was he depressed?

She remembered reading that depression sometimes manifested as anger or aggression. Her chest tightened as she thought about a recent news story detailing the suicide of a local teen. He'd been an 'A' grade student, on the honor roll, and captain of the football team. The suicide had seemingly come out of nowhere, and his parents were understandably distraught that they hadn't seen the signs.

She knocked on the door of Ed's apartment and he opened it, his face guarded and serious.

"Hey," he said. "Come on through. He's in the living room."

Philip flicked his eyes up as she came into the room, then he returned to staring at the coffee table.

Emily took a sharp intake of breath as she saw his face. His left eye was swollen, the dark red already turning to a sickening plum purple. His lip was badly cut and his face was pale.

She sat on the couch next to him.

She wanted to take him in her arms and hold him, but he was stiff, poised as if to defend himself. Reaching out, she put a hand gently on his, and he flashed her a hunted, wary look that made her heart ache.

"What happened?" Emily said in a voice barely above a whisper.

Philip withdrew his hand.

Ed sat on the chair opposite, elbows on his knees as he leaned forward, his brow furrowed.

"You're not in trouble, you know that, right?" He said to his eldest son. "We only want to understand what happened, and if we need to do anything to prevent it from happening again."

Philip took a long, shaky breath, but said nothing, his gaze firmly on the coffee table.

Emily reached out towards him, but he pulled away.

"Darling?" she said, quietly. "Dad told me the nurse called him to come and pick you up. She didn't know what happened, though. Can you tell us who else was involved?"

Philip chewed the inside of his cheek, but said nothing.

Ed stood. "Maybe we should call the school? See if anyone saw anything?"

Philip looked up, panic in his eyes. "No, Dad. Please don't."

"Then tell us what happened," Ed replied.

Philip dropped his eyes again.

"Fine," said Ed, reaching for his phone.

"No, Dad, please. You can't call them," pleaded Philip.

Ed put his phone down on the side table. "Tell us what

happened, then."

Philip squirmed, obviously fighting some internal battle, before he said in a low voice, "It was my fault. It's over now though, so you don't have to do anything. Just let it be. OK?"

"Who else was involved?" Ed asked.

"No one," muttered Philip.

"So you did this to yourself, did you?" said Ed.

Philip looked up at him, his eyes flashing with anger and defiance.

"Just leave it, Dad," he hissed.

"No. I will not 'leave it'. No one is going to beat up my son and walk away without consequences," said Ed, once again reaching for his phone.

"Mom, please?" Philip said, looking at Emily with a pleading expression.

"I'm sorry, darling," Emily said softly, "but I agree with your father. This isn't something we can just ignore. It's too serious, I'm sure you can see that?"

Philip sighed again, the breath shaking his whole body.

"Ok," he said, his eyes fixed on the ground. "But if I tell you what happened, then you have to promise not to go to the school about it, agreed?"

Ed shook his head. "No, son, I'm sorry, but I can't promise that. If there's any chance this might happen again, then I am going to do everything in my power to ensure your safety. That's my job as your father, after all."

Philip's face softened for a second, then he said, "I know, Dad. That's why I don't want you to be mad."

"I'm not mad. I just want to understand what happened. Will you tell us?"

Philip bit his fingernail, a habit both his parents were trying to discourage, but for the moment they let it be. Then he straightened his back, lifted his head, and looked at them.

"Ok, so there's this boy called Damon in my class and he's

a nasty piece of work. Everyone hates him. He thinks he's one of the 'popular' kids, but he's not. He's just a bully."

Emily's eyes narrowed. She knew all about Damon, and 'nasty piece of work' didn't even come close to describing that demon spawn. Damon's father owned a car dealership in town and he was a loud, crass, arrogant man. The mother was equally bad, always gossiping and spreading rumors about people, yelling at the referee at little league games, and complaining that her little angel was being treated badly by teachers and coaches alike.

"He's hated me ever since I stood up to him for bullying Jacob for wearing glasses," Philip was saying. "Last week he called Tanya fat and followed her around at recess, making oinking noises. I told him to stop, but he just ignored me. He thinks that because he's on the wrestling team and he's a lineman that he can push everyone around. I mean, yeah, he's huge, but you can't treat people like that, right?"

Emily and Ed nodded in agreement.

Philip looked down at the floor again. "So, today he started saying something to me and I just lost it. I know it's bad to fight, but I couldn't help myself."

"What did he say?" Asked Ed.

Philip looked at him with a pained expression. "He was calling you a homo, Dad." He said in a small voice.

Emily froze. Ed looked as if he had been slapped.

"What?" Said Emily, feeling dizzy.

Philip chewed his nail again.

Ed was pale, frozen, stunned.

Philip continued in a small, vulnerable voice. "I don't know where it came from or why he said it. He didn't say anything specific, he was just saying the word over and over. Then he started being really explicit, and I just lost it. I ran at him and started punching and kicking him. I think I caught him by surprise because he fell down. But then he got up again and came at me."

Ed shut his eyes and put his head in his hands. He leaned over, elbows on his knees, as if he were trying not to pass out.

"Dad?" Said Philip quietly. "I know you're gay. That's why you and Mom separated, right?"

Emily stared at him, unable to form a response.

"But if you guys are happy then it doesn't matter to me," continued Philip. "Yeah, I was mad when you separated. I couldn't understand it, and I was worried you would start fighting, and we'd all be miserable. But you both seem so much happier now. You're amazing parents, and nothing can change that."

Philip looked at Ed and said, "I couldn't let him say those things about you, Dad. It was so disrespectful, I had to stop him. I'm sorry, but I had to."

Emily held out her arms. "Come here, darling."

Philip folded himself into her embrace and cried as if a dam had opened in him, allowing all his emotions to finally flow freely.

"I'm so sorry, sweetheart," she whispered. "We should have told you from the beginning. We didn't give you enough credit. We should have been honest with you. You are so mature and insightful. And you're right, fighting is never the answer, but I can see why you did it."

Ed lifted his head, tears in his eyes.

"I'm sorry you were put in that position, Philip. You should never feel that you need to defend me. This is all my fault."

"No, Dad," said Philip. "Damon had it coming. He's racist and sexist and homophobic, and he needs to learn that you can't treat people like that or there will be consequences."

Ed rubbed his face with his hand. "I'll go and speak to the Principal tomorrow, explain what happened, and see if they want to take it any further."

"What do you mean 'further'?" Philip said, wide eyed.

"I don't know yet," replied Ed, looking serious, "but you assaulted another student, Philip. His parents may want to press charges."

"I'll go with you," said Emily, her body stiff with anger. "Philip's right. Damon had no right to say what he did, and that kind of behavior can't be tolerated. Yes, Philip didn't handle it in the best way. He shouldn't have made it physical, but that whole family could learn a lesson from this. They're all as bad as each other. I won't let you go in there on your own, Ed. We're a family and we stick together."

Ed smiled at Emily as he held back fresh tears.

She smiled back at him and realized that she felt as fiercely protective of him as she did their son. Yes, the last six months had been hard, but Ed was a good man, and she respected him as much as she ever had.

She felt the tears welling up in her own eyes, and before they could fall, she took a deep breath and said brightly, "Well, that's enough drama for one day. Why don't I go and pick up Sophie and Harry and you guys can order pizza?"

"Pizza? On a Thursday?" Asked Philip.

"Just this once," said Emily. "But don't make this a habit so you can get pizza more regularly, ok?" she said, raising an eyebrow to her son.

Philip looked reproachful but then smiled ever so slightly, before wincing in pain, and putting tentative fingers to his bruised and cut lip.

At that moment, Emily could have happily ripped that evil little Damon to pieces.

Ed walked her to the front door.

"I'm sorry," he said, hanging his head. "What a mess."

She reached out and lifted his chin so he could look her in the eyes.

"Ed," she said, "you have nothing to apologize for. We love you, and we will always defend you. That kid had no right to say what he did." She tutted and shook her head. "Seriously, you're gonna have to hold me back if his parents make anything of this. I will lose my shit if they come anywhere near you, me, or Philip."

Ed chuckled despite himself. "You really are terrifying."

"You bet I am," she replied, and gave him a quick hug before heading out to collect her other cubs.

31

Eden
Friday, September 25th - Santa Monica

Emily touched Brody's arm as they left the conference room.

"Brody? I need a minute."

He turned, flashing a wide, brilliant smile. "Of course, Emily. How can I help you?"

As the room emptied, his smile vanished, and he looked at her, his eyes cold.

"What?" He said sharply, "My calendar is jammed. I don't have time for this."

"But you said I could present the QA strategy at the pitch tomorrow. You promised."

As soon as the words left her mouth, she kicked herself for sounding so immature and unprofessional.

Brody gave her a withering look.

"Things have moved on since we talked, and I feel the message would be better coming from me, OK? More cohesive."

With that, he turned and walked away.

"'More cohesive' my ass," mumbled Emily, as she stormed down the corridor towards her desk.

She knew what was happening. She wasn't stupid. She could see how Brody looked at that new marketing intern, Natasha.

Natasha was tall, blonde and effortlessly gorgeous, and whenever she walked past, Brody would watch her with the hunger of a predator watching its prey.

Had he ever looked at her in that way? Maybe, once. But certainly not anymore. And since the day they sailed to Catalina, the dinner dates and overnight invitations had dried up completely.

Had she done something wrong? Said something out of turn? She couldn't think what it could be. Was he done with her? Could he really be that cold?

Emily ground her teeth at the sheer inevitability of it all. How could she have been so blind? God, she felt like an idiot. And, if she was honest with herself, she felt a little old for all of this.

She dropped her notepad and laptop onto her desk and sank into her chair, weighed down by the thought of her mammoth 'to do' list.

"Hey girl, got plans for lunch?"

Emily looked up to see Kolleen, purse in hand, smiling at her.

"Sure, I'd love to. I have so much work to do, but I need to get out of here for a while, at least."

Emily had come to value Kolleen's friendship more and more over the last month. Kolleen could have washed her hands of her after the way she'd had spoken to her in the staircase that day, but strangely, the honesty of it all had brought them closer together.

"Italian?" Kolleen asked.

"Sounds great. I might have a glass of wine as well," replied Emily.

"I might join you," said Kolleen.

Drinks and lunch ordered, the friends reached enthusiastically for the freshly baked rolls, breathing in the mouth watering aroma before dipping fluffy handfuls into the olive oil and balsamic vinegar that sat between them in a small glass dish.

"Oil and vinegar," Emily thought to herself, slowly swirling the delicious mixture. *"The yin and yang of contradictory connection."*

She thought back to her cozy kitchen in the English countryside, and the alchemy of the soap making process. She ached for that feeling of contentment, the simple pleasure of creating something new from carefully gathered ingredients. She sighed at the memory. Those days felt like a world away now.

Kolleen watched her friend, the weight of concern in her eyes.

"You OK?" she asked. "Things are a bit shaky with the boss-man, aren't they? Are you managing to weather the storm?"

Emily, pulled from her reverie, cringed and put a hand over her eyes.

"Shit, is it that obvious?"

Kolleen made a sympathetic face. "It's just a pattern I've seen before. No offense."

Emily shook her head in resignation.

"You saw all of this coming a mile off, didn't you? Damn, I should have listened to you."

Kolleen's brow furrowed as she reached for Emily's hand, her expression holding nothing but compassion.

Emily took a deep breath and said, "It seemed to be going well until we took a trip to Catalina for the weekend. He's been distant ever since, but I can't work out why."

"Did you fight?"

"No. I mean, I messed up a bit when a rope got caught

around the winch, but nothing was damaged. Actually, it was weird because I found an old photograph of Brody lounging on some sailboat with his arm around a girl. It was stashed in a locker that never gets used. He got all cagey when I asked him about it. You don't think that's what this is all about, do you? An old photograph?"

Kolleen pursed her lips, her eyes narrowing.

"Let me guess," she said. "She was tan, and tall, and blonde, and gorgeous, right?"

"Yes. But this was ages ago. They looked like teenagers, early twenties at most."

Kolleen tutted and looked venomous before saying, "I'd put a million bucks on that being a photograph of the infamous Eden."

"Oh, shit. Kolleen, you're right! I remember now. I asked Brody about it, and he said her name was Eden. Who is she, though? And why would it matter to him so much?"

Kolleen blew out hard, then took a large sip of wine.

"Well, for better or worse, Brody and I go way back. I've known him since he first founded Apex. In fact, I was one of his first hires. When the company was still in its infancy, we spent countless hours networking and schmoozing prospective clients to raise the necessary capital needed for his grand ideas. Late at night, when he'd had too much to drink, he'd end up talking about this girl, Eden. He'd say that she was his 'one true love' and he'd wax lyrical about the color of her eyes and how soft her hair was, blah blah blah. It became a bit of a running joke. They met in high school, and they ran away together instead of going to college. Very romantic, except that she came from money, and her parents were furious. They didn't consider Brody to be the 'right kind of boy' for their little princess."

Kolleen took another sip of her wine and paused as the food arrived. Then she continued.

"So, the two lovebirds flew to the Caribbean and spent the summer sailing charter boats around for rich clients. Brody thought it was forever, but pretty soon Eden got tired of him, and went back to Daddy and his millions, leaving our man alone and brokenhearted."

Kolleen looked thoughtful for a moment.

"He'd always tell us the story of this one special sailboat. I can't remember what it was called, but it was a big wooden boat with white sails. He and Eden sailed it through the night, and he'd always choke up as he described how beautiful the stars were, and how unreal it was to see the luminous plankton glowing all around them. They sailed it into the harbor and then they sat on the dock, holding each other close as they watched the sun come up."

Kolleen shook herself, as if pulling herself from a spell. "Jesus," she said, trying to laugh, "I must have heard that story a million times."

Emily was frozen in place.

"What?" Kolleen asked.

"'Speranza'," said Emily, in a whisper.

"Excuse me?"

"The name of the sailboat. It was 'Speranza'."

Kolleen looked puzzled, as Emily shook her head and smiled at her own naivety.

"I've heard the story as well. Although it was spun a little differently when he told it to me. But it was certainly convincing. I'll give him that."

The confusion on Kolleen's face turned to realization, and then to horror.

"Oh, shit, Emily," Kolleen said, wide eyed, "I didn't know. I swear. I would never have…"

"It's fine. It's not you that's to blame. I'm a grown woman, and I fell for it. I'm sure I'm not the first, and I probably won't be the last. That Brody really can turn on the charm when it suits him, more fool me for falling for it."

Kolleen sat up straight, her eyes flashing with anger.

"Don't you say that. You're not to blame for anything, unless it's judging someone else by your own standards of integrity. Let's not take the focus off who's the asshole here."

Emily, deflated, put her head in her hands.

"I feel like such an idiot. He basically photoshopped the girl out of his most romantic moment and used the story as bait, and I fell for it hook, line and sinker. Maybe I just wanted it to be true. Deep down, I knew things with Ed weren't right, and I was looking for an escape. Brody seemed so damn perfect with his sailboats and his surfing at dawn, and I was willing to believe anything. I wanted to believe it."

Kolleen squeezed Emily's hand in solidarity. "I swear I could chop his balls off, that little shit. How dare he treat you like that? But I'm no saint either. I've seen the way he treats women, and I've always turned a blind eye. No more, though. I'm done with it."

"I should have seen the signs earlier," said Emily. "You know, he asked me about my separation from Ed when it was still a fairly new thing? Someone in HR told him about it."

Kolleen looked horrified.

"Now, that's stepping over a line," she said, her eyes flashing with indignation. "That kind of information is supposed to be confidential, and he used that as part of his plan to seduce you? That's downright unethical."

"He didn't seduce me. Nothing happened that I didn't walk into willingly, and I'm a grown woman able to make her own decisions. But, you're right. Sharing information about my marriage troubles with the owner of the company is deeply unethical. The whole thing is beginning to stink," said Emily.

Suddenly, she looked pained.

"Shit. Now I have to go back to the office and face him. I'm yesterday's news, and he's moved on already. Have you seen the way he's been looking at that new intern?"

"Oh, God. 'Natasha'," Kolleen said, scrunching up her face. "She's the worst. If that kid put half the effort into her work that she puts into gossiping with Serena and Ava, then I wouldn't have to spend every afternoon checking for mistakes in her spreadsheets."

Kolleen put down her wine, her expression turning to one of resolve.

"You know what they say, girl, 'don't let the bastards get you down.' You're going to move on from this and be all the stronger because of it. How do you want to handle it? Whatever you want, I've got your back all the way."

Emily blew out a long breath.

"I need to think. Right now I'm tempted to slink out the back door and never come back, but I won't give him the satisfaction. Give me a couple of days to mull it over, and I'll let you know my plan."

"I'm so sorry it came to this, Emily. Whatever you need, I'm on your side, yes?"

"Thank you, you're the best," replied Emily, squeezing Kolleen's hand in return.

32

Ed
Friday, September 25th - Pasadena

"Hey there, come on in," said Ed as he opened the door to the apartment.

"Thank you," said Emily, hovering on the doorstep. "I'm sorry to derail your plans. I just really needed to talk to you," said Emily, her voice trembling.

As he ushered her in, she moved forward reflexively to hug him, then hesitated, looking into the apartment behind him.

Ed smiled at her, his eyes full of love. "Come here," he said, and pulled her in for a bear hug.

Emily slipped off her shoes at the door and Ed led her into the living room, handing her a glass of wine and ushering her to sit down on the couch.

"Where's Conner? Did you have plans? I'm so sorry to come over at such short notice." She said, suddenly on edge.

"He's at home, and he understands. It's no problem at all. Now tell me what's been going on and why you're so upset."

Emily sighed out a ragged breath and bit her lip.

"I'm an idiot, Ed. That's basically the bottom line."

Ed smiled gently and put his hand on her knee. "I'm probably going to need more than that if I'm going to understand what's going on."

She smiled at him. After the day she'd had, just being in his presence felt like a soothing balm.

She had wrestled with coming here tonight. Her initial rage and the burn of betrayal had long since dissipated, but she still hadn't entirely come to terms with Ed's new life. But as the situation with Brody deteriorated, she had realized how much she missed Ed's friendship, and his calming influence on her. She missed having him by her side, supporting her and offering a voice of reason when she couldn't see through a situation.

She had called him earlier in tears.

After a long and exhausting day at the office and the revelations over lunch, she had been angry, humiliated and lost, and it had been a reflex to reach out to him. Even his voice at the other end of the line had felt like a cool cloth on a fevered brow, and when he'd suggested she come over and talk it through, she had agreed without hesitation.

It was only later that she had thought of Conner and felt her hackles rise.

But still she had come, and Ed was the same warm comfort that he always had been.

"I don't even know where to start," she said. "I suppose I'll start by saying that I've been sleeping with my boss."

She looked at Ed and felt a flutter of guilt, despite the fact that they were separated, and he was with Conner.

"Yeah, I thought that might be the case," Ed stated matter-of-factly.

"It didn't start until we were separated, though. Until after I came over and saw you with Conner... well... you know," Emily trailed off.

Ed nodded.

"I know," he said. "We're both loyal people. I know you would never have cheated on me with anyone."

Emily felt her shoulders drop.

"It started in Vegas, and it was great for a while. But I've recently learned that Brody isn't quite the man I thought he was."

"Did he hurt you?" Asked Ed, his shoulders stiffening, a guarded look crossing his face.

Emily let out half a laugh. "Not physically, no. It's just my ego that's bruised. But it looks like he'd be in trouble if he had hurt me."

"You're damn right!" Ed said. "I'd beat the crap out of that arrogant little surfer-boy."

Emily laughed and leaned towards him. Wrapping an arm around him, she pulled him in for a hug.

"Thank you," she said, quietly. "To be honest, I was worried that I'd never be able to forgive you when you left. I thought I would never heal from it. I'm not saying that I'm completely there with the whole Conner thing, but I think I'm making progress."

Ed looked into her eyes. "I know. And there's no hurry. This is a huge transition for all of us, and it'll take however long it takes."

Emily took a large gulp of the wine and collapsed back into the cushions.

Ed sipped his wine and placed it back on the side table.

"So. We've established that surferboy Brody is a shit, and this I believe whole-heartedly, but what actually happened?"

Emily groaned and shook her head.

"He lied to me, and I bought it like a fool. It's over between us, and he's moved on, but that's not why I'm so upset. I can't keep working for him. It's not that we dated and now we've broken up. I'm an adult, and yes, it would be messy, but I could handle it. It's far more serious than that. I've uncovered some concerning trends that could suggest borderline unethical practices, and that I won't tolerate. I was wondering why he was keeping me out of the pitches to new investors, and now I know why. It's because he wants to move the manufacturing to China and drastically cut costs as we scale up production. I've looked into the manufacturing plants he's recommending, and they barely meet our minimum standards on working conditions. I don't know, it just leaves a bad taste in my mouth. I can't work for a company who values profits over human lives. I'm not going to rush into anything, don't worry, I'm not that foolish, and technically he's not breaking the law, but I'm going to have to make some hard decisions over the next couple of months. I can't be part of something this morally ambiguous. That's not who I am."

Ed's face broke into a wide, glowing smile. "There she is."

"What?"

"There's the warrior I married. I was worried that you'd lost yourself for a while, but I see that you're back again. You've never been willing to compromise your ethics, and you've always fought for what you knew was right. That's why I fell in love with you."

Emily smiled and laughed. Then her smile faded.

"Can I ask you something? But you have to promise to be honest."

"Of course."

"Did you really not know you were gay? How could you not have known something as fundamental as that?"

The smile dropped from Ed's face.

"Wow. That came out of left field."

"I'm sorry, I just can't... understand it. I believe you when you say you weren't lying to me, and that our marriage wasn't a sham, but how is it possible that you never knew?"

Ed reached for the wine bottle and topped up both their

glasses. Then he looked deep into her eyes and said,

"Honestly, Emily, I swear to you that I didn't know. Looking back on it now, I remember there was an incident at school; I had what can only be described as a 'crush' on a boy called Toby. Let's just say that my father made it very clear to me that this wasn't an acceptable path to walk down. If he was still with us, I'm sure he'd claim that he wasn't homophobic, but he did have certain 'expectations' of family life, and what was expected of his son, and he wouldn't have tolerated the idea of me being gay. Plus, I went to an all boys' school, and stuff like that happened quite a bit. I was never interested in dating, and I'd never had a girlfriend before I met you. I fell in love with who you were. I never considered there could be more to it than that."

Emily let out a ragged breath.

"I'm trying to understand, honestly I am. I'm just not there yet."

"I know. I'm still adjusting to it myself. But let's put this aside for now and talk about you. What are you going to do next? What are we going to do as a family?"

Emily rubbed her temples and sighed.

"I really don't know. It's a nightmare. My work visa is based on working for Apex, and I can't see how I can do that anymore. As far as I can see, I have three options. Option one is to stay at Apex and work for an unethical company I don't believe in. Option two is to pack it all in and go back to England. Option three is to find another job. But I'm not even properly qualified for this job. How is anyone going to take me seriously enough to offer me a job, plus sponsor my visa? I am royally screwed, Ed. And if we have to go back to England, how is that going to affect you and the kids? They're settled here, they have friends and they're enjoying school. I'm not sure they'd want to go back to England again even if you offered it to them. And then there's you and

Connor. I'd feel terrible asking you to choose between him and us. Basically, I've fucked everything up for everyone, haven't I?"

Tears streamed down Emily's face. Now that she's spelled it out, not just to Ed, but to herself, she could see just how much she wanted to stay in California. But how? It was impossible.

Ed took the wineglass from her hand and placed it on the coaster. He put an arm around her and whispered,

"It's OK. We'll work it out together. There's got to be a way. Don't worry, we'll work it out as a family."

33

Descanso
Saturday, September 26th - Pasadena

Emily and Chrissy met in the parking lot of Descanso Gardens, and after big, fierce hugs, they walked to the entrance together. Chrissy had bought an annual membership so she could come to this magical place whenever she wanted to, but, of course, she didn't make it here as often as she would like.

The friends wandered the winding paths, shaded from the sun by a thick canopy of leaves. They stopped to inhale the delicate perfumes of the brightly colored flowers, and the scent of fresh cut grass. It was blissful to get out of the heat of the day and relax in the relative cool of the gardens.

"God, I love this place," said Chrissy, shutting her eyes and stretching her arms out wide as she breathed deeply. "It's good for the soul, isn't it?"

Emily arched an eyebrow and said, "If you start spinning around and singing, 'The Hills Are Alive,' I'm leaving, OK?"

"Fair enough. I'll keep it for next time," replied Chrissy, grinning and giving Emily a playful shove.

They continued walking towards the manicured rose

gardens, stopping to watch the miniature train rattle past, carrying its cargo of exuberant toddlers and their accompanying parents.

Chrissy smiled to herself. It didn't seem so long ago that she was riding this very train with Josh and Jackie, chugging through the fragrant wildflowers and past the meandering streams.

When the kids were toddlers, she would bring them to Descanso every week for fresh air and exercise, and to watch the changing of the seasons. The bright daffodils and sweet-scented irises of spring would bloom and fade, making way for the glory of the summer roses. Fall would turn the forest leaves to gold, and winter allowed the shy camellias to step forward. Each season had its special treats, and Chrissy could feel the flow of nature moving forward, like the huge silent hands of an invisible clock.

The highlight of every Descanso day was always the train ride, though, and her babies would stand by the platform clutching their little paper tickets, and hand them earnestly to the driver when the train arrived.

She missed those simple days when they were young, when they would throw their arms around her neck to hug her, and crouch by the pond looking for frogs and turtles, and play hide and seek amongst the trees.

"You, OK?" asked Emily. "You seem very far away."

"Yes. Just time traveling for a moment," replied Chrissy, and the friends smiled at each other in mutual understanding.

"So," said Chrissy, pulling herself back into the present. "You said, and I quote, 'everything is going to shit.' Care to expand on that?"

Emily looked to the heavens, then said, "Long story short, we may have to move back to England."

"What?" Chrissy said, so loudly that a couple pushing a

stroller stopped to look at her. "Hang on just one second. Back up, and start from the beginning, would you?"

Emily huffed out a breath and began to run through the events of the last two months. She told Chrissy about the overheard restroom gossip session, and about Phillip's fight at school. She explained her concerns about the new direction of Apex, about Eden, and finally, about her disintegrating relationship with Brody.

"Oh my God, Emily. So the whole 'Speranza story was bullshit? It was just a pickup line? What a bastard!"

Emily shrugged.

"It wasn't exactly bullshit. I mean, it happened. But in the version Brody told me he conveniently left out the part where his 'one true love' was not a beautiful wooden sailboat, but was, in fact, a leggy blonde who dumped his ass a couple of weeks later."

"Serves him bloody right," said Chrissy, her eyes narrowed.

"The whole thing has been a humiliating disaster, but it has shown me who my true friends are. Kolleen has been honest with me from the start, and she did her best to keep me away from Brody. I just wouldn't listen. And Ed was so amazing yesterday. Yes, he hurt me, and I'm still not completely over it, but I needed him and he was there for me, and that goes a long way."

Chrissy nodded. "Ed's a good guy. Hopefully, you two can find a way to be friends in the long term."

"Yes, I can see that being a possibility now, whereas I couldn't even imagine it a month ago."

"Circumstances change, people change, and relationships grow stronger or break under the pressure."

Emily stopped by the fountain. Running her fingers along the surface of the sparkling water, she breathed in the scent of roses, and stared into the distance to the San Gabriel

Mountains.

"I hope we don't have to leave," she said, quietly. "I love Pasadena. Even though we haven't been here long, it already feels more like home than anywhere I've lived before. I'll miss the mountains."

The tears welled up in her eyes, as Chrissy put her arms around her protectively.

"Anyway," Emily said, pulling herself out of the embrace and wiping her eyes. "Enough about me and the dumpster fire that is my life. What's going on with you? How's the writing? And how's it going with your father? Joe, isn't it?"

Chrissy snorted. "Ha! You wanna talk about dumpster fires? Well, I've got one of my own, and his name is Joseph Graham."

As Chrissy told Emily what had happened, the friends walked through the rose garden and toward the forest of oak trees.

Chrissy could feel the tension melting away as she kicked dry leaves into the air and stomped on them, feeling the crispy crunch running through her in a delicious wave.

She looked at Emily and said, "Do you think I'm weird?"

Emily hooted. "Yes. Extremely. But also, wonderfully. I wouldn't change you for the world."

"I worry sometimes that I'm lost. That I need to grow up and get my shit together. Do you ever feel like that?"

Emily folded her arms, pursed her lips, and raised an eyebrow.

"Really? Have you not been listening to anything I've been saying?"

Chrissy laughed.

"Yeah, well maybe. But from the outside, you and Liz always seem so competent. So put-together."

"Hmmm, so do a lot of people, but I think we're all just trying to find our way."

As they walked towards the Japanese Gardens, Emily asked, "Do you really think your father would try to destroy your writing career? Is he that vindictive?"

Chrissy sighed.

"I don't know. He's incredibly self destructive, so maybe I shouldn't put it past him to focus some of that self loathing in my direction. It's sad, but I think he can't bear the idea of me being successful, especially on my own merits and not as a reflection of him, you know? Did I tell you I called my mom after I spoke to him?"

"No, you didn't. What did she say?"

"She said that there's more to him than meets the eye." Chrissy said, and then after a pause, "I think she still has a soft spot for him. Not that she would want a relationship with him or anything, but I think she feels sorry for him."

"There's no excuse for behavior like that," said Emily.

"No, I totally agree, and I'm not sure we'll be able to salvage our relationship after what he said to me. Only time will tell, I guess. Talking of mothers, have you spoken to yours recently? Does she know you're considering moving back to England?"

"God, no. I'm not adding that into the mix as well. Can you imagine? She'd be overjoyed to hear that I've fallen on my face. I'd never hear the end of it. If we have to move back, then I'll sort out as much as I can before I tell them. And we won't be moving back to the countryside, anyway."

"Where would you move to?"

"London, I think. Or the outskirts, at least. I raised it with Ed and he seems on board, although he'd much rather stay in California, as I think we all would. Actually, I called Liz and talked to her about it a bit, just to ask for some advice. She was so lovely and supportive. I think this new man is bringing out the best in her."

Chrissy grinned. She couldn't help feeling a little proud

that she'd had something to do with this budding romance.

"Yes, they are so cute together. You know that he moved to London to be with her? So romantic! He got a job at a bank in the city just so he can be close to her."

Emily made a face.

"What?" Said Chrissy. "You don't think that's romantic? I do."

"Hmmm, I don't know. Maybe I'm still feeling raw from the Brody debacle, but I'm not sure. We'll have to see how it goes."

Chrissy swatted her arm, put her hand dramatically to her breast and said, "He is her prince and she is his princess. It's fate. It's written in the stars. They will fall in love and live happily ever after in a castle. It's meant to be."

Emily snorted, but in that moment she couldn't help loving her eternally optimistic soul sister.

"I hope it goes well, I really do," she said, "Liz deserves some happiness in her life."

They stood shoulder to shoulder on the wooden bridge and watched the Koi swim languidly in the shade of the cherry trees.

"I'd miss you so much if you leave," said Chrissy. "It makes my heart hurt just to think about it. I never realized how much I needed you guys in my life, and I'm so glad we're friends again."

Emily said nothing. She just smiled and put her arm around her old friend, pulling her close.

34

Whiskey
Saturday, September 26th - London

Tilting her head back and raising her eyebrows, Liz applied the smoky eye shadow to the second lid. The light of the makeup mirror illuminated her face, shining through the evening dusk as the streetlights started to flicker on across London. She compared eyelids and nodded, satisfied. Next, she reached for the mascara.

Andrew's voice came from the living room.

"I'm making myself an Old Fashioned. Do you want one?"

"You know I don't like whiskey, and should you be drinking before they get here? Is that wise?" Liz said, coating her blonde lashes with the sultry black mascara.

"I'm just having one. I need it. I'm dying here," came the response.

"You'll be asleep before 9pm if you start drinking now."

"I'm going to struggle to stay awake, anyway. I'm running on fumes as it is. I don't even know why they're coming tonight. Couldn't we have put them off for another couple of weeks?"

Liz growled and tried to focus on applying her lipstick.

Smacking her lips together, she pouted in the mirror one last time before turning towards the kitchen.

"Andrew, we've had this conversation already. You were the one who invited them, and you told me this would be the best day to have them over for dinner. If it was going to be such a problem, then you shouldn't have committed to it in the first place," she said, trying to control her irritation as she checked on the duck confit.

Andrew's voice came from the living room.

"No, I told you this was the only time I could do it. That's an entirely different thing. I don't think you appreciate how busy this week has been, and next week is going to be even worse. The last thing I want to do is to host friends right now."

Liz, who was searching through Andrew's kitchen drawers for matching silverware, stood up straight and took a

deep breath. Her jaw was wrench-tight and her shoulders ached from the tension of another long week at work. God, she would kill for a cigarette right now. Trying to keep her voice smooth, she said,

"I hate to state the obvious, but these are your friends, Andrew, not mine. And you were the one who invited them. I told you that your first week in a new job would be hell, but you didn't listen to me. I think you were still on an adrenaline high when you spoke to Fiona on Tuesday and invited them over, so don't put this on me, OK? I just confirmed the time with her, that's all. And believe me, the last thing I want to do on a Saturday night is to listen to Reece droning on about the markets, or bloody Fiona's incessant prattle about the latest issue of Tatler, and who she bumped into at the polo match last weekend."

"The polo season is over," said Andrew, adjusting his tie as he walked into the kitchen.

"Well, whatever. I'm sure she'll find some other social

inanity to bore us with."

Liz turned to look at him, and despite her irritation, she was taken aback by how handsome he looked.

Andrew caught her expression, and a smile flickered across his lips.

"You can't help yourself, can you? I'm just too damn gorgeous," he crooned playfully, as he took her in his arms and swept her around before dipping her ever so slightly.

"If you're not careful, I'm going to stab you with a steak knife," said Liz, struggling not to smile.

"Then I will die for love, and it'll be worth it."

"Shut up, you idiot," she said, allowing him to place a kiss on her cheek.

"You cut me to the quick, m'lady," he replied, holding his chest dramatically. "If you continue in this manner, then I may ban you from trying my new celebratory scotch. I bought a very special single malt to toast my first ever soul-sucking city job, long overdue as it is."

"No hardship there. I don't like scotch anyway," Liz said, making a face.

Andrew tried to grab her, but she darted out of his reach.

"Well, that just won't do, will it, now," Andrew said, his eyes dancing with mischief. "Any future Lady Armstrong-Bell needs to appreciate fine scotch. It's part of the indoctrination into the madness. We will begin your training tonight, young lady."

Liz was about to argue, but before she knew it, Andrew had pulled her to him. He took her face in his hands and touched his lips to hers, softly at first, but then with a rising urgency. As her lips parted, she wanted to let go, to sink into him. But she pulled herself back.

"No. We can't. They'll be here in twenty minutes, and I've already done my hair. Plus the duck will burn to a crisp, and nobody wants charred waterfowl with their plum sauce."

Andrew pouted, then gave her a wicked grin.

His cell phone rang, and he reached to grab it.

"Let's hope this is them calling to cancel, then I'm really going to mess up your hair, and to hell with the duck."

Holding eye contact with her, he raised an eyebrow and answered the call.

The grin vanished, and his face went gray.

"What's wrong? What happened?" He said in a tight voice, his eyes wide.

Liz watched as he grabbed the side of the couch and collapsed onto it.

"What is it?" she mouthed to him, but he only waved her away.

"When? Where are they now?" He asked, his voice strangled.

Liz felt a cold fear wash over her.

"I'm coming. I'll be there as soon as I can. Do you have someone with you?"

Liz sat next to him, helpless and lost, trying to piece together what was happening.

"I'll catch the first flight and be there tonight."

Andrew hung up the phone and stared into the distance. He looked as if he might pass out. Liz took his shoulders gently and laid him back against the back of the couch.

He breathed raggedly, his face a mask of horror. Then he turned to her, his eyes wide and filled with tears.

"There's been an accident," he whispered. "It's my father and brother. They've been killed."

Liz just stared at him, unable to comprehend what he was saying.

"No." She heard the words come out of her mouth, but it was as if someone else was speaking. "No, it must be a mistake."

Andrew took her hand and squeezed it hard, his

expression lost and desperate. She could feel him trying to hold on to her, as if he was spiraling into a deep pit, an oblivion from which he would never return.

"I have to go," he whispered. "I have to go home. My mother is hysterical. I need to be with her."

"I'll come with you," said Liz.

"No. I have to do this alone. I'm sorry, Liz, but my family needs me."

He stood, but stumbled and sat back down, his legs unable to hold him.

"You're in no state to go anywhere. You're in shock." Said Liz, her heart hammering in her chest.

"I have to catch a flight." Andrew said in a faraway voice.

"You need a stiff drink." Said Liz. She stood, shaking, and walked to the whiskey cabinet.

She handed him the glass, and he sipped it. Slowly, his breathing steadied.

"What happened?" Liz asked.

"I'm not sure. My mother wasn't making much sense. All I could make out was that there'd been an accident, and they'd been killed. She said the plane went down. Oh my God, Liz."

Andrew turned to her, the color draining from his face again.

"They took the Cessna to the Highlands to go fly-fishing. That's the plane I took you up in when we flew to Montrose for our picnic. They invited me to go with them this weekend, but I said I couldn't because you and I had plans. I would have been with them, Liz. I should have been with them."

Liz squeezed his hand so tightly it hurt. Pain to cut through the terror, through the disbelief. Pain to keep them both from spinning out of control.

"I'll drive you to the airport," said Liz in a calm, steady voice. "Go and pack some things while I book you a flight, then I'll drive you to Heathrow. Is someone with your mother?"

"Yes. Charlie, the estate manager. And Julia as well, and Ann, our housekeeper."

"OK, I'll call the house and ask Charlie if he can come and pick you up from Edinburgh airport. Ann and Julia can stay with your mother."

"Thank you, Liz." Said Andrew in a flat voice.

He stood and walked on shaky legs to the bedroom.

Liz watched him go and then gripped the kitchen countertop, digging her nails into the granite.

"Just keep it together, Liz," she told herself. "Just for a little while longer. Get him to the airport, on to a flight, and home safely. Then you can fall apart."

She took a long, shaky breath and reached for her laptop.

As she blinked away tears and tried to focus on the flight booking page, she pushed away the thoughts that screamed to be heard.

"Andrew could have been on that plane. Whatever happened to his father and brother could have happened to him, too. He could be gone. Forever."

She couldn't bear it. Even the thought of it made her sick to her stomach, and she almost crumpled under the weight of the guilt as relief washed over her knowing that at least he was still with her.

35

Debts
Saturday, October 3rd - Kallenford

"How's he doing?" asked Liz from the backseat, as Charlie drove them through the rain-washed streets of Edinburgh and out into the countryside.

Charlie tutted and shook his head, answering in his thick Scottish accent.

"Och, they're still both very shaken up, so they are. Her Ladyship hardly speaks or eats, she just stands at the window of her private drawing room looking oot to the end of the driveway. It's as if she's expecting their car to come around the corner at any minute. And his Lordship is nay better. He's like a ghost, so silent and sad, going through the motions with all that awful paperwork, but he's only half there."

Liz looked out of the window as the rain ran down the glass in rivulets, blocking her view.

"His Lordship," she repeated to herself. For a second she'd wondered who Charlie was referring to before she realized he meant Andrew. She couldn't imagine Andrew as 'his Lordship'. Her bright, happy, carefree Andrew. But now he was. That mantle had been laid on his shoulders whether or not he wanted it, and her heart ached for him.

As they pulled up to the front of Kallenford Castle, the building and grounds looked drab and lifeless. It was as if the building itself were mourning.

"Wait one second, madam," Charlie said, as he stepped out of the car and shook open an oversized umbrella.

Holding it high, he opened the car door, allowing Liz to step out.

"Now, mind the puddles, madam, while I see you safely inside." He said, holding the umbrella over her head.

"But Charlie, you're getting soaked," said Liz.

"Pay no heed to me, madam. I'm used to the weather."

"Nonsense. There's plenty of room for both of us," she replied, grabbing his arm and pulling him under the umbrella.

At first he stiffened, then relaxed and smiled at her.

"You're a special one, madam. He picked well, if it's not too presumptuous for me to say."

Liz grinned and bumped him gently with her shoulder.

Inside the entrance hall, they shook off their wet coats and Charlie took them to the boot room.

Ann, the family's faithful housekeeper, was there to greet her, and she offered her a painful, faded smile.

"Madam?" she said. "His Lordship requested that I provide you with some slippers to wear around the house. All the family wear them. I hope these will be acceptable?"

Liz thanked her and, removing her shoes, she slipped on the soft baby pink slippers.

"May I walk you to the library? His Lordship is just finishing up some business, but he will be with you shortly."

As Ann opened the heavy wooden door, Andrew looked up from where he was sitting behind an ornate wooden desk.

He looked haggard, as if he had aged ten years in the last week alone.

At his feet lay an old black Labrador, and opposite him sat a young man wearing a sharp suit, but whose sympathetic expression put Liz at ease.

They both stood as she entered.

As her eyes met Andrew's, his expression grew warm, and the faintest smile cracked the sides of his pale lips.

"Hey," he said in a voice so heavy and weary. "It's so lovely to see you."

He walked to her, hugging her tightly and sighing, before kissing her on the cheek.

"Can you give us five minutes? We're finishing off some paperwork, and then I'm all yours."

"Of course, take your time," Liz said.

"I'm so sorry. I'm forgetting my manners. Liz, this is Aarav; he's our solicitor. He's here to help me wade through the necessary agony that is inheritance tax law."

Aarav bowed slightly.

"It's a pleasure to meet you, madam," he said in a crisp voice.

"Thank you. You too," said Liz, feeling somewhat awkward.

Ann, still standing in the doorway, cleared her throat and said, "Can I bring tea for anyone?"

Andrew's eyes lit up.

"Yes please, Ann, I would love some. Earl Grey. Aarav, can I tempt you?"

"No, thank you. Thank you for the offer, though."

"Liz?" asked Andrew, turning to her.

"Yes, please. That would be lovely," she said, looking at Ann.

Ann gave her a smile and pulled the door closed behind her.

As Andrew signed the last of the documents, Liz took a seat in a large leather chair by the crackling fireplace and took the opportunity to look around.

The library was large and impressive, with paneled walls leading to high ceilings covered in intricate moldings. The hand painted wallpaper, its pattern now barely visible, spoke to the faded opulence of the room, and the chairs, sofas and rugs were somehow both threadbare and luxurious, moth-eaten yet elegant, with deep hues of red and gold. The solid wooden bookcases seemed to groan under the weight of a thousand leather-bound books, centuries of knowledge collected by this aristocratic family.

The walls were hung at regular intervals with embellished gold frames containing paintings of what Liz could only assume were various Armstrong-Bells from the past. Stern looking gentlemen with bristling mustaches and beards stood draped in rich fabrics, their hounds at their feet. These were interspersed with paintings of pale, melancholic women with long elegant necks, who stood demurely, staring off into the distance. One particularly fierce Earl wearing the clan tartan that Liz recognized from Andrews' birthday party, appeared to be staring directly at her with his beady little eyes. It made her shift uncomfortably in her chair, and for a wild moment she considered apologizing for her presence in this private family library, which he appeared to be adamantly against.

Of course, she'd been aware of the size and grandeur of Kallenford Castle. She had, after all, seen it many times from the outside. But it dawned on her that she had only been inside its walls once, on the night of the surprise birthday party, and then only in the great hall and the formal drawing room.

She wondered how many rooms the castle had. Mentally retracing her steps, she tried to do some quick calculations. The grand entrance hall had at least four doors leading off it, one to the drawing room where the party had been held, one into this library, one to the ballroom, she believed, and that left one other. Where could that lead?

Then there was the huge sweeping staircase leading to the upper floors. From the outside it was clear that there must be at least three floors, so, fifty rooms? Maybe more?

Ann returned with the tea tray, and Liz sat up, smiling and whispering a thank you.

As she poured, she could hear Andrew saying,

"Good. Thank you so much for all your help. Let's talk again tomorrow." The two men stood and shook hands.

They walked together to the library door, where Charlie was waiting to see Aarav out, the old dog trailing faithfully behind Andrew as they went.

Andrew turned to Liz, his face relaxing as she stood, and he took her in his arms.

"I can't tell you how glad I am to see you," he whispered into her ear, and she felt her whole body glow.

He kissed her, pulling her close to him as if he were drinking deeply after being lost in the desert.

"Are you ok?" she whispered. "I've been so worried about you."

"Let's sit," he said, pouring himself a cup of steaming tea from the silver teapot. "To be honest, no. I'm not. But I'm better for seeing you, though."

She squeezed his hand as the old dog lay down at his side, looking up at Liz with eyes of liquid sadness.

Andrew tousled the dog's ears, and with a sigh, it settled across his feet.

"This is Sally," said Andrew, the heaviness returning to his voice. "She's my father's dog. Or was. I guess she's my dog now. Poor old Sally, you're suffering, old girl, aren't you?"

Liz stroked the dog's head as they sat in silence.

Eventually, Liz said, "Charlie told me your mother is finding it very hard."

Andrew dropped his eyes.

"She's in a bad way, Liz. I think I might need to get a nurse to come and care for her. She won't eat, she hardly sleeps, and she won't talk to me or even Ann."

"She's in shock. It's understandable. She's just lost her husband and one of her children. I'm sure that would be unbearable for anyone."

Andrews' brow furrowed as he ran his hands through his hair distractedly.

"It's not just that. The estate is in a much worse financial state than anyone knew."

"How bad?"

Andrew looked up, his eyes dark.

"Bad. My father was never a businessman, and he tended to ignore problems in the hope that they would go away. It seems he's been in a financially precarious position for almost five years now, and no one in the family knew. Our accountant has been tearing his hair out, but my father wouldn't listen to him. He even tried talking to my brother last time he was home from maneuvers, but you know what James was like. He idolized our father and he would never hear anything against him."

"Is it manageable? How much are we talking about here?"

Andrew stood up and began to pace.

"Seriously, Liz, I don't know. That's what scares me. We're in a hole, a deep one, and the more I look through the paperwork, the deeper it gets. We could sell some of the land, but that's a finite resource, so even if we did, the money wouldn't last forever. The estate owns roughly 6,000 acres of land, half of it farmland. That has a total market value of approximately seven million pounds. The rest of it is hill country worth about four and a half million in real estate development costs."

"Holy shit, Andrew! That's a fortune!" Liz said, almost choking on her tea.

Andrew shook his head.

"No, actually it's not. I know it sounds like a fortune, but this castle and its grounds are a financial albatross. The castle itself is over 14,000 square feet, 82 rooms in total if you include the cellars, the kitchens, and the stable block, and most of the building is almost three hundred years old. The insurance alone on a property like this is crippling.

We did a full walkthrough yesterday to check the condition of the entire castle. We went into rooms that no one has been into in months, and we realized that there's been a flood in the corner of the east wing. There's mold all over the 17th century tapestries, and now the ceiling is unstable. The entire roof might need to be replaced, and this is a listed building, so god only knows how much it will cost to bring it up to working order in accordance with the Scottish Heritage Directorate.

Our accountant told me that the operating cost of a property like this, including maintaining all the out-buildings and cottages, could be as much as a million pounds a year, so if we sold all the land this year it would only pay for the upkeep for 11 years. If we ran the castle on a tight budget we might be able to stretch the money out, but what if we have children? I'd be leaving them in an impossible financial situation, and I can't do that."

Liz swallowed at Andrew's free use of the word 'we', and the assumption that they would have children to leave the castle to.

Andrew continued, "I told my mother we'll probably need to open the castle to the public, or maybe even sell it while it's still in a good structural state. I think that's what pushed her over the edge. Maybe it was insensitive to say it. Maybe I should have waited until she was stronger, but none of this is my fault. I'm just left to pick up the pieces."

He turned to her, tears in his eyes, fighting to keep his

composure.

"Come here," she said softly, opening her arms, and he collapsed into her, sobbing.

"He hasn't even had time to grieve," she thought to herself as she held him tightly, feeling his body shake against her, and her heart ached at the realization.

"I can't do this, Liz. I can't," he sobbed.

"Yes, you can. You have to, and I'll help you." She whispered in response.

36

Funeral
Saturday, October 10th - Kallenford

"Liz? Can you help me with these cuff-links?"

Andrew stepped out of the bathroom and handed Liz the silver links. Tiny works of art showing the family crest buffed to a shine by Ann. He wore a simple black suit with a white shirt and black tie. He looked so handsome, and she felt her heart aching for this carefree boy who had turned into a man overnight, shouldering a burden he never thought would be his.

Liz fixed the cuff-links into place, then looked up into his weary eyes as he smiled down at her. The soft blue of his irises reminded her of sea mist on a chilly winter's day.

"You doing ok?" she whispered.

"Yeah. It's going to be a long day, though." He replied.

"I know." She put a hand on his arm and squeezed.

He turned to the mirror, pulling the suit jacket over his broad shoulders and adjusting the white pocket square.

"I couldn't sleep last night, so I read through the accident report again. I can't understand it, the seat never did that before. I flew that Cessna hundreds of times and the runner always worked perfectly. Why would it have slipped and jammed like that?"

"Darling, don't do this to yourself," Liz said. "You have enough to deal with today without thinking about the accident."

"But I've run the whole thing over and over again in my mind," he said, brow furrowed as he pulled his fingers through his hair distractedly. "My father did all the pre-flight checks correctly and everything was fine. Then, as they took off and ascended, the seat rolled back hard on its runners and jammed so he couldn't reach the controls. Why would it have done that? Maybe he'd adjusted it and not inserted the pin correctly? It seems unlikely, though. The investigator said that both he and James' seatbelts were unbuckled, so they were obviously trying to reach forward and grab the control column, but the plane was banking hard to the left. They just couldn't pull up in time."

Liz put a hand on his arm and he looked at her, his eyes haunted.

"Do you think they knew?" he said quietly. "Did they know they were going to die? Or did it all happen too fast? The coroner and the investigation team don't know if they were killed instantly or... I hope they were. I hope they were dead before the fire started."

Liz stepped forward and wrapped her arms around him. She needed him to stop, for both their sakes.

"Please, Andrew. It's too much. You can't keep doing this to yourself."

Andrew held her at arm's length, looking at her with fear and desperation.

"It could have been us, Liz," he said in a haunted whisper. "It could have happened the day I flew us to Montrose. I could have killed you."

"Stop," she said, pushing him away so she could look him

in the eyes, her chest heaving with grief. "You need to stop this, now. This isn't helping, and you're going to destroy yourself if you keep thinking this way. It's not your fault. None of this is your fault, ok? We need to grieve, and then deal with what comes next, but blaming yourself doesn't lead anywhere good."

Andrew took a deep, shaky breath and stood tall.

"You're right. We have guests waiting downstairs and the cars will be arriving soon to pick us up. I guess I'm 'Lord Kallenford' now, whether I want it or not, and I have duties and responsibilities to attend to."

Arm in arm, they walked from the bedroom, down the corridor, and to the top of the grand staircase.

Andrew's mother joined them, her face pale and fragile, pain radiating from her. Andrew gently took her arm and led her down the winding wooden staircase as Liz followed behind.

Friends and family were gathered in the entrance hall below, a group of maybe twenty mourners. Hundreds had wanted to come and pay their respects, but Andrew's mother had asked that it be an intimate affair.

Liz recognized some of the faces below, but most were strangers to her. She searched the crowd for Julia, but couldn't see her.

Ann caught her eye and nodded in support. Her characteristically rosy cheeks were sunken and sallow, her mouth, normally turned up in a smile, was pinched. She had been with the family for over twenty years, originally as a nanny to the boys, but recently as the housekeeper and linchpin of the estate's remaining staff. Since the accident she had been going about her duties in silence, robotic, refusing to sit down or rest in case the weight of her pain overwhelmed her completely.

As Andrew and his mother descended, the mourners

looked up towards them. James's fellow officers from the Royal Lancers clicked their heels to attention and saluted with white-gloved hands, their serious eyes fixed on Andrew from under the brims of their red caps. Backs straight and shoulders back, their black uniforms spotless, dotted only by gleaming gold buttons, and finished with bright scarlet stiff collars.

Liz could see the pain and pride in their eyes, and she understood how much this father and son had meant to their regiment.

As Andrew and his mother reached the bottom of the stairs, they were surrounded by murmurs of condolence and support.

The great front doors of the castle were opened, and the mourners stepped out into the sharp sunlight of the frigid Scottish October day.

As her heels crunched on the gravel, a chill wind caught at Liz's black dress, making her pull her black jacket tightly around her.

The hearses led the way slowly across the driveway as the crowd walked behind them. As they did, the bagpipes played a beautiful, mournful rendition of 'Flowers of the Forest'.

Liz felt her chest heave as the tears rose in her eyes. The resonance of the pipes flowed through her body, searching out her deepest grief and pulling it to the surface. She could taste the sweet pain of sorrow as the vibration stirred something deep in her soul.

They made their way down the one track lane that led to the family chapel; a small stone building, partly hidden by the ancient oaks and long grass that surrounded it.

The hearses came to a stop, and twelve officers stepped forward. Gently, they lifted the mahogany caskets, both draped with the Union Flag, onto their shoulders and began the slow march into the chapel.

There was a warmth by her shoulder, and she felt Andrew's hand reach for hers. They locked eyes for a moment, before he turned away once more to support his mother's elbow as they followed the coffins into the chapel.

In the front row Andrew sat upright, his jaw tight, holding his mother's hand in one hand and Liz's in the other. Liz shifted in her seat, uncomfortable in the unusual surroundings, having not set foot in a church for decades.

The minister solemnly welcomed the gathered congregation, and they stood to sing the first hymn.

There were readings from several family members, but Liz was too focused on Andrew to listen. She knew how he felt about giving the eulogy, and she was worried that he wouldn't make it through without breaking down.

She stiffened when she heard his name, and watched as he stood, bracing himself as if he were walking into a strong wind. He squeezed her hand hard before dropping it and reaching for his notes.

He stood behind the lectern, looking out over the gathered mourners. Taking a deep breath, he cleared his throat and began.

"'The clock of life is wound but once,
And no man has the power,
To tell just where the hands will stop,
At late or early hour.'
Robert H. Smith.

"Not one, but two clocks stopped abruptly a short while ago, and the silence is deafening. I am adrift in time and space with no compass to guide me. That rhythmic metronome of love and support that guided me through my childhood is quiet now, and the world seems empty without it.

"My father and brother were many things to many people. A major, and a lieutenant. A husband, and a son. A father and a brother. They were commanding, holding the respect of their regiment and all those around them, but they were also deeply caring and loving. My father was a simple man at heart. He enjoyed gardening and cooking, and he taught me about herbs. One of my earliest memories is of him crouching next to me in the herb garden in the grounds of our home. He rubbed a mint leaf between his thumb and forefinger, and his eyes lit up with pride and joy when I said that it smelled like summer. He loved me and Jimmy to distraction, but above all, he adored my mother, as she did him. They were childhood sweethearts, and they grew together as one."

Andrew cleared his throat again and continued.

"And Jimmy. Oh, Jimmy. I know you hated me calling you that, but that's who you were to me. My older brother and my North Star. I remember when I was ten years old, throwing a ball in the house, and I smashed a priceless vase. Jimmy came to investigate and found me trying to hide the pieces under the dresser. He took my hand and looked at me closely before saying, "You made a mistake, but it's better to admit it and take the consequences than to lie. A good man always stands for the truth." You were wise beyond your years, and always so patient with my reckless ways.

"1 Corinthians, 13:11 says, 'When I was a child, I spoke like a child, I thought like a child, I reasoned like a child. When I became a man, I gave up childish ways.'

Although I am indeed a man in years, I admit that, until this tragedy, I had the privilege of remaining a child at heart. To follow my passion for ironwork, to climb trees and watch the sunset over the fields, to feel free and loved and safe. And this was because I had my father and my brother by my side, guiding me, protecting me, and leading me. Now I must give up my childish ways and become a man. I only hope I can be half the man my father and my brother were. We will miss your strength, kindness, and integrity. We love you."

Liz bit back tears as Andrew returned to his seat.

His mother took his hand and squeezed it tightly, pride for her youngest son breaking through the sorrow like the sun breaking through the clouds.

Another hymn followed, and finally the commendation and farewell led by the minister. Then they all stood and filed slowly out of the chapel.

The remaining members of the regiment had formed a line between the chapel and the small mausoleum that would be the final resting place for the caskets. They held their rifles at their sides.

As the officers emerged with the caskets, there was a pause, and then a sharp, barked order;

"Present arms." In one fluid movement, the officers held their weapons out in front of them.

"Reversed arms." In unison, the muzzles were turned to the ground.

The final order was barked, "rest on your arms reversed."

Muzzles and eyes were both lowered, and a single bugle began to play the beautiful, mournful notes of 'The Last Post'.

The sound resonated through the ancient forest around them. The wind whipped the last of the autumn leaves off the gnarled oaks and they fluttered to the ground as if the trees were weeping for the loss of the two great men.

The procession stopped at the metal doors of the mausoleum, and six officers stepped forward. They lifted their rifles to the sky and fired three volleys. The sharp crack of each shot made Liz blink.

As the caskets were entombed, Liz shivered, the chill wind and emotional exhaustion catching up with her. She felt Andrew's arm slip around her shoulder, his warmth and strength steadying her as she looked up into his eyes.

"You OK?" He asked softly. She nodded. "Thank you for

being here. It means the world to me," he said, looking at her so intently that she dropped her eyes.

As the sun set across the fields and forests, the mourners made their way back to the castle as the sound of the bagpipes playing 'Amazing Grace' echoed through the grounds.

The comfort of the grand entrance hall was a welcome respite from the unforgiving October wind outside, and Liz was able to release the vise-like grip she had unconsciously adopted to brace herself against the cold.

She shook the blood back into her arms, and flexed her fingers, then she found herself ushered into the drawing room by the ever-attentive Ann.

The fire blazing in the hearth cast a warm glow across the room, making it feel almost merry. Various hors d'oeuvres were set on the heavy wooden table in the corner, and as she breathed in the smell of delicious food, a young woman carrying a silver tray of drinks offered her a hot toddy.

The heat from the glass spread through her fingers, and she hugged it to her. She breathed in the scent of lemon, whiskey, cloves and honey, and as she sipped the golden liquid, it ran like a welcoming molten stream down her throat and through her body.

She closed her eyes and breathed deeply; the tension slipping from her weary body. Opening them again, she saw Andrew, standing by the fireplace, smiling at her, the light of the fire playing across his face.

He'd stood on that very spot on the night of his birthday party, and she felt a sharp pang as she realized that on that night both his father and brother had been next to him.

He was smiling now, despite the solemn occasion, and the atmosphere felt lighter than it had done for days. Andrew called for a toast to his father and brother, and everyone raised their glasses in response. As per Scottish tradition, the mourning would now be replaced by the telling of tales of those that had been lost, and a celebration of their life.

Soft laughter filled the room, and soon tears of joy from happy memories began to mingle with the tears of sorrow.

Liz sipped on her second whiskey of the evening, surprised at how much she was enjoying it, as she listened with amusement to a wild tale of a stag hunt gone perilously wrong. Just at the climax of the story, she felt a touch on her arm and turned to see Julia, her face ashen and drawn, standing beside her.

"Julia, are you alright? You look exhausted. Come, take a seat and I'll get you a drink," she said, standing and offering her chair.

"No, I need... Liz, can you come with me? Quietly, though, and don't let his Lord or Ladyship see you," said Julia, her eyes wide and haunted.

Liz stood, the warmth of the whiskey and the fire draining from her.

Julia turned and walked towards the door and out into the entrance hall. Liz followed in silence.

Once they were in the entrance hall, Julia turned to face Liz; the tears streaming down her face.

Liz started to speak, but Julia held up a warning hand to stop her.

"Julia, what's wrong?" Liz insisted. "I haven't seen you all day and now you're white as a sheet. What's going on?"

Julia lurched to the side as if her knees might give out, and instinctively Liz reached out to support her.

"Liz. It's Joe. He's... gone."

Liz looked at her, uncomprehending.

"Joe who? Gone where? Julia, I think you'd better sit down for a minute."

"No!" Julia snapped, "It's Joe. Joseph Graham. Chrissy's father. He's... he passed away earlier today. I was there, but I couldn't do anything to stop it."

Liz shook her head, trying to clear her mind. She was struggling to process Julia's words, struggling to pull herself from the warm, comfortable fog the whiskey had created in her mind.

She finally collected her thoughts enough to say, "Let's sit down, Julia, so you can start from the beginning and tell me exactly what happened."

37

Duty
Sunday October 11th - Kallenford

Liz sat in the echoing stillness of the library, the silence broken only by the steady tick, tick, tick of the grandfather clock in the corner. A throaty pendulum, marking time as it had done for centuries, oblivious to the turbulence around it.

She laced her fingers together and squeezed hard as she stared at the old-fashioned telephone on the huge, ornate desk in front of her.

She shut her eyes and breathed in the familiar smell of leather and old books, then opened them again, bracing herself for the conversation ahead.

She reached for her cell phone and texted Chrissy to check she was ready to take the call.

Her phone buzzed in confirmation.

She picked up the phone on the desk and dialed her old friend's number.

The line rang, and Chrissy answered.

"Hey you, what's with all the dramatics? You alright?"

"Are you in a quiet place? I don't want you to be

disturbed. You're not out shopping or anything, are you?"

"Seriously Liz, you're scaring me. Are you sick or something? What's going on?"

Liz sucked in air, struggling not to drown in the dark waters of all this grief.

"Chrissy, it's Joe. He... he passed away last night."

There was silence on the other end of the line.

"Chrissy? You there?"

"Yeah."

Liz waited, giving Chrissy time to form a response.

Eventually, her tone flat, Chrissy said, "What happened?"

"He had a heart attack. Julia went over yesterday afternoon to check on him on her way to the funeral. His drinking had been getting out of control, and she said he'd been particularly belligerent last week, even throwing a mug of tea at her. They'd argued, and she'd stormed out. She called the next day, and the next, but he'd been ignoring her calls. She hadn't seen or heard from him for a couple of days and she was starting to worry, so she popped by yesterday to check on him. When she knocked on the front door, he didn't answer. It was locked, which was unusual, so she used her spare key to open it, and went inside. She called for him but he didn't answer, so she walked around the house. She went into the drawing room and found him on the floor. He was gasping for air."

"Oh, shit," said Chrissy in a whisper.

"She called the emergency services straight away, and they were there within minutes, but by then he had stopped breathing."

Liz was speaking slowly and clearly, as much for her benefit as for Chrissy's, recounting the incident exactly as Julia had told her.

"They did everything they could, but by the time they got to the hospital, it was too late. I'm so sorry, Chrissy."

Liz could hear Chrissy's breathing change as the enormity of the situation hit her.

They sat in silence for a moment, both struggling to process what had happened.

Then Chrissy asked in a timid voice, "Did he ask for me? At the end?"

Liz squeezed her eyes shut, her chest constricting as she answered.

"No, Chrissy. But Julia said he couldn't speak. It happened so fast. She doesn't think he was in any pain."

Another silence, then Chrissy said,

"What happens now?"

Liz swallowed.

"It seems he left instructions with the town lawyer. He'd told his doctor that they should be carried out in the event of his death. He asked that he be cremated with no one in attendance, no service, no announcement, no press. And he named you his sole beneficiary."

Liz heard Chrissy take a sharp intake of breath.

"Chrissy, you need to come to Kallenford and go through all his possessions. I'll help, of course, but there will be decisions that need to be made."

"I understand." Chrissy's voice came, shaky and small. "I don't know how to feel. I mean, six months ago I didn't even know he existed, and we haven't exactly had the best of relationships since then, but…"

"I know," said Liz, in a soft tone. "He was your father, for good or for bad."

Liz wished she could reach through the phone and wrap her arms around Chrissy. Hold her close so they could shelter from this storm together. She was exhausted from all this death, all the emptiness. She had to keep going, though, just a little while longer, then she could rest.

"Chrissy?" She said, "Let me know when you can come

and I'll make arrangements for Charlie to pick you up from the airport."

"Charlie?" Chrissy asked.

"He's the estate manager. And I'll ask Andrew if you can stay here at the castle while you're visiting. I'm sure it won't be a problem."

"Thank you, Liz. Let me talk to Scott and I'll let you know my plans as soon as possible. I should go now. I miss you. I'll talk to you soon."

The phone rang off, and Liz held the receiver a while longer, listening to the dial tone before placing it carefully back on the stand.

She sat again in the stillness, only the tick, tick, tick of the great clock breaking the otherwise deafening silence.

Eventually she stood, rubbed her aching neck, and walked towards the drawing room.

The castle was a cavernous, echoing shell, so empty without the vibrance of the two eldest Armstrong-Bell men who would never again walk through its many rooms and corridors. It was as if the very building itself was mourning their passing, sagging under the weight of the grief that permeated it.

At the door to the drawing room, she stopped, lifting her head and dropping her shoulders, trying to compartmentalize the grief from the two separate losses. She had told Andrew of Joe's passing, but she was determined not to burden him further when he was already so exhausted.

As she stepped towards the door, she noticed it was already slightly open. She stopped, taken aback, as she heard the sound of Lady Katherine's voice, raised in uncharacteristic defiance.

"But Andrew, you must see that this is about more than just you, now. It breaks my heart, but you must face facts. You are the Earl of Kallenford, and with that title comes a weight of responsibility that I worry you aren't prepared for."

"You're damn right I'm not prepared for it. I never imagined I would be in this position, and I never wanted this. Can't you see that the only way I can get through it all is to have Liz by my side? I can't do it without her."

Liz heard the sigh from Lady Katherine, frustration mixed with pain.

"Darling, Liz is a lovely person, and I have a great fondness for her. Under different circumstances, I could see the two of you being very happy together, but the loss of your father and brother changes everything, and you have a duty to protect your heritage."

There was an edge to Andrew's voice now, a tone that Liz had never heard before. "How can you even be thinking about this right now? We only buried them yesterday, for god's sake."

"Believe me darling, this is the last thing I want to be talking about, but we don't have the luxury of time. I see how much Liz means to you, and I worry that, in your vulnerable state, you may make decisions with your heart rather than with your head. Please, darling…"

"Don't touch me," Andrew said in an acid tone. "I can't believe you're suggesting I whore myself out to the highest bidder."

Lady Katherine tutted, "Now, don't be so dramatic. I am merely suggesting that we find you a more suitable match. You and Liz come from different worlds, and love can only take you so far."

"Ha," Andrew spat. "You married for love, why can't I?"

"Oh sweetheart, yes, I loved your father very much, but we also had shared experiences. We both grew up with wealth and position, and because of it, we understood each other deeply. Marriage is more than an infatuation, it's a contract, an understanding of shared values and obligations, and it won't work if it's not built on a solid foundation."

Andrew's voice cracked as he said, "But... I love her."

"I understand, darling."

There was a silence, and Liz, still standing behind the closed door, held her hand tightly across her mouth to muffle the sound of her sobs. Her body shook, but she was pinned to the spot, unable to pull herself away.

"Come, sit with me," said Lady Katherine softly. "Andrew, I wish with all my heart there was another way, but the debts your father left are too large, and the death duties and inheritance taxes are crippling. The estate won't survive without a sizable injection of money, and you won't be the first member of the family to be pragmatic about a mutually beneficial pairing. It saved Kallenford once before, and now it must again."

Andrews' voice came, broken and drained, "I can't give her up, mother. I love her."

"You've always been a romantic, believing in soulmates; finding that one person you are destined to be with. I saw you the night of your party, the way your face shone when you saw Liz. You looked at her as if she was the only person in the universe that mattered. And I've seen you turn your life upside down for her, but may I ask you a question?"

There was a pause before she continued.

"Has she ever told you she loves you?"

A deathly silence followed, and in that moment, Liz felt her world fall apart.

"Not yet," said Andrew in a small voice. "But I know she does. She just hasn't said it out loud yet, but she will, when she's ready," he said, the pain seeping through his voice.

"Yes, well, maybe it's time to step away, my darling. It's for the best after all," said Lady Katherine in a comforting tone.

"I can't be here right now," said Andrew, with urgency in his voice.

Liz jumped, the adrenaline pumping through her body, giving her the ability to move again. He was coming to the door and she couldn't let him see her there.

She stumbled, wiping the tears from her eyes, and threw herself back through the open doors of the library and out of his line of sight.

As she turned, she saw Ann across the entrance hall, their eyes locked, shared alarm on their faces.

Ann's eyes flickered to the drawing-room door as Andrew emerged.

"Hi Ann. Have you seen Liz?"

Her face did not betray her as she said in a casual tone, "Good afternoon Lord Kallenford, no, I'm sorry, I haven't seen her all day."

"Ann, please, I've asked you a thousand times. Just call me Andrew. That is my name, after all."

"Oh dear, no. That wouldn't be proper at all," Ann said, dropping her eyes as her cheeks flushed a deep red.

Andrew huffed in frustration before saying, "Well, in that case, please tell my mother that I'm going down to the stables. I need to get out of this drafty old pile for a couple of hours."

Liz heard his footsteps disappearing towards the kitchen and pictured him slipping out the side door onto the cobbles and around to the stables at the back of the estate.

Her eyes moved back to Ann, who was walking across the entrance hall towards her.

Ann reached out a hand and squeezed Liz's arm, her eyes sorrowful.

"These are hard times for the family, and everyone will be forced to make adjustments. Just know that you are loved, my dear," and with a final squeeze, she turned and walked towards the staircase.

"Could she have known what Andrew and his mother

were talking about?" wondered Liz. "Am I so naïve that I'm the only one that couldn't see where this was heading?"

Later that evening, Andrew was quiet, staring out of the window as he sipped his single malt.

Liz stepped behind him, slipping her arms around his waist. She felt him stiffen ever so slightly at her touch.

"You alright?" She asked. "I mean, considering the circumstances, how are you doing?"

"I'm fine. Just tired," he replied. "I went for a long ride earlier and now I'm aching. Not used to the exercise, I suppose."

"Mmm. And how's your mother? How is she coping with everything?" Liz asked, sensing the distance between them.

Andrew stepped away from her, cleared his throat and said, "You know what, Liz? I'm pretty exhausted. I might just turn in for the night if that's OK?"

And with that, he walked away.

38

Ethics
Friday, October 16th - Santa Monica

It was dark outside by the time Emily finally stood up from her desk. She'd been avoiding this moment all day, but now she had to do it. It was time.

She inhaled deeply, and with her mouth dry and her heart thumping, she headed to the elevator and up to the top floor.

She walked along the darkened corridor towards Brody's corner office.

Hesitating, she stopped at a large window to check her reflection and fix her hair.

Below her she could see the twinkling lights of Santa Monica as the city shifted from slick, fashionable startup hub to an upmarket, bohemian destination. Soon the trendy bars and restaurants would be filled with thin, beautiful, successful millennials, sitting at tables that were too close together, listening to live music that was too loud to hear over.

She knocked on Brody's door.

"Hey. Come on in, I'm almost done here," came Brody's response, his voice as sweet as honey.

As she opened the door, his welcoming smile dropped.

"Oh. Emily, I'm sorry, but I'm about to head out. Whatever it is, it'll have to wait till tomorrow," he said, his voice now frosty.

Emily swallowed hard.

"Actually, no. I need to speak to you now, I'm afraid. I have some… concerns."

"Now? At 7pm on a Friday night?"

The truth was, Emily had been waiting all day for the chance to speak to him. He'd been in back-to-back meetings from early that morning, and she didn't want to just grab ten minutes in between investor calls. This conversation could not be hurried. It was too important.

"Brody, I've been looking at the proposed manufacturing plants in China, and they don't meet our safety and quality standards."

"Seriously, Emily, can we discuss this on Monday?"

"Are you aware that the company you're recommending to manage our operations out there subcontracts a large percentage of their bottling production? And that those subcontractors have extremely questionable safety records? Some of them won't even release their factory audit results."

Brody stood up from his desk and slammed his laptop shut with such ferocity that it made Emily flinch.

"This isn't the right time to discuss this, Emily, and I'd appreciate it if you didn't march into my office as I'm trying to leave for the evening and throw unsubstantiated accusations at me. It may shock you to hear this, but you are not involved in all the decisions this company makes, nor are you privy to all the information we are using to make those decisions. Now, if we are done here, then I'll say 'good night,'" he said, showing her the door.

Emily's heart was hammering, but she stood her ground.

"No. You're not going to brush me off again, Brody. You

put me in charge of Quality Assurance, now let me do my job."

Brody snorted a laugh as he walked around the desk towards her.

"This is a fucking joke. Who do you think you are telling me how to run my business? This is just the kind of bullshit I was afraid of when I agreed to let Kolleen hire you. She saw you as some sort of 'Jiminy fucking Cricket'; the conscience of the business or some shit like that. I told her you'd be nothing more than a pain in the ass."

Emily could feel her cheeks burning and her breathing become shallow. The adrenaline pumped in her ears as he came closer.

"Why did you even agree to hire me then, if you were so concerned?" She said, trying to keep her voice level.

Brody leaned in towards her so she could feel the warmth of his breath in her face. She would not step back, though. She refused to let him win.

In a low, menacing tone, he said, "Because you were a distraction. You were different from the other girls. Older in years, but in some ways so much younger than them. I wanted to see how you would change when you had the room to grow. But I think you've peaked now, sweetie, and you need to get back in your box and let the big boys play. Maybe you should have stayed in England making your soaps in that little house of yours. Maybe then you'd still have a marriage, eh?"

Emily slapped him across the face, then blinked in shock and stumbled backwards.

Keeping his eyes on her, Brody rubbed a hand against his reddening cheek and laughed a low, growling laugh.

"I'll give you that one, I guess, but now I have somewhere to be, so you better get out of my way," he said, pushing past her towards the door.

"I quit," said Emily, her voice cool, belying the free-fall panic she felt inside.

He stopped. Then turned to face her again.

"No. You don't. You don't have the guts."

"I will be handing in my letter of resignation tomorrow morning, after I've cleared out my desk."

Brody barked a laugh, then looked at her closely.

She was shaking now, but she held his gaze.

"What would you do? Go back to England with your tail between your legs?"

Emily swallowed and said, "Well, that's none of your business, is it? And now I'd better be going. Have a lovely evening, Brody. I'm sure whatever poor woman you'll be lying to tonight is expecting you. Mustn't keep them waiting," she said, and pushed past him and towards the door.

She strode down the hall, nervous that he would follow her, grab her arm and swing her around, but no, there were no footfalls behind her.

She pressed the button for the elevator, and as it opened, she almost bumped into a leggy blonde wearing an impossibly short silk dress.

She smiled despite herself, despite the irony of it all.

"Hi, Natasha. He's just finishing up. Have a lovely evening."

"Um, thanks. You too, I guess," said Natasha, flashing a bright smile, a sharp contrast to her combative smokey eyes, narrowed with suspicion.

"You have nothing to worry about, kid," thought Emily as she rode the elevator down. *"You're welcome to him."*

By the time she got to her car in the underground parking garage, however, the adrenaline high had worn off and she realized just what she had done.

Shit.

Maybe she could go crawling back, cap in hand tomorrow and ask him for her job back?

No, things had gone too far, and as she stood in the dark garage, the tears streamed down her face.

What was she going to tell Ed? How could she have been so impulsive? She didn't have the luxury of quitting on a whim like that. She had other people's lives in her hands, other people's futures.

With a heavy sigh, she got into her car, turned the engine on, and pulled out of her parking space, turning towards the freeway to start the long journey home.

As she joined the 405, her phone buzzed. The caller ID lit up in the darkness.

It was Brody.

For a moment, she considered not answering it. But then, with her heart pumping in her chest, she hit connect.

She could hear Brody's voice oozing through the speakers of her car like liquid gold.

"Hey, Emily. I wanted to say how sorry I am for earlier," he said, the muffled sounds of a lively bar in the background. "I shouldn't have said what I did. It's been a long week and I'm exhausted. You were right to get mad at me, but I'm hoping we can put this behind us and start afresh on Monday?"

"I meant what I said, Brody. At least about how ethical these particular Chinese partners are. I can't just turn a blind eye to this."

"I know, and I hear your concerns. Can we talk about them on Monday?"

Emily squirmed before saying. "Sure. Monday."

"Great. Now you have a fantastic weekend, yes?"

Emily started to reply, but before she could speak, the line went dead. It was clear that Brody was in a hurry to get back to whatever he had been doing before he called her.

"I wonder if he called me while Natasha was in the

restroom? Or buying a round of drinks?" she thought to herself. Wherever that skinny model had been during the call, it was clear that Brody hadn't wanted her to know that he was calling Emily.

A small, vicious smile played on her lips as she toyed with a thought.

"I wonder what he would do if I texted him right now and told him to ditch her. If I told him, I'd meet him at his apartment and give him the night of his life. Would he drop her for me?"

She shook away the thought.

Brody would just love the idea of two women fighting each other for his attention. No, she wouldn't give him the satisfaction of even entertaining the idea.

As she weaved through the traffic, she thought back to the events of the evening.

So, she still had a job.

That was a relief, wasn't it?

But if it was such a relief, then why did she still have a bad taste in her mouth and a knot in her stomach?

39

Photographs
Saturday, October 17th - Kallenford

Chrissy's flight arrived into Edinburgh airport late on Friday evening, and Liz was there to greet her.

"Didn't you say you were sending Charlie to pick me up?" Chrissy asked as she hugged her old friend.

"That was the plan, but I wanted to come myself. I insisted," Liz said, squeezing her tightly.

They drove through the drizzling rain straight to the castle, and Liz carried Chrissy's bags up the huge winding staircase to a spotless bedroom with a cozy floral print comforter.

"Wow, Liz. This place is massive, isn't it?" Chrissy said, wide eyed. It was the first time she'd set foot inside Kallenford Castle.

"It is indeed," said Liz with a weighted look.

"How's Andrew doing? It must be awful to lose your father and your brother so suddenly like that."

Liz swallowed hard.

"It's been hard on the whole family. Andrew's doing OK, but he has a lot on his mind right now."

"And here I am, imposing at such a dark time," said

Chrissy, looking guilty.

"Not at all," said Liz. "You've lost your father as well, and even though the two of you weren't close, you have your own grief to work through."

They headed to the kitchen, where Andrew greeted Chrissy with a wan smile and an enormous hug.

"It's been a tough couple of weeks, hasn't it?" he said to her, his blue eyes misty with fatigue.

"It has, indeed. If there is anything I can do, then I'm here for you, Andrew," Chrissy said in a soft voice.

"Thank you. And the offer goes both ways, of course," replied Andrew.

After a light dinner, they all headed to bed. Chrissy slept as well as could be expected for someone battling jet lag, but in the morning she was ready to tackle the task at hand - sorting through the contents of Joe's hunting lodge.

The two friends stood in the doorway of the drawing room, surveying the mess.

"What can I do to help?" Asked Liz, taking in the piles of books and papers that covered every surface and most of the floor. "I wouldn't even know where to begin," she said, looking to Chrissy for guidance.

Chrissy sighed heavily and bit her lip.

"I know. There's a lot to do. I guess you could start upstairs if you don't mind, and pack up all the clothes? We'll take them to the charity shop in town. We can do the same with everything in the kitchen, unless Julia wants anything from in there. I'll go through all his papers and see if I can put them in some sort of order. I wonder if anyone would be interested in the old transcripts of his published work? I should probably put those aside."

Liz put a hand on her dear friend's arm and squeezed.

"Let me know if you need to take a break, or if you want tea or coffee or anything, OK? And remember that we don't have to do everything today. You take your time, take as long as you need."

Chrissy managed a faint smile and nodded in appreciation.

It was hard to know how she felt at this moment, standing in the lodge that her father had called home for so many years. A father she didn't even know existed a year ago.

Was she upset at his sudden passing? Yes. But she'd found as the days had gone by, she was grieving more for the relationship they didn't have than for the one they did.

At first she had grieved for the perfect father, the one she had always wished for, a man Joe could never have been, even if he had been in her life.

But now she wished that he'd have been honest with her, shared who he was, with all his strengths and flaws. She grieved for the missed opportunity to get to know him better. Yes, he had been volatile, and often downright vindictive, but part of her yearned for the time they could have shared together.

She sifted through the papers on his desk.

A final notice for an unpaid electricity bill, dated several weeks ago.

A newspaper clipping about a fishing boat lost at sea. Maybe an idea for a new story? She would never know.

An old envelope stained with coffee, with several words scrawled on it. She could decipher the word 'munitions', then something illegible, then possibly the word 'grindstone'. What was he thinking when he wrote these snippets?

She came upon a notebook with the word Christina on the front page. Hesitating, she held it still for a moment, not sure whether she wanted to open it and read the contents. She was pretty certain whatever it contained would not be flattering. Taking a deep breath, she decided to take a look.

Again, Joe's scrawls were almost impenetrable. "With

handwriting like this, he would have made a great doctor," she thought to herself, with a grin.

She could make out a couple of words, though. 'Insightful,' 'refreshing' and 'mature' sprang out at her, much to her surprise. There was a line in all caps that read, 'EXPECTS IT ALL TO BE HANDED TO HER. GOT TO FIGHT HARDER.' She raised an eyebrow. "Now there's the Joseph Graham I came to know and love," she thought.

She checked herself.

'Love.'

Had she loved him? Or was it just a throwaway comment?

As the day wore on, Chrissy started to make some sense of the chaos around her. By the afternoon, she had made her way to a large bookcase in the corner.

Her eyes scanned the rows of novels that filled the first three shelves. A collection of classic tomes, mostly hardback, written by authors that Joe had revered. There were at least five Hemingway novels, McCarthy, Steinbeck, Yates and Ellison were also present, and far from gathering dust, like most literary collections, it was clear that Joe had both read and cared for these novels like the precious items they were.

Chrissy pulled a thin, beautifully bound book from the shelf. It was old and fragile, and the title and author were no longer visible along the spine. She examined the red leather binding, and the faded gilt decoration. Opening it carefully, she found that it was a first edition of Sylvia Plath's poetry.

Interesting.

Hemingway and Steinbeck Chrissy could believe, that seemed very in keeping with Joe's style, but Plath? Maybe Trish had been right. Maybe there was more to Joe that met the eye after all.

On the top shelf of the bookcase, almost out of reach, Chrissy saw what appeared to be several old photograph albums. She pulled them down, coughing as a thick cloud of dust came down with them.

She walked to the desk, and pulling out Joe's chair, she took a seat.

Brushing off the remaining dust, she opened the large, heavy leather cover of the first album.

It contained a series of black and white photographs, some fixed in place with mounted corners, some loose.

Chrissy picked up a grainy photograph which showed a teenage boy standing proudly next to a prop plane. Turning the photograph over, she saw, written in ink on the back, the words 'Arthur, aged 17, 1937.'

Who was Arthur?

She turned the sleeves of the album slowly and carefully, examining the photographs. They showed various scenes of family life; summer vacations with the smiling faces of adults and children sitting on a checkered blanket, enjoying a picnic by the beach. A young boy learning to ride a rusty old bike, his brow furrowed in concentration while his father held the back of the seat to steady him.

Chrissy wondered who these strangers from the past could be. Most of the photographs had no caption, suggesting that the person who lovingly mounted them could not have imagined a time when the identities of these people would be lost.

There was one large family portrait that had a caption written in elegant script beneath it. In the center, sitting on high-backed chairs, were the mother and father of the group. Next to them stood three children of various ages, and in the mother's lap sat a toddler. The caption read,

'August 2nd 1954. Arthur Graham - aged 34. Agnes Graham - aged 30. Arthur Jr. 'Arty' - aged 8 (deceased). Lynda - aged 5. Mary - aged 4. Joseph - aged 2.'

So this was Joseph Graham as a cherub faced toddler in his mother's arms?

Chrissy wondered why the caption read 'deceased' next to Joe's older brother's name.

She continued to turn the pages of the album and noticed that there were no more photographs of 'Arty' after 1954.

Moving on to the next album, Chrissy sensed she had shifted in time.

Now here was Joseph Graham at age 19, dressed in his Naval Academy uniform, his smile self assured to the point of being cocky. The next couple of pages showed photographs of Joe larking around with other military men, and then the background changed to jungle and Chrissy guessed these photographs were from Vietnam. Although, again, there were no captions.

"I wonder who printed and mounted these later photographs?" she thought to herself. "Not Joe, surely. So then, who?"

After Vietnam, the photos became erratic. No more careful mounting. Now the prints were merely jammed into the crease of the pages to hold them in place. Faded color photographs of Joe wearing bell bottoms and silk shirts, his arms thrown around various women, his smile tight, his eyes dull.

The last photograph showed Joe in a gray suit, a pink flower in his lapel, his arm around the waist of a fresh-faced young girl wearing a flouncy wedding dress.

Joe's first wedding day.

As Chrissy looked into the eyes of that young writer, she could already see the hard edge forming in him. The first glimmers of disenchantment, the emergence of the bitter Joe she had come to know.

But why had he become so consumed with hatred? Nothing in any of these photographs suggested anything other than an idyllic life. What had happened to Joe to turn him into the acidic person he had become?

Just then, Liz walked through the door of the drawing room.

"Hey, Chrissy. I found these old journals under Joe's bed. Do you want to take a look through them?"

Well, now. Joe wrote journals, did he? Maybe this could shed some light on why Joe became the man he did.

40

Icarus
Friday, October 23rd - Kallenford

"Take as long as you like," said Liz from the doorway of the study, "and give Trish my love, yes?"

"I will do," replied Chrissy as she settled herself behind the huge wooden desk and prepared for her call.

She had spent the last several days engrossed in Joe's journals. The more of the hunting lodge she and Liz had cleared out, the more journals they had found. They were everywhere, in closets, under beds. They even found a couple in the airing cupboard under some old towels. Joe was indeed a prolific writer, and he had spent much of the last ten years of his life reexamining his history and his beliefs about the world. Now she had pieced together a coherent narrative about his life. She wanted to share it with Trish.

She dialed her mother's number.

"Hi, darling," Trish answered. "I'm just pouring myself a cup of tea, and then I'll be all yours. So, you found some journals, did you?"

"Yes, quite a few, in fact," said Chrissy, raising an eyebrow. "We could fill a small library with the number we found. I wanted to talk to you about Joe, if that's OK? I'm not sure why, I just feel I need to tell his story, even if it's only to one other person."

"Hmm," said Trish, and Chrissy could picture her nodding. "And the cremation is tomorrow, correct?"

"Yes," said Chrissy in a quiet voice.

"I'm assuming Joe didn't want anyone in attendance?"

"Yes. How do you know?"

"That was his way. No fuss. No 'wringing of hands'. He would have felt it was insincere."

"You knew him well, didn't you? Maybe better than most."

"I'm not sure anyone really knew Joseph Graham," Trish said, and Chrissy heard her swallow. "Anyway, tell me what you found out."

Chrissy inhaled and then began.

"Well, digging through the journals and cross-referencing them against the old photograph albums, I've pieced together most of Joe's background, or at least his own version of it.

Joe's father, Arthur Graham, loved to fly and wanted to become a pilot. However, Arthur's father didn't think it was a fitting career, and instead he pressured his son into joining the Naval Academy and training to be a doctor. Arthur was twenty-one and stationed at Pearl Harbor when the bombs fell. He saw more than any man ever should, and he suffered from nightmares and various maladies from that day on. Consequently, he was a distant father, and Joe always yearned for his approval."

"Is that why Joe joined the navy? To gain his father's approval?"

"I think so. It seems that Joe tried to become a pilot first, and fulfill his father's dreams, but he had a slight visual impairment that prevented him from flying. He felt as if he'd let his father down, so he joined the Naval Academy instead, hoping to redeem himself. Unfortunately, he was discharged after only three years because of an injury, and this cemented his father's opinion of him as a disappointment."

"But that wasn't his fault, surely?"

"I agree, but it seems his father didn't feel that way. Joe was always an afterthought to Arthur. He had never been the favorite son; that honor had gone to Arthur's first born and namesake, Arty, but Arty died tragically at the age of eight when he found his father's gun and accidentally shot himself. He was killed instantly. According to Joe, his father always made it clear that Joe could never fill the shoes of poor old Arty, lost too soon."

"That's so unfair. How do you compete with a ghost?"

"Exactly. I can see now how the seeds were sown for Joe believing he would never measure up. No amount of praise or adoration from the masses would ever fill that emptiness. Reading through his journals, I think Joe's happiest times were when he was working as a war correspondent in Vietnam and Afghanistan. All the servicemen loved him, and he was something of a celebrity. He would spin tales and buy rounds of drinks, and although he was always in trouble, it seemed like he was happy."

Trish chuckled, "Yes, he talked about those times with such passion and enthusiasm."

"He wrote a lot about you as well, Mum," said Chrissy quietly. "He loved you to distraction. In fact, I think you were his one true love."

There was a pause, then Trish took a deep breath and said, "We met at a magical time. A time out of time, where we could be our true selves without the expectations and pressures of real life. I know you don't like it when I talk about these kinds of things, but we saw into each other's souls, and that kind of connection stays with you forever."

Chrissy sat in silence for a moment. Normally she would

roll her eyes in disgust when her mother started talking about 'hippie stuff', but on this occasion, she could see the truth of it.

"It's strange," Chrissy continued. "It seems like the more famous he got, the more miserable he became. He loved his writing, at least initially, but he hated the attention it brought him. It was as if he despised his fans and his followers. He found them simping and clawing, as if they were sucking the creativity right out of his veins, leaving him nothing but a dry husk. It was such a strange relationship. He was desperate for the adoration, the validation that came with the accolades and awards, and if he didn't get them, he would rage and spout venom about being unappreciated. But equally, when his talent was acknowledged, he would do everything he could to reject and demean it. It must have been like living inside a hurricane of emotions, never satisfied, never fulfilled."

Trish sighed, then said,

"He was a true Icarus. Reaching for the sun, needing its glory and brilliance, while at the same time being consumed and destroyed by it,"

There was silence for a moment, both mother and daughter lost in their thoughts.

"Was it inevitable?" asked Chrissy. "That he would self-destruct?"

"Now that's the million dollar question, my angel," said Trish. "Who knows what's destined, and what happens by chance? Do you believe in destiny? Or do you find it restrictive to think that your life has a predetermined plan from which you cannot deviate, even if you wanted to? Personally, I believe in destiny. For instance, I believe I was meant to meet your father that weekend at Glastonbury, otherwise, you would not be here. I also believe that you were destined to meet him and spend time with him before he was gone. He taught you something, helped you in some way, even if it's not yet clear what that was. Would you agree?"

"Maybe. But it was only for such a short time. Only a couple of months. I wish it could have been for longer."

"Sometimes the people who have the biggest impact on us are only in our lives for the briefest moment. It's not the length of time that matters, it's how they touch you, how they change you."

"I guess," said Chrissy, struggling with a sudden, unexpected urge to cry.

"Are you ready to let him go now, darling?" asked Trish.

"What do you mean?" replied Chrissy, confused.

"Isn't that what all this has been about? Coming to terms with it? Finding peace? 'Getting closure', as they say nowadays."

"I suppose it has," said Chrissy. "It's strange. There are so many versions of Joseph Graham, aren't there? There's the Joe I sat with and struggled to learn from during my first visit to Kallenford, the one so bitter and vindictive, lost in resentment and drowning in bourbon. Then there's the Joe the newspapers saw; the acclaimed bestselling author, who became a recluse. There's the disreputable liar that Scott's college friend uncovered, and then the son, just trying to please his distant father, hiding his truth in his private journals. Which one is the 'real' Joe? Which one do we believe?"

"They're all the real Joe. Or they were, at least. Every life is like a diamond. Different lights create different reflections, but all are beautiful in their own way."

"Thank you, Trish. I'm glad I was able to get to know him better, and to talk to you about it. I think you're right, this was an exercise in letting go, and I'm ready to say goodbye to him now."

"I'm glad to hear that. I love you, my angel, and I'm always here for you when you need me."

"I know. Thank you, mum. I'll speak to you again soon."

Chrissy hung up the phone and sat back in the high-backed chair.

Joe was gone. But at least she'd had the opportunity to get to know him, or as well as anyone had ever known the myriad faces that made up the famous author who was Joseph Graham.

41

Parting
Saturday, October 24th - Kallenford

The day had a muted, still quality, the colors faded as if washed with a gray film. Winter was approaching, and the countryside was getting ready for its slumber. The ground was hard, the trees bare, and there was no birdsong to be heard. Even the blustery wind had calmed, leaving only a sharp chill in the air.

"I think this is the right place," said Chrissy, her voice heavy with sorrow, as she looked out over the fields towards the river.

"It's perfect," whispered Liz. "Very peaceful. Andrew said the deer graze here in the dawn when the mists are still hanging low, and the song thrush's nest in the trees over there, so in the spring you can hear their song. Come summer, these fields will be filled with wildflowers. It will be beautiful."

Chrissy squeezed her eyes shut and swallowed. The dull ache that had sat in her chest for the last couple of days sharpened, and every breath felt jagged. The emptiness weighed on her, making her movements labored. She was exhausted, unable to pull herself out of the pervasive fog of emotion that engulfed her. She was too drained to even cry.

"Do you want me to do it?" asked Liz gently, putting a hand on Chrissy's arm.

"No. I will," replied Chrissy, and she bent to pick up the urn.

Unscrewing the lid, she took one last deep, shaky breath, before scattering her father's ashes onto the grass in front of her.

The friends stood in silence, their arms around each other, listening to the faint sound of the river rushing in the distance.

"It's done, then," Chrissy said, her voice distant and monotone. "He's gone."

Liz's heart constricted. She struggled to find the right words to say to take the pain away. She wanted to reassure Chrissy that everything would be alright, that Joe wasn't gone, that he was in heaven looking down on her, and they would meet again one day. But she didn't believe that, and she couldn't bring herself to make hollow promises, even to save her friends' heartache.

"I don't even know if I'll miss him," Chrissy said quietly. "I just feel numb."

She shivered, and Liz said,

"Let's get you home and in front of a warm fire, shall we?"

They turned and walked back through the fields towards the castle.

As they walked into the drawing room, a fire blazed in the hearth. This was Ann working her magic, and Liz could have hugged her for it. The family had been through so much recently, but at least they had the love and support of Ann, Charlie, and Julia.

She settled Chrissy into a chair by the fireplace and tucked a woolen blanket around her waist and legs.

"Do you want a hot toddy?" she asked, "It has whiskey in it, which sounds gross, I know, but it's actually quite delicious, and it might make you feel better?"

"No. Thank you," replied Chrissy, her voice empty.

Ann stepped through the door and quietly signaled to Liz to get her attention.

"How's she doing?" she mouthed.

Liz made a face and mouthed back, "Not so great."

Ann made a pained expression.

"Can I get you anything?" she whispered.

Liz could only shrug and shake her head. She didn't know how to fix this. She felt hopeless.

Kneeling down in front of Chrissy, she placed her hands on her friend's knees and said quietly,

"Chrissy? I'm going to go upstairs and pack up your things, OK? I don't want you to have to worry about that between now and when we leave for the airport. There's no rush, though. We don't have to leave for another couple of hours. You just sit here and stay warm. I won't be far away, I promise. If you need anything at all, just ask Ann, do you hear me?"

Chrissy nodded, almost imperceptibly, as she stared into the flames.

Liz pulled herself to her feet and walked towards the door, giving Ann a weighted look as she went.

Ann caught her arm as she passed, her eyes filled with tears.

"Miss Elizabeth, please, are you absolutely sure? I know it's not my place to comment, but I'm asking you to reconsider."

Liz forced a smile, patted Ann's hand, then walked away.

Charlie helped her to carry the bags downstairs and load them into the car.

As they were heading back inside, Andrew met them at the

front door.

"All ready for the trip?" He asked, a smile lighting up his face. "If you make good time, you should be back in time for dinner. I've asked Ann to see if she can get some fresh steaks from the village. I thought we could have steak and roasted vegetables. What do you think?"

"Andrew, can we talk for a moment?" Liz said.

"Of course. In fact, I've been wanting to talk to you all day. Shall we go to the study and leave Chrissy in peace?"

Liz nodded, and they walked across the entrance hall.

There were papers strewn across the desk in the study, and Andrew swept them into a messy pile.

"I've been meaning to file these away for days, but they just keep coming. It's like fighting back a snowdrift in the Arctic," he chortled. "I had some good news today, though, at least." He seemed excitable, almost jittery, and Liz wondered if it was overstimulation from the exhaustion. "Our breeding mare is pregnant! It's fantastic, and it means we might be able to turn a profit from the stud farm after all. Oh, and we have a meeting next Tuesday with the tenants from Polwick Farm about next year's crop rotation. I was wondering if you would join us? I would very much value your opinion."

Liz walked to the window and looked out over the manicured grounds to the fields beyond. The early evening light had begun to soften the pall grey sky, painting it with a delicate watercolor palette of lilac and peach.

A delicate misting of rain brushed against the ancient windowpane, and as she touched her fingers to the freezing glass, she watched a bird dart towards the sanctuary of the trees.

"Liz?" Andrew said, walking up behind her. "I know I've been distant over the last week or so, and I'm sorry. But I've been thinking things through, and I've come to a decision. The last month has been the worst period of my entire life, and I'm not sure I would have survived it if it wasn't for you. Liz? Will you look at me for a second? I need to ask you something."

She didn't move.

"It's raining," she said, quietly.

"Liz?"

"It's raining, again. Just a little. Somehow, the soft rain makes the countryside even more beautiful."

Andrew frowned, but continued.

"Liz? I know today has been awful. In fact, the last two weeks have been awful. I'm heartbroken for Chrissy, and I wouldn't normally do this under the circumstances, but this can't wait any longer."

He touched her arm.

"Liz? Please look at me."

She turned to look at him, her eyes cloudy with grief.

"I need to ask you something," he said, swallowing hard. "I'm going to ask you something extremely important. Something that may change our lives."

His fingers brushed his trouser pocket.

"Do you love me?" he asked, his eyes burning into hers.

"Andrew, please…" she said, her voice cracking as she tried to turn away.

"Can you say it, Liz?" he asked, reaching for her hand. "Can you say it out loud? Liz, please," his voice faltered, pleading. "Please, tell me you love me."

She turned to look out of the window again, tears streaming down her face.

"Andrew," she said in a hollow voice. "I'm leaving. Tonight. I'm not coming back from the airport. After I've seen Chrissy to her gate, I'm flying back to London. I don't think we should see each other again."

Andrew gasped, and she heard him reach for the back of the chair for balance.

She couldn't turn around. She couldn't bear to see his face at that moment.

There was a deathly silence in the study, broken only by the ticking of the grandfather clock.

Then Andrew said in a broken voice,

"Why?"

Liz swallowed back the tears. The swell of heartbreak threatened to crash over her and consume her utterly. She dug her fingernails into the palms of her hands, using the sharp pain to keep her focused on what must be done.

"We both know this is the only way, Andrew. The only possible way forward. This is bigger than either of us. You have a duty to protect Kallenford and your heritage, and I can't be the one to threaten that. I can't offer you what you need."

She could hear his breath coming faster and a wrench of pity mixed with fear passed through her.

"No," he shouted, his voice strangled, his desperation ripping through her heart. "I won't give you up. I can't! I don't care what anyone says. I never asked for any of this, and I don't want any of this. All I want is you."

She heard the sobs racking his body, and as she turned she saw him, crumpled in a chair, as if she had landed the final blow to a wounded, dying animal.

She began to reach for him, then stopped herself. Her breath, ragged now, came in short bursts, catching in her throat as if she were drowning. She desperately wanted to hold him, to protect him from all this pain.

But she couldn't.

All she could do was to turn and walk away.

42

New Model
Thursday, November 19th - Santa Monica

"I don't want to go back in," said Kolleen, slumping her shoulders as they got to the automatic sliding doors of the Apex building. "Can't we just walk down to the beach and sit under the pier with our feet in the sand? This toxic culture is sucking the life out of me."

"I hear you," said Emily, "and I'm sorely tempted to, but if I don't work on those new figures, then Brody will kill me."

"Fine," grumbled Kolleen. "But I'm counting down the minutes to margarita-time."

Kolleen was right, it had been a lovely lunch, and, as always, spending time with Kolleen was the only part of the day that Emily enjoyed anymore. She wasn't eager to walk back into that snake pit either, but it was her job, so she gritted her teeth and pushed the button to call the elevator.

As the doors slid open and they stepped out, the giggling that had been going on between Serena and Ava stopped abruptly, and the two leggy twenty-year-olds stared, wide eyed, at Emily and Kolleen.

"Yes?" Snapped Kolleen. "Can we help you?"

Ava gave her a withering look and turned to whisper under her breath to the cat-eyed Serena.

"What do those two fetuses possibly find to gossip breathlessly about all day, anyway? It blows my mind," ranted Kolleen, as she stomped down the hallway. "I wish Brody would fire them both, but they provide too much eye candy. We all know that's why they're still here."

Emily snorted.

"Just breathe deeply. Don't let them know they get to you. It only makes them worse."

"They're very existence 'gets to me.' Emily, can we just go to the beach and drink cocktails, please?"

Emily grinned at her friend and shook her head.

"Sadly not, old pal. We are grownups, and that equals jobs, taxes, and all sorts of other pain and suffering. Now get to your desk and start being productive."

Kolleen pouted and headed off to her desk.

Emily was scrolling through emails when a folder slammed down on her desk, making her jump. She looked up to see Serena standing above her, a chilling smile fluttering across her lips.

"Brody wants you to redo these slides with the updated figures. He needs them for this afternoon," she said, curtly.

"For the investor meeting," thought Emily. *"Yet another investor meeting that I am not invited to."*

She sighed with frustration.

"Can't Natasha do it?" She asked.

Serena pursed her lips and raised an eyebrow in answer.

Oh shit, yes. Natasha had left last week to 'explore other opportunities', whatever that meant. It seemed that things had not worked out as she had expected with Brody.

"Well, not Natasha then," said Emily, "but,… the 'new Natasha'. What's her name, again?"

Serena narrowed her eyes and said,

"I think you mean Reagan, and I don't think calling her 'new Natasha' is very respectful, you know."

"Sure. Whatever, Serena," Emily said, feeling her blood boil. "So, Reagan, then. Can't she do it?"

"She's still 'getting up to speed' with how everything works around here. She's not ready to take on any workload quite yet," hissed Serena.

"Oh, for god's sake," said Emily. "She's been here for over two weeks now. When is she actually going to start doing any work?"

"You'll have to ask Brody that," replied Serena, her face tight and her eyes flashing. "In the meantime, please update the figures, and have them back to me by 3pm." She turned and walked away.

Emily waited until Serena was out of sight before she flicked to the Word document she had open on her laptop.

She read through the contents for the thousandth time, then closed it once more.

"Emily?" Came Brody's voice from behind her. She jumped. How long had he been standing there?

"Oh. Hi," she stammered. "I didn't see you there. Serena just brought me the folder. I'll have the figures for you by 3pm at the latest."

"Thanks, but I wanted to speak to you about something else," said Brody, his voice low. He looked around them to check that there was no one within earshot. Once he was comfortable that they would not be overheard, he continued. "Something very concerning happened last night."

"Oh? What was that?"

"Kolleen came to speak with me about some concerns you have been sharing with her. She asked me some very pointed questions about our manufacturing strategy and our plans for globalization."

Emily swallowed.

Brody continued. "I would appreciate it if you did not attempt to derail my business and question my ethics behind my back. We discussed your concerns already, and I specifically asked you not to share your thoughts more widely. This is a very delicate time in the growth of this venture, and your irrational and unsubstantiated claims could ruin everything if they reach the ears of the investors. Thankfully, Kolleen is a close friend of mine and so I was able to do some damage control, but if I hear that you have been speaking to anyone else about this, then I'm afraid your job might be at risk. Please remember that sharing information like that is a breach of confidentiality, and I wouldn't want to be forced to get HR involved."

Brody's eyes were cold, and although he was trying not to let it show, Emily could tell he was furious.

"Do you understand me?" He said, leaning towards her over the desk.

"I do. Perfectly. It won't happen again, Brody," said Emily, holding eye contact.

"It better not," he spat, as he stood and paced off.

Emily took a deep breath, opened the Word document once more, and hit 'print'.

She folded the paper and put it in her purse. Then she headed for the restroom to freshen up her makeup.

Swinging the door open, she saw Reagan looking into the wall of mirrors. She was reapplying her lipstick, and she dropped her eyes when she saw Emily.

Emily stood next to her and fished in her purse for her face powder.

Looking in the mirror, she made eye contact and said warmly, "Hi Reagan. How's everything going? Are you settling in, OK?"

Reagan swallowed and said,

"Yes. It's really great. Such an amazing opportunity."

Emily smiled and said, "I'm glad. It can be a little overwhelming at first, but if you need anything, just ask, and I'll see if I can help."

Reagan blushed and said,

"Thank you, Emily. That's very generous of you, especially because... well, you know... because of your history with Brody."

Emily's breath caught in her chest, but she didn't allow her expression to alter.

"How do you mean?" she said, as casually as she could manage.

"Oh, well, um. I'm sorry. I shouldn't have said it like that," Reagan stammered, obviously flustered by this conversation. "I just meant that you and Brody were... well, together for a while, weren't you?"

Emily's jaw tightened, but she continued to look in the mirror, as if checking her mascara.

"That is true. But we're not together anymore, so it's no longer relevant."

"Well, but... you see. Brody and I are... well... you know... seeing each other."

Emily tried not to react to this news.

"That didn't take long did it, Brody?" she thought to herself. *"So Natasha wasn't the only one who wanted to 'explore other options', it seems."*

Emily snapped the lid back onto her lipstick and turned to Reagan. She seemed so painfully young and eager, and Emily felt a maternal stab despite herself.

"Just be careful, yes?" she said softly to Reagan. "Watch out for yourself."

Reagan smiled brightly before saying,

"Thank you for your concern, but Brody is just wonderful. I know things didn't work out between you, but I am pretty excited about where this could be heading, you know? I get him, you see? He's shared things with me that he's never told anyone before, and he's a sweet, caring, hopeless romantic behind all those brains."

Emily felt her stomach contract.

You poor, sweet, naïve child.

She turned to walk away, but then she stopped and turned back.

"Reagan? Did he tell you about his night sailing under the stars? Did he tell you about 'Speranza?"

Reagan's face went pale.

"Yes, but.. how?…" she looked stricken.

"I'm sorry, darling, but it's all a dream," said Emily. "Ask him about Eden. Ask him for the truth."

As Reagan stood staring at her in shock, Emily turned and walked out of the door.

She walked down the hallway to the elevator doors and pressed the button for the top floor.

Brody wasn't in his office, and the top floor was empty. Everyone was in yet another investor meeting.

Emily took the folded paper from her purse and placed it on his desk. By the time he read it, she would be gone.

She had spent the last couple of days putting everything in order. She wouldn't be letting anyone down, she'd made sure of that, but she couldn't stay at this company a moment later.

She would pull Kolleen aside quickly on her way out and tell her, then she would walk out of the Apex offices forever.

"But what are you going to do?" Kolleen had spluttered. "You don't have another job to go to. Are you absolutely sure, Emily? It's not too late. You could go and get the letter right now before he sees it."

"No, I have to go. It'll be OK, Kolleen, everything will work out, somehow."

Kolleen had no other words, so she just hugged her friend tightly, and walked her to the door.

43

Offer
Friday, November 20th - Pasadena

Chrissy glanced at the time on the dashboard and made a face. The traffic on the freeway had been at a standstill because of the car wreck caused by the earlier rain, and consequently they were now running late for their various extracurriculars.

Jackie sat slumped against the back passenger window, her face thunderous, her anger palpable.

"My coach is going to kill me," she muttered under her breath. "Why does this always happen?"

Chrissy could feel her blood pressure rising. She tried to keep her voice steady as she replied,

"It doesn't always happen, Jackie. You haven't been late for practice for months, and we can't help the traffic."

Jackie flashed a glare in her mother's direction.

"You don't understand. Everyone else will be there already, mom."

"You say that like this is my fault," said Chrissy through her teeth. "How am I supposed to control this?" She said, gesticulating at the traffic that was snarled all the way to the exit ramp.

"Yeah, Jackie," said Josh who was sitting in the passenger seat with his earbuds in. "Give mom a break, she can't help the traffic."

"Thank you, Josh," said Chrissy, giving her son a grateful glance.

"Oh fuck off, Josh. You make me sick. If you don't stop acting so superior I'm going to tell mom all about..."

Just then Chrissy's phone rang through the car speakers, and Gabriella's name flashed up.

"Shush," said Chrissy, waving a hand at both of them. "I need to take this, so please be quiet, alright?"

She took a deep breath and answered.

"Hi Gabriella. It's lovely to hear from you."

"Hi Chrissy," came Gabriella's crisp voice. "Is this a good time to talk? I'm about to head out of the office for the weekend, but I wanted to share some news. It's not urgent, however, so we can catch up on Monday if you'd prefer?"

Chrissy wrinkled her nose. She and Gabriella had been missing each other's calls all day, and she was on tenterhooks to know what this 'news' was.

"No, let's talk about it now," said Chrissy, signaling to exit the freeway.

"Well," began Gabriella, "I received an email earlier today from a small publishing house. They are interested in making you an offer for your novel."

Chrissy's heart leapt, and she squeezed the steering wheel in excitement.

"That's fantastic news! What do we do now?" She asked, watching the traffic lights as she waited for them to turn green.

"Now, hold on a second," said Gabriella in a smooth tone. "We'll need to look over the offer and see if it's what you want. They are a niche publishing house, and my agency hasn't worked with them before, so we will need to work out terms that are acceptable on both sides."

"Hmmhmm, sounds good to me," Chrissy said, pulling into the parking lot of the gymnastics complex and waving at Jackie to get out.

"I asked them to email me a typical contract to look over. It seems reasonably straightforward, standard boilerplate stuff," Gabriella continued, "we'll need to work through the terms of acceptance of course, advance payment, royalties, etcetera."

"Sorry, Gabriella, give me one second," Chrissy said, muting the line and shouting to Jackie as she walked towards the doors of the gym,

"Jackie, don't you have a sleepover at Cherie's house tonight? Your bag is in the trunk."

"Oh, shoot, yes," said Jackie, turning on her heels and heading back to the car. "Thanks, mom."

"Mom, we have to go," said Josh looking irate, "I'm gonna be late for track practice if we don't leave right now."

"Um, Chrissy?" Gabriella's voice came over the speaker. "Would it be better to discuss this next week when you aren't so busy?"

Chrissy shushed Josh and signaled Jackie to hurry up before she unmuted the phone.

"No, it's fine. I'm good. What were you saying about an advance payment?"

There was a pause before Gabriella said in a measured tone,

"I'll put everything down in an email for you, so you can read it through later. The editor said one thing that I think we'll need to investigate further. She said that they want to make some changes to the manuscript."

Chrissy frowned.

"What changes?" She asked, weaving her way through the

traffic towards the track field.

"She didn't specify. She said it was nothing unreasonable, though, and that most debut authors need to be open to a level of instruction in order to polish their manuscripts to the shine required for publication."

Chrissy pulled up next to the athletics field and mouthed her goodbyes to Josh.

"Mom, don't forget to email my coach with that order form for my new track uniform," Josh said through the open passenger door.

Chrissy nodded and, with her jaw clenched, she said in a whisper, "I did it earlier today. Now go. I'll see you at pick up."

The tension headache pulsed in her temples, but at least both kids were where they should be, now.

"Chrissy?" came Gabriella's voice again.

"Sorry, yes, I'm here," said Chrissy, slumping in her seat.

"I just wanted to say, congratulations. This is your first offer from a publisher. This is a big deal."

Chrissy smiled as it hit her. Gabriella was right, this was a very big deal, and her eyes filled with tears.

"I don't want you to get ahead of yourself, though," said Gabriella in a stern tone. "This might not be exactly the right fit for you, only time will tell on that front. But either way, you should be proud of what you've accomplished so far."

"Thank you, Gabriella," said Chrissy, feeling both relief and exhaustion flood through her body. "Have a lovely weekend, and let's talk about it some more next week."

"Sounds good. I'll email you over all the details now so you can read through them. I'll answer any questions you have when we speak next week, and then we can begin negotiations with the publisher. Have a wonderful weekend, Chrissy, and I'll speak to you soon."

As Gabriella hung up, Chrissy filled her lungs with air and

allowed herself a moment of peace in an otherwise insanely hectic day.

She picked up her phone and scanned through her emails, opening Gabriella's when she saw the subject line, 'offer from publisher'.

Scrolling through the document she grinned to herself, it was all legal jargon that meant nothing to her. Words like 'grant of rights' and 'separate accounting', 'options' and 'right of first refusal', she was glad that she had Gabriella to lead her through all this.

But what this meant was that she'd done it. She was going to be a published author.

Smiling, she looked up into the purest of blue skies, and whispered a thank you to both Rachel and her dearest friends Liz and Emily, without which none of this would be happening.

It was their story, after all, that Gabriella had read and loved, and that the publishing house now wanted to publish.

Chrissy was becoming an author, her dream was coming true, and she had her friends to thank for it.

Her butterflies.

44

Sunday Roast
Sunday, November 22nd - London

"Can I top up your wine, Liz? How's it all going in here?" Asked Lauren, strolling into the kitchen with the bottle of pinot noir.

Liz wiped her furrowed brow and said, "It's good. I think. And yes, more wine would be great, thanks. I think we're almost there, so can you check if Cynthia and Naomi have finished setting the table?"

"Will do," replied Lauren. "And shout if you need anything, yes? It all smells delicious."

Liz smiled widely until Lauren's back was turned, then she downed the glass of wine and squeezed her eyes shut. What the hell had she been thinking, offering to cook Sunday lunch for everyone? She wasn't a cook. She barely knew how to make toast, and yet here she was preparing what amounted to a Christmas dinner.

The oven alarm beeped, and Liz checked her scrawled and splattered sheet of timings.

Slipping her hands into the oven gloves, she opened the oven door and pulled out the roast beef. Sticking it with the thermometer, she nodded to herself before setting it on the carving board and covering it with silver foil.

"Well, bloody hell," she thought to herself in amazement. "I think it's actually coming together."

The final piece of the puzzle was the Yorkshire puddings, and as she slid them into the oven, she surveyed the destruction that surrounded her.

This meal had cost her a fortune. It wasn't only the meat and vegetables and other various ingredients that she'd had to buy, but all the necessary equipment as well. The baking trays, the serving dishes, the silver foil and thermometer. As the queen of takeout and delivery, she'd had none of these so-called 'kitchen essentials' and she wondered how she'd survived as long as she had without them.

But now everything was ready, and Lauren was right. It did indeed smell delicious.

And so began the great procession of dishes from kitchen to dining table, and Liz felt quite emotional when she saw the spread she had created.

Buttered carrots and honeyed parsnips, succulent beef alongside crispy roast potatoes, and fluffy Yorkshire puddings, with delicious onion gravy to pour all over everything.

"It's amazing, Auntie Liz," said Naomi, bouncing up and down in her chair in anticipation. "Can we eat it now? My stomach is growling."

"Me too, girl," said Liz with a huge smile. "Let's do this!"

Liz sliced the beef, and everyone helped themselves to mounds of the steaming, delicious food.

"Will wonders never cease?" said Cynthia, beaming at Liz. "You're a natural cook, darling. Who would have known it?"

Liz was too tired, too full, and too content to make a smart remark, so she just shrugged and smiled and took the compliment in the spirit in which it was given.

After lunch, everyone rolled themselves to the living room to lounge on the sofas.

"Don't worry about the dishes, darling," said Cynthia. "Lauren and I will clean everything up later, but I'm too full to even move right now."

"Me too," said Lauren, "but yes, we'll do it together, won't we, Mrs. Cavendish?"

Cynthia smiled at Lauren and said, "I wish you would call me Cynthia. Mrs. Cavendish is so formal."

"Ok. If you're absolutely sure?"

"Of course I am. Like you said, we're practically family, my dear."

The rest of the afternoon was delightfully peaceful. Naomi sat on Cynthia's lap and they read her new favorite story together, while Lauren told Liz all about her job and the highs and lows of pediatric nursing.

Once Naomi was satisfied that she had read the book enough times, she jumped down from Cynthia's lap and wandered off to get her iPad.

Cynthia reached for her newspaper and settled back into her chair.

Liz was dozing off, dreaming of fresh carrots and parsnips, a deep sense of pride and contentment surrounding her like warm fluffy clouds, when she felt a hand on her arm.

Her mother was sitting next to her on the couch, her face pale, her expression unreadable.

"What?" Liz said, trying to pull herself back to full consciousness. "What's wrong?"

"Oh, darling," said Cynthia. "I wasn't sure whether I should show you this, but I think you should know."

She handed Liz the newspaper.

Liz saw the headline, and her stomach dropped.

* * *

'Earl of Kallenford: Engaged.

Once dubbed the most eligible bachelor in the UK, Lord Andrew Arthur Armstrong-Bell, 14th Earl of Kallenford (aged 35) announced his engagement yesterday to Isabella Maria Orsa (aged 31) after returning from a romantic getaway to her hometown in Italy earlier this week.

"We met through a mutual friend, and we hit it off straight away," he told reporters. The couple plan to marry next summer at Lord Kallenford's home estate in Scotland.

"I am so happy that my son has finally found love after such a trying time," said Lady Kallenford, Andrews mother, and recently widowed dowager, who lost both her husband and eldest son in a tragic flying accident in September of this year.

The Orsa family originally made their fortune in the logging and timber trade, but are best known for their domination of the global cosmetics industry.

We wish Lord Kallenford and his bride-to-be all the best for their future together.'

Liz stared at the photograph of Andrew standing with his arm around a beautiful, dark-haired young woman.

She tried to look away, but she was transfixed.

Andrew was smiling, but he looked somewhat stilted, as if he were hosting a formal function. The young woman was stunning in an imposing, somewhat haughty way. Her large dark eyes held the expression of someone who had always been given exactly what she wanted, and lord help anyone who got in her way.

Liz tried to picture Andrew kneeling next to her, showing her the otter's den in the riverbed, or a new fawn, unsteady on its legs. Would this elegant Italian beauty run next to him through the wild flowers in the meadow? Would she climb a tree to see the ruins of the old pele tower?

She turned away, biting back the tears, trying to push the thoughts out of her head. This was a pointless folly and she wouldn't torment herself anymore.

"I'm so sorry, sweetheart," whispered Cynthia, seeing the pain on her child's face.

"It's fine," said Liz, swallowing hard. "It's for the best. It's what the family needs, after all. A huge injection of cash will secure the future for Kallenford Castle and lift the weight of debt off Andrew's shoulders."

Cynthia looked at the ground before saying,

"Do you think that's why he did it? For the money?"

Liz couldn't answer. Suddenly, she felt dizzy, and she sat down heavily on the couch.

Of course it was. Surely? He needed an heiress with a fortune, and here she was. Italian aristocracy, with a pedigree not even Andrew's mother could fault.

That's why he proposed to her, wasn't it?

Or…

Liz couldn't escape the dark thoughts that clouded her mind.

Could it be that Lady Katherine had been right all along? Maybe marriage was about more than just infatuation? Andrew and his new fiancée would have shared experiences. As the children of noble families, they would no doubt know the same people, move in the same circles. They would look at challenges through the same lens. They would have more in common than she and Andrew ever had.

Liz felt her heart ache as she realized that the Andrew she had known, the one who watched the seasons change with the innocence of a child, was gone now, swallowed up by the responsibilities of his position. Isabella wouldn't need to marvel at the silver flash of a trout jumping in the river. That wasn't her role. She wasn't Andrew's playmate, after all. She was his equal in managing a legacy that went back hundreds of years.

And then the worst thought of all. What if he actually loved her?

Liz couldn't bear it. The thought alone burned into her very soul.

She stood abruptly and stumbled to the kitchen while saying in a faltering voice,

"I'm going to sort out the dishes. I don't need any help, I just need some time alone."

"Ok my darling, but if you need me, then please just call," said Cynthia, wishing she could do more to help her heartbroken daughter.

45

Giving Thanks
Thursday November 26th - Pasadena

Emily ruffled Doogie's ears as he looked at her inquiringly, his head on one side and his tongue hanging out. He looked as if he was smiling at her, and she grinned at him and said,

"Are you having a nice Thanksgiving, Doogie? I sure am,"

Doogie barked in confirmation, danced around in a little circle, and settled at her feet.

The day could not have been more perfect. After a chilly spell earlier in the month, today had been unseasonably hot, so the kids had gone swimming before Thanksgiving dinner was served. Even Josh and Jackie, who were constantly at each other's throats these days, appeared to have called a truce, and the five children all played in the pool together, whoops of glee echoing through the house where the adults sat, chatting and drinking beer.

Now Scott was in the kitchen in his role as head chef, which he loved. Chrissy was more than happy for him to manage the culinary side of the festivities as she plied Emily and Ed with more drinks and nibbles, while trying to control the overly excited Doogie.

The smells coming from the kitchen were mouth-watering. Scott had already made three types of pie; pumpkin, apple and pecan, and they were laid out on the large dining room table amongst the beautiful Thanksgiving decorations.

Chrissy came through to the living room and sat on the chair opposite Emily.

"You happy?" she asked, as Doogie leapt up from Emily's feet and ran to his master.

"Extremely," said Emily with a deep, contented sigh. "Thank you again for having us today. You really didn't need to open your home on Thanksgiving."

"No, it is truly wonderful to have you all here. It's made the day even more special that we're able to share it with you all."

Emily closed her eyes, the warmth in her heart overflowing.

"It's lovely to have both the families together like this. It's something I pictured when we first agreed to move here. I'm not even going to think about where we might be next year, because this, right here, is enough."

Chrissy tried not to let the smile slip from her face. The uncertainty of Emily's future had been pricking at her today, but she was determined not to let it spoil their time together. No one knew what the future held, and there was no point spoiling today by worrying about tomorrow.

"Scott says the turkey should be ready in about 20 minutes, so I'm going to call the kids in to get dried off and dressed," she said brightly, jumping up from the chair. "Can I get you anything else?"

"No, honestly, I'm perfectly content right here. Are you sure there's nothing I can do to help, though? Poor old Scott must have his hands full in there all by himself?"

Chrissy waved a hand in dismissal. "No, he's fine. He'd much rather be left alone to manage it all. He loves it, really, the crazy man." She smiled and headed into the backyard to call the kids.

Emily sipped the last of her beer and sat back in her chair. What a crazy year it had been. So many ups and downs, so many life changes. But today they were together and happy.

She thought of Ed, who had volunteered to act as lifeguard while the children were in the pool. He was a good man, and they had come a long way in getting to know each other again since that fateful day in June. She was blessed to have him as the father of her children, and thankful they had navigated such a difficult time, and come out stronger on the other side.

She thought of the future, and what that could bring.

Would they have to go back to England?

Would their roles be reversed again if they did? With Ed working at Emily at home looking after the children?

She knew in her heart that whatever was to come; she was a different person now than the woman who had arrived in California less than two years ago. She had begun to discover who she was. She had started to 'spread her wings' as Chrissy would say, and although she had played the fiery phoenix for a while, maybe she could find a way to fly that felt more like her true self.

At that moment, the children crashed through the open French doors in a deafening wave of noise and merriment, padding wet footprints all over the beautiful wooden floors. Emily tutted and ushered them upstairs to get changed.

As she and Chrissy exchanged looks of loving exasperation, Emily's cell phone began to ring.

She reached into her purse to get it and saw Kolleen's name on the display.

"Hi there!" Emily said. "What a lovely surprise! Happy Thanksgiving."

Kolleen's voice came, warm and joyful. "Hey, girl. And the

same to you! I know you're probably in the middle of dinner, but do you have a second?"

"Of course. We have about fifteen minutes until Scott serves up the turkey. Is everything alright?"

"It is, indeed. And I might have some news that will make your Thanksgiving even more special."

"What?" said Emily, her stomach fluttering with anticipation. "Come on, tell me, you can't keep me in suspense like this."

Kolleen laughed a deep, throaty laugh, then said, "Do you remember that cosmetics company we were talking to about best practices for manufacturing small batch lines?"

"Um, yes?" Emily said, trying to recall the meeting that now felt like a lifetime ago.

"They reached out to me to ask if you were on a contract with Apex, and if so, when it ended. They asked me if I thought you might consider working for them as a consultant once you were done with the Apex launch. Apparently, their COO was extremely impressed with your attention to detail, and how intuitive manufacturing processes seemed to be to you. All I told them was that you might be available, and that I would see if you'd like to speak to them further about the opportunity."

"Oh my god, Kolleen. That would be amazing. I loved that business and their ethos around sustainability. Thank you so much!" said Emily, the tears welling up in her eyes.

"Don't thank me, girl. This is all you. I knew things would work out for you. You are such a strong, honest person, and you deserve all the luck in the world. I'm so happy this might mean you can stay in California, and we can still hang out."

"Can you email me the details? I'll call them next week and see if we can set up a meeting. Thank you, you're the best!"

Just then, Scott appeared in the doorway to the living room and said like an old town crier,

"Come one, come all, dinner is served."

A cheer came from upstairs, and the wildebeest came trampling down the staircase towards the dining room.

Emily laughed and said over the uproar,

"Kolleen, I gotta go before the locusts descend and there's nothing left to eat. Thank you again, and I'll call you next week."

Plates piled high, everyone cheered as Scott carved the turkey.

Chrissy proposed a toast.

"To good friends and new opportunities."

Emily added,

"To best friends who have your back, no matter what."

They raised their glasses and then tucked into the delicious meal before them.

46

Merry Christmas
Sunday December 24th - Mission Ridge Ski Resort,
Pasadena, & London

"I won't be long," said Emily. "I'm going to jump on a call with Liz and Chrissy, and then I'll be out again to play. Have fun, you guys!"

She walked up the wooden stairs of the ski chalet, banging the snow off her boots as she went.

As she reached the door, she turned to look at her beloved family.

Sinewy fir trees framed them on either side, standing stark against the crisp white snow, their dark evergreen limbs sprinkled with a powdery white embellishment. The children played together, jumping in and out of the fresh snowdrifts, laughing and screaming as they threw snowballs at each other and made snow angels. Ed looked on, his cheeks and nose ruddy with the cold, occasionally throwing snowballs of his own, much to the kids' glee.

Emily sighed with contentment at the scene. What a perfect Christmas this was going to be!

None of them had been skiing before, so the first couple of

days had been quite a challenge, but now they were easily snapping their boots into the ski's, and sliding on and off the ski lifts. The alpine chalet they had rented for the week had begun to feel like a second home, and everyone was in love with the cozy sanctuary that provided easy access to the slopes.

As she opened the front door and stepped through into the rustic living room, the warmth washed over her. She could smell the wood-smoke from last night's fire, when they had roasted marshmallows together, and watched their favorite family movie.

Kicking off her snow boots, she headed to the kitchen to make herself a nice cup of tea. She inhaled the glorious aroma of toast from the morning's breakfast mixed with the fresh pine scent from outside, and she knew that from this moment on, this combination would always remind her of Christmas.

With a piping hot mug of tea in her hands, she sat in the breakfast nook, looking through the window at the virgin blanket of snow that surrounded the chalet.

She FaceTimed both Liz and Chrissy.

Liz answered first.

"Hey, Emily. Happy Christmas! How is it? How's the powder?"

Emily laughed, and said, "It's amazing! I don't think we'll ever want to leave."

Chrissy connected next.

"Hi guys, and merry Christmas to both of you! Ooh, Emily, are you liking the resort? Isn't it just gorgeous? I'm so jealous," she said with a huge grin on her face.

"Totally!" exclaimed Emily. "It's unbelievable that this ski resort is only a three-hour drive from Pasadena. I feel like I'm in another state. Or another country, even."

"How's the skiing going?" asked Liz. "Are you getting the hang of it?"

Emily wrinkled her nose and shrugged.

"Kinda. Ed is a natural, and the kids are dominating the bunny slopes. Me, less so. But I'm thoroughly enjoying the 'après-ski' part of the vacation, so it's all good."

"We're all missing you back here," said Chrissy.

"Is it hot there in Pasadena?" asked Liz.

"It's not swimming pool hot, but it's still pleasant to sit out in the sun. I'm sitting on the patio right now with a glass of chardonnay, watching a few fluffy clouds float across the blue sky. This would be a fantastic day for a hike. It's not too hot, and the skies are clear. Do you remember the day we went up to the Angeles Forest and looked out across the mountain ranges? That was such a wonderful moment, and I'm so glad we got to share it."

Liz sighed.

"Yes, although it feels like a lifetime ago now, so much has happened since then. I might need to come out and visit again soon. I'm in dire need of some vitamin D. It's been so dreary and gray here for weeks now. I love the cold, but this is getting a bit much, even for me."

"You're always welcome," said Chrissy. "We'd love to have you come and stay again. Are you spending Christmas with Lauren and Naomi?"

The smile dropped from Liz's face, and she said,

"No, sadly not. We haven't seen much of them since they moved in with Gary. I understand, though, and I'm not taking it personally. They're trying to build their new family, and they need time and space to do that. So it's just me and mum for Christmas this year."

"Oh, Liz. That's a shame," said Emily. "We're thinking that we might go back to England for Christmas next year to see family and friends, it's been a while after all, so maybe we could get together then, if not before?"

"I'd like that," replied Liz.

"And," Emily said, hesitantly, "Chrissy told me the news about Andrew. I'm so sorry. That sucks. If you need anything, or you want to come and visit to get away from it all, then please just reach out. Our home is always open to you."

Liz smiled, but her eyes flickered with pain.

"Anyway," she said, brightly. "When do you start the new job? Are you excited?"

Emily beamed.

"January 2nd. And yes, I can't wait to get my teeth into it. I've already had a couple of calls with a guy from their compliance team, a nice chap called Patrick, who has been very helpful in getting me up to speed with all the current agreements. We're going to work closely together for the first couple of months, and do a full documentation review before we build out the strategy going forward. He seems quite sweet. We were talking about hiking, and he offered to take me out for a couple of mountain biking trips in the Sierras if I want to. He's a mountain biker, you see."

"Is he, indeed?" said Liz, her eyebrow arched.

"Oh my god, Liz. Let's not start all this again, shall we?" said Emily, her lips pursed.

"Hang on," said Chrissy with a devilish grin. "I'm going to top up my glass of wine if you guys are going to start fighting again. It's been a while, so maybe you're due for a bust up? Weren't the last big fireworks on July 4th last year, ironically?"

They all laughed, thinking back to those special days last summer when this whole journey had begun.

"Hey, Chrissy," said Liz. "How's everything going with your publisher? When will your magnum opus be flying off bookshelves around the world? I can't wait to buy a copy."

Chrissy snorted and made a face.

"I wouldn't hold your breath," she said. "I think this publishing deal might not happen after all. Initially, they said they wanted to 'propose some changes' to the manuscript. It quickly became apparent that what they meant by that was to rip it apart and fundamentally change the story."

"So you said no?" asked Emily, sipping her tea.

"Actually, I was open to the idea. What do I know, after all? I'm just a new writer with no track record to prove that what I write is actually any good. It was Gabriella who put her foot down. She was adamant that they not 'eviscerate my work' as she described it. She said that if I took all their suggestions, my manuscript would be wholly unrecognizable, and my voice would be lost."

"That's interesting," said Liz, tucking her feet up under her and pulling her blanket up to her neck to ward off the cold. "So, what's the plan now?"

Chrissy shrugged, deflated.

"Who knows? I wallow in anonymity, unpublished and unsung like most other writers? Gabriella says we should hold out for a publishing house that can see the value in the manuscript, but maybe it will never get picked up. We'll just have to see, I guess.

"I don't believe that," said Emily, looking out over the glistening snow. "I think Rachel brought us back together for a reason, and that reason is bigger than we know. Yes, our lives have changed dramatically, but I don't believe our journey is done. I think there's still something waiting for us, the real reason we came back together."

"Wow, Emily," said Chrissy. "You're starting to sound like Trish."

"Don't you feel it, though?" insisted Emily. "Like we're at the beginning of something huge? It's as if the adventure is only just beginning."

Maybe it was the magic of the season, but as each of the friends thought about the year to come, they had to agree that

Emily was right. There was something on the horizon calling to them.

But what?

'Rachel's Butterflies Trilogy'

The story of 'Rachel's Butterflies' continues in 'Butterflies Rising.'

Please visit my website for more information and to receive updates on all my latest books!

www.vickichilds.com

Vicki Childs Online

Thank you for reading 'Kiss the Sun', the second book in the 'Rachel's Butterflies', trilogy. I hope you enjoyed it!

Reviews are the lifeblood of a novel, especially for independently published authors, so I would be incredibly grateful if you would take a moment to leave a review on Amazon for me.

Also, please sign up to my mailing list on my website at www.vickichilds.com to ensure you are the first to hear about new releases and special offers. I promise you will only hear from me when I have something important to share.

Finally, come hang out with me online at:

www.vickichilds.com
Facebook.com/vickichildsauthor
https://www.instagram.com/vickichildsauthor

Acknowledgements

As I continue on my journey as an author, I am deeply humbled by the constant and unwavering support of some amazing individuals.

Thank you to my long-suffering husband, Richard, you are my soulmate and the inspiration for Scott.

To my wonderful, inquisitive children Nicholas and Eleanor, for believing in me, and bringing joy and light to my life.

Thank you to my mother, Alex, who shared her love of reading and stories with me from a very young age. You opened my eyes and my heart to the wonder of books, and changed the course of my life because of it.

Thank you to my two closest friends Pippa and Joe who inspired this continuing story. Your love and support over the years has taught me the true power of friendship, and allowed me to see my own butterfly wings.

And finally to my beta readers and advocates, Bradley Brady, Rebecca Sakamoto, Birgitt Van Wormer, Lynne Childs, Aine Waldron, Karen Kneely, Elisa Wilson, Jane Militello, Crystal Gace, Katy Brown, Tiffany Debnath, Cynthia Culver, Jerri Johnson, Catherine Orezzi, Janelle Pamer, and Shirley Ridsdale.

Thank you for your considered feedback and insight, without which 'Kiss the Sun' would not be the book it is today.

This book touches on the painful topic of suicide. If you or someone you know is in crisis—whether they are considering suicide or not—please call the toll-free Lifeline at 800-273-TALK (8255) to speak with a trained crisis counselor 24/7.

If you are in the UK call Samaritans at 116 123

About the Author

Vicki grew up in England, not far from Windsor Castle. She studied Psychology at the University of Surrey and spent most of her career working in talent acquisition and training. She relocated to California with her husband in 2008, just before the birth of their first child. After calling Pasadena home for almost fifteen years, she now lives in Windermere, Florida with her husband, two children, two dogs and two cats.

Made in United States
North Haven, CT
05 December 2023